As Randa unlocked her front door, she saw her dog bolt to the kitchen for his water bowl. She shook her head as she watched him from the living room, then glanced at Justin as he closed the door. "Would you like something to drink?"

Justin grinned. "How about some juice?"

Randa nodded and started to walk to the kitchen, but Justin grabbed her hand. Pulling her body to his, he kissed her for the second time. He'd never been the kissing type, but for some reason, he couldn't get enough of Randa's soft, full lips. "Later," he mumbled against her mouth.

She knew she had two choices. One, she could ignore the feel of his stiffening manhood against her, or two, she could give in. As he thrust his tongue deeper inside her mouth and pressed her tighter against his growing need, she decided to go with the latter option.

"Justin?" She moaned his name. Her only answer was a pair of hands roaming down her back and cupping her round bottom in a gentle squeeze.

His hungry kisses swept down her neck and she felt a familiar ache in her core.

BOOK YOUR PLACE ON OUR WEBSITE AND MAKE THE ARABESQUE ROMANCE CONNECTION!

We've created a customized website just for our very special Arabesque readers, where you can get the inside scoop on everything that's going on with Arabesque romance novels.

When you come online, you'll have the exciting opportunity to:

- View covers of upcoming books

- Learn about our future publishing schedule (listed by publication month and author)

- Find out when your favorite authors will be visiting a city near you

- Search for and order backlist books

- Check out author bios and background information

- Send e-mail to your favorite authors

- Join us in weekly chats with authors, readers and other guests

- Get writing guidelines

- AND MUCH MORE!

Visit our website at
http://www.arabesquebooks.com

CAMPAIGN
FOR LOVE

CELYA BOWERS

BET Publications, LLC
http://www.bet.com
http://www.arabesquebooks.com

ARABESQUE BOOKS are published by

BET Publications, LLC
c/o BET BOOKS
One BET Plaza
1900 W Place NE
Washington, D.C. 20018-1211

All Kensington Titles, Imprints, and Distributed Lines are available at special quantity discounts for bulk purchases for sales
promotion, premiums, fund-raising, and educational or institu-
tional use. Special book excerpts or customized printings can
also be created to fit specific needs. For details, write or phone
the office of the Kensington special sales manager: Kensington
Publishing Corp., 850 Third Avenue, New York, NY 10022,
attn: Special Sales Department, Phone: 1-800-221-2647.

BET Books is a trademark of Black Entertainment Television,
Inc. ARABESQUE, the ARABESQUE logo and the BET
BOOKS logo are trademarks and registered trademarks.

First Printing: November 2004
10 9 8 7 6 5 4 3 2 1

Printed in the United States of America

DEDICATION

This book is for my mother, Celia Mae Bowers Shaw Kenney, who didn't get to see this glorious occasion.

ACKNOWLEDGMENTS

I would like to thank my mother, who taught me knowledge is everlasting, much like her spirit.

To my readers: Melody Alvarado and Judy Brown, thanks for the criticism. To John Brown, thank you for having a cousin named Randa.

To Darwyn Tilley, Jeri Murphy, Sheila Kenney, Earl Kenney, Yolanda Tilley, Celya Tilley, Shannon Murphy, thank you for your undying support and for keeping me going when the glass is half-empty.

To my brother, Kim Kenney, thank you for being Darius.

To my critique group, the Arlington K/A Writers Group: Diane Kelly, Simon Rex-Lear, Gay Downs, Charles McMillen, Vannetta Chapman, and Urania Fung, thanks for all those gentle reminders about sentence structure and keeping me focused.

A big thanks to everyone who encouraged me to keep writing. I thank you from the bottom of my soul.

ONE

Miranda Stone smiled as the waiter brought a bottle of champagne to the table. "Bea, I can't believe we're going to be working together. I just didn't think this was possible after, you know. . . ." Her voice trailed off and her eyes darted.

Beatrice Carrington looked deep into her friend's face. "Randa, it wasn't your fault that you got fired." She paused as the waiter poured the bubbly liquid into their glasses. "Think of this as a new beginning. I know you won't be a director anymore, but as an assistant, you'll have more free time. Isn't that what you wanted?"

Randa nodded and Bea continued. "This is your second chance at happiness, and you deserve it. So I don't want to see any more tears. This is a celebration." She reached across the table and patted her friend's hand.

"I know, Bea. I'm thankful that you got me the job, and I won't let you down. I know Sloane, Hart, & Lagrone is a prestigious advertising firm. And that Mr. Crawford . . ." Randa fanned her hand at her face, reminiscing about Darius. He was the only Black executive at the firm and his smooth brown skin reminded her of a milkshake with extra chocolate. "Whew! He was very nice and very nice looking, too. It's a shame that he's getting married Saturday."

Bea gave a wicked grin, but remained silent.

"I know you, Bea," Randa said, fixing her friend with a you-better-tell-me look. "What are you not saying?"

Bea set her glass down and looked across the table at Randa. A diehard gossip, she just couldn't keep her mouth shut any longer. "Well, Darius has been through the ringer these last few months, too. His sister Darbi married Curry, his best friend and co-worker, ten months ago."

Randa tried to contain her surprise but failed. "Isn't he white?"

"You're a fine one to talk," Bea reminded her since she seemed to have forgotten. "Your ex is white. Yes, Curry is white and Darius's sister is black. But it was love, and Darius couldn't stop it."

"That's beautiful," Randa said, remembering the look of satisfaction Darius had when he spoke of his family. She recalled seeing a picture of a honey beige, curly-headed infant on his desk. It must have been his nephew. "Oooh, Bea, I almost forgot," Randa blurted. "I meant to ask you if you'd heard anything about my new boss. When I interviewed with Darius, they hadn't selected one yet." She pulled her champagne flute to her lips and took a sip.

"He started this week. His name is Justin Brewster, he's from Oregon or somewhere, and he doesn't really talk much to mere assistants. You've got your work cut out for you." Bea smiled as she raised her glass in a toast. "While I'm on the subject, I guess I should mention that he's not too bad to look at, either."

Randa burst into a fit of giggles. "You are too much, girl. I'll appreciate the eye candy, but dating a man I work with or for is not in my game plan."

Bea joined in her laughter and made a belated toast to Randa. "This is to your new job and your second chance. May it be everything your previous job wasn't."

They clicked flutes and downed the remainder of their champagne.

Justin Brewster stared out of the window of his two-story townhouse. The past year seemed like a bad dream. He feared he would soon wake up and his ex-wife, Lisa, would be demanding that they visit one of her friends for brunch. God, how he hated brunch with her friends.

Shaking his head back to reality, he remembered that he didn't live in Portland anymore, he wasn't married to that horrible woman, and he didn't have to worry about his ex-wife's friends and their sick competitive spirit, which had driven him into a mountain of debt.

Now he lived in Arlington, Texas, and had just started a new job. He laughed as he walked through the bedroom, kicking empty storage boxes out of his way.

Because of Lisa, he'd moved away from his friends and family to get a fresh start. Sloane, Hart, & Lagrone was a prestigious ad agency that had recently redesigned its marketing, advertising, and public relations departments. The position he'd been hired for was brand new, and they had wanted Justin to start immediately. So soon, in fact, that he didn't even get time to pick his assistant. His boss, Darius Crawford, assured him that they had a more-than-competent woman in mind, but Justin didn't like the fact that he knew nothing about her.

When she started on Monday, Darius would be on his honeymoon, leaving Justin with a woman he didn't know, to tell her about a job he wasn't quite sure of. He hoped his assistant was nothing like his annoying, whiny ex. He wasn't up for going through hell a second time.

Monday morning, Randa approached Justin's office, wishing her workday was already done. Her day had started out badly and was growing progressively worse by the minute. First she had taken the wrong exit in busy downtown Fort Worth rush hour traffic, then she had ripped her brand new stockings as she got into the elevator. Now, she would be late meeting her new boss, a man Bea had already warned her about. She regretted not going home and crawling back into bed.

Sucking up her misery, Randa put on her best sunny disposition as she exited the elevator. She walked with pride until she reached the marketing department and saw her boss. Bea had lied. This man was way more than mere fine; he was damn near Denzel.

The brown-skinned man, who appeared to be in his late thirties, sat behind his large desk and shook his head in dismay as Randa approached his office. She had to steady herself in her stilettos as she took in the contours of his massive upper body. He had removed his suit jacket, and though he wore a sleeved white tee under his dress shirt, his rippling biceps were still quite evident and were accented by his navy blue suspenders.

She realized she was staring at him and looked away, composing herself before she knocked on his open door. "Mr. Brewster, I'm Miranda Stone, your new assistant. I'm sorry I'm late, I—"

Justin held up his large hand to stop her. "No need to explain, Mrs. Stone. The only result I'm concerned with is that you're here now," he said curtly. He ushered her inside his office and closed the door.

"I took a wrong exit," she explained. Bea hadn't lied about him being a piece of work. Randa could already tell his personality left a lot to be desired.

"I understand, Mrs. Stone. I apologize for my rudeness." He took a deep breath, calming his body before he spoke. Miranda wore a short skirt, made to appear even shorter by the very high heels she wore. He noticed she had legs that even Tina Turner would envy and tried not to stare. The last thing he needed was a sexual harassment charge. "I realize this is a new job, and it's easy to get lost in unfamiliar territory. Your regular work hours are from eight to five." He handed her a business card. "If you find for some reason you can't get here at eight, please call me," he continued. "Since Mr. Crawford hired you and is now on his honeymoon, you will have to fill me in about yourself."

He took a seat behind his desk, effectively widening the gap between them. Justin's tone indicated to Miranda that it was futile trying to explain her attempts to get to work on time. He was clearly a no-nonsense type of man. With a resigned sigh, she sat down and told him her background.

She explained that two months prior, she had been fired from her job at Fuentes, Gonzales, and Balmerston Advertising after sixteen years. "They wanted a different image," she began. "After Mr. Balmerston died last year, the company decided to gear their advertising personnel to the growing Hispanic market. I'm fluent in both Spanish and French, but they still fired me." She gave a lengthy explanation so he wouldn't think she was incompetent.

"That's discrimination. They fired you because you're black," he said, disgust clearly etched in his voice. His brown eyes focused on her face, urging her to continue.

"The official reason was my productivity level had

decreased." Miranda looked down at her hands. She'd told herself a million times that getting fired wasn't her fault, but she still felt bad about losing her job.

"Had it?" Justin sipped his coffee and pretended to be nonchalant. Miranda had sat back in the chair, making herself comfortable, and crossed her legs. He wondered if she knew she was exposing nearly all of one smooth brown leg to him.

"No, I helped form that marketing department," she said, anger seeping into her voice. "That was my first job out of college and I had been a faithful, good employee."

"I'm sorry that happened," he offered coldly. He was strangely attracted to this young woman who sat before him, and he didn't want her to realize he was interested in her. After all, she was his assistant. He stared at her blankly as she wiped her eyes. "Are you okay, Mrs. Stone?"

She blew her nose with a tissue from his desk and looked up. "Actually, it's Miss Stone. I'm sorry, it's been a rough two months. I lost my mother to an aneurysm just after I was fired." She dabbed her eyes, so as not to upset her flawless makeup. "I promise to keep the tears to a minimum."

Men! She had just told the saga of her life and he sat there, stone-faced, like she had just told him the day's weather.

"I completely understand, Ms. Stone," he said, keeping his voice even. "I'm recently divorced myself. I know that doesn't compete with your loss in any way, but I understand the hurt of losing a loved one. Why don't you take a few minutes to collect yourself and then we'll discuss your duties?"

Miranda nodded. After a visit to the ladies' room, she felt much better. She walked back into Justin's office and braced herself for the next round. Taking a seat in the chair she'd previously vacated, she took out her notepad and pen, ready to get to work.

Justin took a deep breath. "Ms. Stone, I would like to apologize for my earlier behavior," he said sincerely.

"That's quite all right, Mr. Brewster," Randa assured him in a thin voice. She crossed her legs again and rested her notepad in her lap. "I understand I was late and upset your morning routine. I will make my best effort not to let it happen again." She picked up her pen and poised it in her hand. "You were going to assign my duties," she prompted. He wanted professional, and that was exactly what he was going to get. She smiled in satisfaction.

He stood and paced the small office. "First, please call me Justin. Everyone is pretty informal around here." Justin continued to walk up and down.

"That's fine, Mr. Brew—er, Justin. Actually, my friends call me Randa."

"All right, Randa." The words rolled off his tongue like a melody, and he liked the sound of her nickname. "Let's go over your duties." Justin sat behind his desk and began reading from a list.

After an hour, he had detailed her job specifically so that there was no margin for error. Randa watched his eyes as he spoke. They were a brilliant black, but they had a certain sadness about them. *What did he have to be sad about,* she wondered. *He probably left his wife and skipped town, not paying any child support to the brood he'd left the poor woman with.*

She shook her head; he didn't look the type to shirk responsibility. Those shoulders looked like they could carry the weight of the world. Randa's mind drifted to all the positions those strong shoulders could put her in before she chastised herself for fantasizing about her boss. He was too uptight to think of half of the poses she'd come up with, anyway.

She refocused on what he was saying and waited until he dismissed her to walk back to her desk. As she sat in front of her computer, she was grateful for the solitude. Taking a few personal items from her purse—her photos of her niece and nephew, a picture of her recently deceased mother, and an oversized coffee mug with Mickey Mouse on it that Beatrice had given her—she arranged them on her desk. Reaching back in her bag, she pulled out a day planner that her brother Karl had given her. His words still rang in her ears as she began transferring the notes from her meeting with Justin to the notebook. "It's okay to take a lower-paying job," he'd said. "You'll have less hours to work and more free time to spend. That's not a bad deal. Starting over at 38 may be more fun than you expected."

Randa sighed at that thought, thinking of the many changes her life had endured over the last few months. She'd traded in her sporty Mercedes for an Infiniti, sold her very expensive custom-designed five-bedroom home, and purchased a modest three-bedroom house in Arlington instead. The house she didn't regret; she never really needed all the space anyway, and she'd only bought it because she was happy to be able to afford it. The car, however, was another story. She really missed her Mercedes.

Luckily, she had invested well over the years and wasn't in a financial crunch after she adjusted her standard of living. That said, going from a six-figure salary to an assistant's pay would take Miranda some time to get used to.

* * *

Friday morning, as Randa prepared a report for her sullen boss, she smiled. Randa decided that instead of moping about her new salary, she would begin enjoying what life she had left. She had wasted so much of it working long hours, eating fattening food, and not having a relationship. She intended to change all that now.

After she collated the report and left copies with both Curry's and Darius's assistants, she walked back to her desk. Once seated, she noticed Justin heading toward her. She ruffled papers, pretending to look busy so he wouldn't bother her. He barely acknowledged her before walking into his own office and closing the door.

She breathed a sigh of relief. As she opened her planner to look at the day ahead, she pledged not to let Justin ruin her good mood. Reading her e-mails, she heard his door open slowly. *What now?*

"Randa, could you come in my office?" he requested in his deep baritone voice.

Before she had a chance to answer him, Justin was already back at his desk. She walked into his office and took her usual seat across from him. She noticed he'd put pictures on his desk, but they weren't of his wife, kids, or girlfriend. A single photo of a mature African-American couple stared back at her as he began to speak.

"Randa, I feel that we may have got started off on the wrong foot this week." He looked at her intently, waiting for her response.

Boy, is that the understatement of the year! She nodded in agreement, watching how well he was wearing that suit. The man was a jerk but Randa had to admit he did look good.

Justin replaced the grim look he'd worn on his face for the past week with a smile. It was a small one, but it was enough for Randa to see his straight, even teeth. Good teeth were very important to her. "I would like to take you to lunch today to make up for my bad mood this week. Is that alright?"

She could refuse, since she had already made plans with the other assistants. On the other hand, a lunch outing might give her the chance to find out why he looked so sad all the time. She decided to accept. "That will be fine, Justin."

"Great. I'll meet you at the elevators at noon then." He picked up a report and started reading it, promptly ending their conversation.

Randa was a bit taken aback by his rudeness, but she left his office without saying a word. Back at her computer, she checked her e-mail and found two more requests for reports. Happy for an excuse to leave her desk, she walked down the hall to retrieve the information.

At noon sharp, Justin stood at the elevator, but Randa was nowhere in sight. He watched as several of the assistants left for lunch, and was about to ask them if they'd seen her, when he heard Randa's voice.

"Hope you weren't waiting for me," Randa said, walking up behind him. "Mr. Sloane caught me in the copy room. He asked me to give you this." She handed him a brown folder.

"Thanks," he said. He'd been waiting for that report all morning.

Randa offered a genuine smile before she spoke, hoping some of her goodwill would rub off on her boss. "I'll put this on your desk while you ring for the elevator." She took the folder back and hurried off before he could respond.

She returned just as the elevator arrived, and

they rode to the ground floor in silence. Justin was determined to find out more about his assistant, since he'd noticed that she spoke easily with everyone but him. As they walked across the street, both pretending to be interested in the street scene they saw every day, he tried to keep his eyes off of the fit of her suit but failed. She was wearing her customary short skirt and stilettos, and her long legs distracted him once again.

After they were seated across from each other and her legs were covered by the tablecloth, Justin's thoughts finally returned to business. "How are you liking your job? Any questions so far?" He took a sip of his hot tea and watched as Randa opened several sugar packets. *Surely she won't put all of them in her glass,* he thought.

"It's finding its way, I guess." She emptied the sugar into her glass of iced tea. After she took a sip, she opened several more packets. "I was so used to working 70-plus hours, it's been a little bit of an adjustment." She paused when she noticed Justin looking at her beverage. "This is why I always order soda. I can never get tea sweet enough."

Justin decided that sweetened tea had to be a Southern thing; he preferred his a little bitter. "I don't put anything in mine. You should try it some time." He couldn't stop himself from grinning at her. "I didn't realize you worked so much before. I bet you could do my job with your eyes closed," he continued, silently challenging her. He wondered how long she would be happy being his assistant, since she was used to so much more responsibility and power.

"I doubt it," she said shrugging her shoulders. "They do things differently here. Plus, I'm content being an assistant. I've done the working-long-hours thing. I would like to try the other side of the coin for a while." She stirred her tea and sipped it. "Perfect."

Justin smiled at her again. In the past ten minutes, he'd smiled more at Randa than he had at Lisa during the last ten years of his marriage. There was something about her that put him at ease. He liked the way her hazel eyes shone in the fluorescent light and the way her hips filled out the short skirts she wore. He felt his groin tightening and forced himself to think of something that didn't have anything to do with the way she looked.

"Are you from Texas?" he asked.

She smiled proudly. "Born and raised. You?"

"I'm from Portland, Oregon. I moved here for the job."

"You miss your friends and family?"

"Yes. I do, especially my parents and my brother. They were my rock during the divorce." He felt a pang in his stomach and squashed the memories of his miserable marriage. For the first time in a long while, he felt happy and he didn't want thoughts of Lisa to ruin it.

"I'm sorry, Justin. I know how awful divorce can be, whether it's amicable or not." She saw a flash of pain in his eyes and without thinking, reached across the table and squeezed his hand.

TWO

After a few weeks, Justin began to loosen up around the office. He had finally begun to see the light at the end of the tunnel. By the time Darius returned from his honeymoon, Justin better understood his job and was getting along much better with his assistant. What few questions he still had, his boss cleared up during their weekly meetings.

Surprisingly, Darius also talked with Justin about his working relationship with Randa. Justin hoped that Darius had not heard how awful things initially were between him and his assistant through office gossip. He sat in Darius's large corner office and listened quietly.

"Randa is a huge asset to the firm," Darius said, looking Justin squarely in the eye. "She knows a lot about marketing and advertising. I hired her as an assistant, but I know she has great potential. She has a heavy background in marketing. Try to give her more than assistant duties." Darius noticed Justin's less-than-pleased expression and clarified his statement so that there was no misunderstanding. "As directors, we should try to encourage our assistants as much as possible. So many times we are in meetings or on business trips, and they handle a lot of our job in our absence. They are a reflection of us."

Justin nodded, and after speaking with Darius for

a few more minutes, left the large office. As he
walked back to his desk, he noticed Randa walking
to the copy room. His eyes followed her form as she
rounded the corner and he noticed, not for the first
time, that she had a nice figure with curves in all the
places he liked.

He wondered about her as a person, as he walked
down the hall. Why would someone so qualified take
an assistant's job? Over lunch during their first week,
she'd said that she wanted more time to herself, but
Justin, being the workaholic that he was, couldn't
understand that logic.

After he was settled at his desk, Randa appeared at
his doorway. Her slender hand was poised for knocking when he looked up. He grinned; she was a fine
physical specimen. "Yes, Randa?" he asked, con-
sciously keeping himself from admiring her physique
any further. He watched her put her hand down and
walk into his office. Her short skirt reached to
midthigh today.

"I'm going to lunch," she announced, enjoying
the way his face lighted up when he saw her.

Justin noticed that she already had her purse slung
over her shoulder. "When you return, we need to go
over the monthly report for Darius and Curry." He
knew that would take up the rest of the afternoon,
and he figured he could get to know her then. He
told himself that it was for strictly professional reasons.

Randa nodded, acknowledging his request, and
walked away. She was back at his doorway in an instant
with a stack of papers in her hand. "I've already outlined and graphed it, showing the relationship to the
other departments for cost purposes." She placed the
printouts on his desk. "If you want to make any
changes, I will be happy to do them after lunch."

Justin sat flabbergasted as he watched her walk

away. So many questions about his super-efficient assistant ran through his mind, but none of them had to do with work. How old was she? Kids? Divorced? Living with someone? They were all questions he shouldn't be asking himself.

As Randa browsed through the designer outlet boutique, she smiled. She knew she shouldn't have been shopping, but she needed to get out of the office, and the store was just down the street.

For the first time since she'd been employed at Sloane, she noticed Justin's cologne that morning. That day, his muscles seemed to bulge a little more, and his booty looked even tighter in his dress slacks. His handsome smile had imprinted itself on her mind, and so far, showed no signs of leaving.

She continued to browse, dismissing the thoughts of his biceps or whatever else might lay under Justin's nice-fitting clothes. As she picked up a pink pantsuit, she remembered her purpose for shopping. Randa had an outrageous number of suits and a few formal dresses, but she had no casual clothes. Now that she had the time to be casual, she would need new outfits to accommodate her new lifestyle.

As she looked through the racks, she spotted Curry, one of the firm's directors, and his wife shopping. Randa recognized her from the pictures on Beatrice's desk and observed them as they wandered through the clothing racks. By the way they held hands as they shopped and favored each other with lovey-dovey gazes, Curry appeared to be very much in love with his wife. It was a look that seldom occurred in lonely people's lives, she reminded herself.

She continued to observe them and was close enough to hear when Curry tried to convince his wife to try on a sexy bikini. "Come on, honey," he pleaded. "You'll look great." He held the bikini against his wife's slender frame. "I'll have to beat the guys in Cozumel off with a stick."

Reluctantly, his wife took the bikini into the dressing room. Randa continued with her shopping until she heard Curry's wolf whistle. Again, the couple had her attention.

"Honey, you look great," he told his wife as he circled her, inspecting the swimsuit from every possible angle allowed in public.

Randa agreed; the bikini seemed to be made for her body. She held back a wave of emotion as she watched Curry sweep his wife into a kiss right in the middle of the swimsuit department. That was the kind of love that Randa knew she had missed out on when she was slaving away at F&G.

Randa forced herself to continue shopping. She picked out shorts and skirts with coordinating blouses. At the checkout counter, she ran into Curry and his wife.

"Randa, this is my wife, Darbi," Curry said, introducing the two women. "Honey, this is Randa, the new super-assistant I told you about."

Darbi smiled as she shook Randa's hand. "Don't let them work you too hard. I know Darius can be all business sometimes."

Randa almost forgot that Curry and Darius were related by marriage. "So far, everyone has been really nice to me. I like it a lot."

Curry nodded at Randa, ending their conversation as he and his wife moved to an open cashier. Randa watched them as Curry paid for her purchases. Beatrice was right, they were nauseatingly happy together.

After a quick bite to eat, Randa headed back to

her cubicle. Knowing she didn't have time to put her bags in her car, she put them behind her desk. She knew her brother would be so proud that she was finally loosening up.

Randa noticed Justin getting into the elevator with Darius and was thankful she would have another hour of peace and quiet. Then she noticed a piece of yellow legal pad paper on her desk. Her boss had left her a full page of things to do while he was gone. "I'm supposed to do all this in one hour?" she muttered.

She looked over her list of tasks and noticed he hadn't even thanked her for the report she had completed well ahead of time. Slowly, she calmed down and focused her attention on the list again.

After she finished her third task, she noticed an envelope on her desk. She sent a small prayer heavenward when she saw it was in Justin's horrible handwriting. Cautiously, she opened it and found a greeting card from him. A gift card to her favorite bookstore landed in her lap. Randa figured she must have misspelled something and he was probably suggesting that she buy a dictionary or something. She could not have been more wrong. Holding up the card, she read it to herself. He'd written: *Miranda, thanks for all your hard work on the report. It was flawless! Thanks again, Justin.*

She smiled and put the card in her drawer. *Perhaps he wasn't a total jerk after all,* she thought.

When Justin returned from his power lunch, Randa wasn't at her desk. He wondered where his assistant had gone to this time. Soon, she appeared with an enormous stack of papers. Seeing her, he immediately walked over and attempted to relieve her of the weight.

"Randa, let me help you," he offered, reaching to take the papers.

"Justin, I can manage, thank you," Randa said in an irritated voice. She held the papers closer to her.

Justin sensed he had upset her, but he wasn't sure why. He figured she was one of those independent women and as long as he was a man, he would never be able to please her. He wondered why he even wanted to please Randa. *She* was *his* assistant. Wasn't it supposed to be the other way around? He found himself apologizing to her anyway. "I'm sorry. I was just trying to help, not set the women's movement back," he offered, making light of her reaction.

She handed him the pages and walked to her desk, watching as he placed them down gently.

Justin looked up from the bundle and addressed her. "Could you stay late tonight?" he asked. "I have a late meeting with a potential client and would like you to attend."

"Why?"

Justin barely held back a retort. Most assistants would have been happy that their boss wanted to include them in on a client meeting. Not Randa; she had to have a valid reason for giving up her free time.

"Because you're my assistant and I think you would be valuable to the meeting," he said tersely. Plus, Darius and Curry had suggested he bring her.

Randa shrugged her shoulders. "Well, I was going to the SPCA to look for a pet. But I guess I could do that some other time." She sighed and sat in her chair.

"The meeting is at six in the conference room," he said, not hiding his displeasure very well. He paused at his doorway, exhaling loudly. He and Randa had to work together closely, and there was no sense in having bad blood between them. Turning to her, he said, "I was thinking we could have dinner afterward. Strictly boss and employee, no strings attached."

"I wasn't about to suggest that they were," she said curtly. She knew he expected her to feel honored he'd invited her to the meeting, but she wasn't happy having to change her plans at the last minute. "Dinner will be fine." Randa bent her head down, noting the change on her calendar.

Justin walked to his office to prepare for the meeting with the potential client. This was his big chance to prove himself, and he was excited at the prospect. He went over his notes several more times, until he had his presentation perfect. It was his first big break and he was understandably nervous, more so than usual. Just then, he wondered whom he was trying to impress—himself, his boss, the potential client? Or maybe it was his new assistant?

Later that evening, Randa walked into the meeting and was surprised to discover that she would be the only woman in the room. She took the first vacant seat she spotted. Unfortunately, it was next to Justin.

As they waited for the potential client, Randa noticed Justin's cologne playing havoc with her senses. Each time they accidentally touched, her legs brushing against his as she crossed them, or his elbow hitting hers as he reached for his rolling pen, she felt a shock. If he smiled at her, she knew she'd be a goner.

Soon the meeting was under way. To Randa's surprise, the potential client they were meeting with was one of her former employer's biggest clients. Jose Gutierrez walked into the room and broke into a fierce grin when he saw Randa.

He walked to her side, bending to kiss her cheek.

"Hello, Ms. Randa," Jose stated enthusiastically. "I wondered where you had gone. I'm so happy to see you."

Randa stood and hugged the distinguished gentleman. "Mr. G. It's great to see you, too!"

Everyone at the table looked at them. Finally, Mr. Hart spoke. "You know her, Joe?" he asked, pointing to the new employee at Sloane, Hart, & Lagrone.

"We go way back. Randa was the brains behind all of my ad campaigns. When Gutierrez's Pizza couldn't generate any business, I went to Fuentes, Gonzales, and Balmerston for help. There I met Miss Randa. She suggested the name change to Joe's Pizza." He squeezed her shoulder affectionately before he said, "I couldn't believe those idiots let her go."

Joe sat in the empty seat by Randa, taking her hand and kissing it. "I will hire your firm as long as Randa works on my campaign," he said, still holding on to her.

Randa coughed and wiggled her hand away from Joe. Although she would have loved to work on the campaign, she didn't want any special treatment. "Mr. G, I'm an assistant here," she whispered, then pointed to Justin. "He's the director of marketing, and my boss."

Darius interceded. "I don't see why Randa can't work on the campaign, Mr. Gutierrez. She can help Justin since he's new to all this. I know *she* has excellent ideas."

Justin bristled at the last statement. There he was, thinking this meeting would be his chance to shine, and his assistant had upstaged him.

"Please call me Jose," Mr. Gutierrez said. "Randa helped build my pizza chain into the mass of franchises that it is now. As long as Randa works on my campaign, you've got the account."

"Done!" Darius agreed without so much as consulting Justin.

Soon Jose rose, bid his new advertising firm goodnight, and left the room. It was only 6:30.

The members of the advertising, marketing, and public relations teams each congratulated Randa, and she could tell they saw her in a different light now. Darius shook her hand and smiled as he spoke. "I knew you were a gold mine when I met you! I know you'll do a great job." He turned toward a gathering of partners and joined their conversation as they walked into the hall.

Soon she and Justin were the only two people left in the room. Randa had noticed the look on his face after Darius's comment, and she knew he would be upset with her. He was a decent guy when he wanted to be, but his insecurities were a deal breaker. Randa gathered her things and prepared to leave for the night, assuming Justin would renege on his dinner invite.

Instead he followed her to the door and asked, "How about the Italian place down the street for dinner?"

"You don't have to, Justin," she offered. She knew he was upset and tried to give him the out he needed.

"No, I want to. Plus, it's Friday night."

Randa nodded. "Italian sounds fine. I'd like that. Just let me grab my purse."

Justin enjoyed the motion of her short skirt as she hurried toward her desk. He exhaled deeply, coming to terms with the events of the meeting. Sure he was upset that he hadn't received his moment of glory, but he could only be so angry. The bright side was he would get to work even more closely with Randa.

Five minutes later, she met him at the elevator.

"It seems we're always meeting by the elevator, doesn't it?" she said, her excited energy bubbling over. Randa didn't want to admit it, but she was happy Justin hadn't canceled their date. She caught herself referring to their dinner plans as a "date" and reminded herself, not for the last time, that he was her boss.

He smiled at her, something he was starting to do more often. "Yes, it does," he said, pushing the button.

After they were seated at the restaurant, Randa thought he would ask her a million questions about her past with Jose or her former job. Fortunately, she was wrong. Justin leaned back in his seat in an almost relaxed pose, grinning. He actually seemed to be enjoying himself.

She wiped her mouth with a napkin. "Okay, what is it? Is my lipstick crooked? Do I have something on my teeth?"

He shook his head, leaving his smile in place. "No. I was just floored at what happened in the conference room, and, to think, my assistant was the reason for it. You're just as amazing as Darius said you were."

A compliment? From Justin? "Why, thank you," she said, using her best Southern belle voice.

"I was all ready to hit them with everything I had, and you stole my thunder," he teased.

Randa didn't know how to respond. Justin was smiling, so he couldn't be angry with her. All of a sudden, she felt overheated and reached for a glass of water. She coughed as she tried to think of something to say, but Justin beat her to it.

"It's okay. It kind of makes up for our first rocky days, don't you think?" He picked up his glass and toasted her. "To the woman with vision."

* * *

Saturday morning, Randa awoke with a sense of direction. After being surprised by Jose, and then by Justin taking her to dinner, she felt maybe it was time for the relaxing part of her life to begin. No more of those horrid seventy-hour workweeks when she seldom saw her neighbors, let alone daylight.

As she dressed in shorts and a T-shirt, she decided she would get a dog that day. It was something that she'd wanted for a long while, but until recently she'd never had the time. She wanted a dog that wouldn't knock her down when she came home, but she didn't want one so small that she would accidentally sit on it, either.

She entered her kitchen and began making breakfast. Her ringing phone interrupted her coffee pouring.

Bea's voice rang over the line. "I hear you wowed them at the meeting last night. I bet Justin was fit to be tied," she said, adding a snicker for emphasis.

Randa couldn't help laughing as she remembered how she shocked not only Justin, but most of the other directors as well. "It was a former client from F&G. Then I had dinner with Justin. He talked only of business. No saucy details about his divorce. Sorry, Bea." Randa knew her friend was an incorrigible gossip and had called to get the goods. Switching subjects, Randa told Bea, who lived up the street from her, about her plans for the day. "Well, I'm going to pick out a pet later. Want to come?"

Beatrice laughed and told her no. "Animals belong outside," she quipped.

* * *

Randa grimaced as she was led through the kennels of the Arlington Animal Shelter. There were so
many cute dogs and cats and she wanted to take all
of them home with her. She knew she would have to
start small and with only one. "Do you have any puppies?" Randa asked the man she was following.

The attendant nodded and led her down another
corridor of kennels. Randa saw the one she wanted
instantly. He was a brown and white Pembroke Corgi
with brown eyes that tugged at her heart. "I'll take this
one," she said, pointing to the medium-sized dog.

The attendant nodded and retrieved the brown
and white puppy, handing the barking, wiggling animal to Randa. She laughed as she was covered in
doggie kisses. Finally she had found a friend, one
that wouldn't know or care that was fired from her
last job. She laughed and handed the dog back to
the attendant, who placed it back in the cage. She
followed the man to a small office where she filled
out the shelter's application form. She noticed a
sign on the wall that read "Volunteers needed."

"How do you become a volunteer?" Randa asked
as she filled out another stack of papers.

"Just fill out the paperwork. We do a background
check, and then there's an orientation session on
Wednesdays," the attendant answered in a dry, non-
caring voice. "A lot of people sign up eagerly and
then don't come."

Randa shook her head. "I love animals. You'll be
trying to get rid of me." She continued to scribble,
filling out the extensive list of questions. "Are there
Saturday shifts available?"

"Yes, mornings and afternoons. We always have
animals that need tending to."

Randa smiled at the thought of being surrounded
by lovable animals all morning. "Good, I would like to

sign up for Saturday mornings, then." She handed the stack of forms back to the attendant.

He looked over her pet agreement and asked about her work schedule and exercise habits. When she answered all of his questions to his satisfaction, he said, "Well, Miss Stone, looks like you just bought yourself a Corgi." He provided a crate big enough for the dog, a bag of dog food, a flea collar, and a leash. "I'll see you at orientation. We begin at 7:00 P.M. sharp."

As Randa drove away from the shelter, she felt the knot of tension she'd been feeling since the meeting yesterday begin to subside. She glanced at her new puppy in the passenger seat and listened as he barked over and over. "Don't you worry," she said, patting his back. "I'll take good care of you."

THREE

Saturday afternoon, Justin walked through his town house, the silence slowly driving him insane. After fifteen years of marriage, he was used to having someone around, and he felt very alone on weekends without the distraction of work to occupy his mind. He debated going to the park in his neighborhood, but he didn't think he would be able to handle seeing couples together.

After customary calls to his brother and parents, neither of whom answered their phones, Justin knew he would lose his mind if he stayed inside another minute. He put on his running shoes and grabbed his keys from the table by the door.

As he ran, his mind drifted to his ex-wife and the last time he saw her. He tried to shake the feeling that he had let someone he loved go, but he'd realized that he couldn't live the life that Lisa desired. He didn't want to always be worried about who had what and how they could do better. After the third mile, Justin snapped back to the present and returned to his town house.

As he walked inside, his phone rang. He picked it up, and before he could even say hello, his brother, Jason, began speaking.

"You need a dog." Jason had heard the pathetic message Justin left on his answering machine.

"I work too much for a dog. It would be alone too much," he reasoned. He had also thought of a pet for companionship, but decided it wouldn't be fair to the animal.

"How about a cat? They're independent and don't need to be walked," Jason said, laughing.

"I'm a man. I can't have a cat. What would the neighbors think?"

"Well, you need something to occupy your mind. I don't want you feeling guilty about divorcing Lisa or moving to Texas," Jason urged.

Justin smiled. If it hadn't been for Jason, he would have been a poor man after the divorce. But luckily his brother had convinced him to invest some funds in his name and because of that, they weren't included in the divorce settlement.

"At first, I did miss her even though we had been separated for a year before the divorce. But it was the best thing for both of us." Justin didn't want to admit that he'd been thinking about her earlier. He reasoned that he was getting over her, though. More and more, Randa was beginning to take over his thoughts.

Jason paused before speaking. "Lisa came to my office the other day. She wanted to know where you had moved. I didn't tell her, but that won't stop her for long. Don't forget what she did to you. Remember the bad times as well as the good."

"Always," he replied. Justin knew what Jason was implying. Jason had saved him from a lifetime of debt and helped him get the job in Texas. "I'll be careful."

After hanging up with his brother, Justin began to think of more ways to enjoy his weekends. All too soon, his time would be filled with new clients and ad campaigns.

* * *

After Randa made a stop at the vet's office and the pet store, she finally returned home. She busied herself unpacking more boxes and hanging pictures as she tried to choose a name for her pet. Finally, she decided on Zack, an abbreviation of her deceased father's name. She patted the puppy on the head, telling him his new name as he ate his meal.

Much later, she fixed the dog a pallet for the night. She'd bought him a doggy bed, but it was still encased in plastic and she didn't feel like putting it together. "I guess I had better take you out for a walk, huh?" she asked, remembering that he'd been holding his bladder for several hours.

She giggled as Zack looked at her, his puppy-dog eyes pleading with her to go ASAP. She went to her room and changed into shorts and a T-shirt. After locating the leash, they headed for the park.

Obviously, Zack was so happy to be free. He started running as soon as Randa unleashed him. She chased him for a while and then decided that he would return when he was tired. Walking at a slower pace, she relaxed and enjoyed the view.

Randa sat down in front of a tree and watched a family. The man played catch with his son as the woman and daughter prepared the food. They looked so happy, Randa thought. She wished she had the last sixteen years to do over. Her prime dating years had been spent behind a desk or in a meeting room.

She sighed as she rose from her spot and glanced around the park for Zack. Soon he was by her side, panting very hard. "Well, I see you had your first lap of doggie freedom!" she said, quickly attaching his leash before he started on a second lap. "I hope this won't happen again." She bent down to rub his fur.

Zack looked at her, begging for forgiveness. If she didn't have children, Zack would be the next best thing, she decided. Randa smiled and gave him another rub.

Justin watched Randa on Monday morning, determined to make sure she knew her place in the next meeting. He was fully aware that he was being childish, but he couldn't allow her to upstage him once again. He smiled in insecure satisfaction as she sat quietly in her chair and listened to him, Darius, and Curry toss around ideas about the campaign. He listened in surprise when she began to speak without being addressed.

"Yes, Randa, what is it?" Justin asked, clearing his voice of all signs of annoyance. It was becoming more obvious to him that she was Curry and Darius's golden child, and he didn't want them to think they weren't getting along.

"Well, since it's summer, why not start with radio ads first? Most people are in their cars during the summer, and they listen to the radio at least occasionally. I would also think about billboards, too."

Darius smiled. "That sounds very promising. How do radio spots run? We haven't used that medium in a while."

"Well, it depends on how heavy we want to advertise," Randa explained. "I would suggest mornings to get the commuters, the afternoons to get the kids, and maybe even early evenings to get the people that are too busy to cook."

"Great, Randa. You and Justin can work on that part, while Curry and I work on some ideas for TV commercials."

Randa smiled and watched as Justin took detailed notes. She leaned toward him and smugly whispered, "I have all this on tape, Justin." She could tell by the look on his face that he was angry with her, but she wasn't going to play the silent, docile role just to keep from bruising his male ego.

Defiantly, Justin kept writing. He had to keep his fingers moving. If he didn't, he might have found his hands around her throat. His assistant had just upstaged him. Again!

After a second week of working late, trying to pull the details of the radio project together, Justin was at wit's end. Randa annoyed him like no one ever had, but still he couldn't stop himself from noticing everything about her as if he were seeing her for the first time. The perfume she wore drove him mad. Then when she put her shoulder-length hair up in a ponytail after hours, he saw she had a pretty, elegant neck. The most endearing, albeit insane, thing about her was the way she called her puppy when she was going to be late. Justin sometimes wondered if he should have the name of the nearest psychiatric hospital on hand, just in case.

He smiled as he listened to Randa's phone conversation with her answering machine.

"Zack, it's Mommy," she whispered into the phone. "I'll be late, honey. Don't pee on the couch."

Randa smiled as she hung up the phone. Sensing Justin's presence, she turned around with a smile on her face. This man was a pain in her ass, but she was determined to kill him with kindness.

Justin's heart began to throb, along with another part of his body, as she looked up at him. In all his days, he had never seen eyes so beautiful.

"Yes, Justin?" she asked, tired of waiting for him to speak.

"Are you hungry? I was thinking we might order pizza. My treat," he added.

"I should really be getting home. I can only imagine how many times Zack has peed on the furniture."

He loved the way Randa just said whatever was on her mind without a buffer. Justin had become too accustomed to a woman who didn't say what she was thinking during his marriage.

"What's a little while longer? Besides, you've already checked in with him," Justin teased her. "Come on, we could have some food and talk about the campaign results." He wanted to get to know his assistant and was tired of everyone else interacting with her more than he did.

"All right. What kind of pizza? I'm kind of picky about food."

Justin laughed. "How can a woman who puts half a bag of sugar in a glass of tea be choosy about food?"

Randa watched him as he poked fun at her and was pleased that he'd remembered that detail. "I can," she asserted. "Years of being single have allowed me to do what I like." She paused to arch an eyebrow at him. "I only like pepperoni. Thick crust."

Justin could tell she was used to having things her way. "Okay, Randa. Since you have done such a great job on the campaign, I'll order what you want." Justin picked up the phone and dialed the local pizza delivery service. After he placed the phone back in its cradle, he faced her. "It should be about thirty minutes."

They stared at each other in awkward silence. Justin had wanted to get to know her, but now he didn't know what to say.

Randa spoke first. "So tell me, Justin, how long were you married?"

"Fifteen years," he said, copping a seat on the

edge of her desk. He tried to keep the regret out of his voice, but as usual he couldn't stop it.

"If it's too painful to talk about, you don't have to answer," she consoled. "I didn't mean to bring back bad memories."

He sighed thoughtfully. "No, you didn't. Actually, I've been thinking about Lisa lately. That's my ex. I miss her sometimes."

"Why did you divorce her, then?" she blurted. She gasped and placed her hand over her mouth, knowing she had crossed the line.

"My, you are direct with other people's lives, aren't you?" He found the honesty of her thoughts and feelings refreshing, not offensive.

"No, it just seemed your mood changed when you mentioned her. Sounds like you still love her."

"Well, I really didn't want to divorce her, but she was bleeding me dry." He tried not to think of all the money he had lost.

"Ever heard of a budget? A financial advisor, perhaps? Separate accounts?" She looked at him as if he had just condemned the entire female species. "You could always have said, 'No, we can't afford it.'"

"You didn't know Lisa. If I said no, that only made her want something more. She was competitive with her friends. If they got something, she had to get something better."

"But, if you couldn't afford it—" Randa began, pausing midsentence. "I'm sorry, that's really none of my business."

"Well, it does help me to talk about it. You can't imagine how hard it is to say no to a spouse."

"I have been married before," she corrected, slightly irritated that he'd made that assumption.

"But you're Ms. Stone," he insisted, accenting her title.

"I know. I resumed using my maiden name after my divorce."

Justin was intrigued. Could they share battle stories? "How long were you married?"

"About two years, twelve years ago. He was a client, and we hit it off."

"Why did you divorce? If he was a client, he must have been loaded." Justin picked up a pen from her desk and began to twirl it in his fingers.

"Not every woman marries for a meal ticket, Justin. Besides, I have my own money."

"True," he amended. "So why the trip to divorce court?" Justin's gaze went to the door. The security guard had arrived with their pizza. After he reimbursed the guard, the woman left.

Justin went to the nearby kitchen and gathered drinks, plates, and napkins before he pulled up a chair to Randa's desk and took a seat. "You were saying?" he reminded her as he opened the pizza box. Randa Stone appeared to be full of surprises.

"He wanted a stay-at-home wife. You know, one of those minivan-driving, soccer-watching, tennis-playing women that drink martinis in the afternoon while the nanny raises the kids. In the beginning, he said it didn't matter, but it did. I guess he was competitive, too. Out of his circle of friends, I was the only wife who worked outside the home."

"My wife would have loved that," Justin chimed in with a chuckle. "She was always complaining that I should make more money so she could stay at home. What made you divorce?" Justin asked as he took a sip of canned iced tea.

"What made *you* divorce?" Randa countered. She picked up a slice of pizza.

Justin couldn't answer. He watched Randa play with the melted cheese as she twirled it around her tongue, then held a large slice in the air before taking a bite.

If the sounds coming from her mouth were any indication, the pizza was good. Those noises, however, were beginning to awaken something in him. Finally, he noticed she was staring at him, waiting for an answer. He cleared his throat and said, "Sorry. When I discovered how much we owed."

"How did you find out?"

"When I went to gather our bills for the financial advisor a few years ago. My brother had been trying to warn me for years about her spending habits, but I would never believe him. Finally, the light clicked on. When I confronted her, she said it was my fault." Justin shrugged, like it was no longer a big deal, but he could still see Lisa's face as she blamed him.

"Gareth and I divorced because he was having an affair," Randa admitted. "I caught them in bed together in my king-size bed." She picked up a second slice.

Infidelity is one thing, but to have the nerve to bring another woman into his wife's bed is intolerable, Justin thought. "I'm sorry, Randa," he said sincerely. "That had to have been shattering to see your husband in bed with another woman." He could only imagine her hurt.

"I never said it was a woman." Randa had a little smirk on her lips.

"Oh my God!" Justin exclaimed, unable to contain his surprise.

"Yes, in my bed. He was a blond Adonis."

"No way." Justin didn't think he could handle any more surprises.

"Well he was blond, too. They made a nice couple. They still do."

"You were married to a white man? Please tell me you're kidding!"

"What's the big deal? Curry's married to Darbi. Does it make me less black now?"

"Of course not, but—"

"Gareth is a nice man. He just lived two lives. On the one hand, he wanted a wife and kids, on the other, he was gay. When he finally came out of the closet, he was much happier. We're still good friends. I'm even friends with Josh, his life partner. Gareth still sends me flowers on my birthday and every Valentine's Day."

Justin was stunned at Randa's easy acceptance of the facts. "Lisa didn't want children. They would have deterred her shopping," he quipped. "I don't regret divorcing her; I really regret that I had to sell everything I owned to get out of debt. I bet you made a good settlement on him."

Randa smiled. Why was Justin *always* thinking of money? "No, we had an amicable split. I didn't need or want his money."

Justin nodded. "Lisa tried her best to play the poor-wife routine. She even started crying in court," he recalled. "Luckily, the judge saw through it."

"Must have been a man."

"No, it was a woman," Justin said thoughtfully. "She even gave Lisa a lecture on being independent."

They both laughed uncontrollably.

An hour later, Randa stopped by Justin's office to let her know she was leaving. "Goodnight, Justin. Tonight was fun." Randa gathered her things and headed for the elevator.

Justin caught up with her just as the doors opened. "I'll ride down with you." He gazed at her, wondering if she was feeling the same way about him that he was beginning to feel about her.

"Tonight was a nice departure from my usual routine of watching Blockbuster movies."

He kept his distance in the elevator once he noticed the mace can on her key ring. Randa shifted to the opposite corner.

"I just can't imagine you renting movies all by yourself. You know, I'm horrible about returning movies on time. I just started buying them when they came out," she rambled.

"Lisa was like that." Instantly, he regretted saying her name in front of Randa again. He didn't want her to think he was still hung up on his wife, even though he'd admitted as much over dinner. Why did he keep saying things he didn't mean to say?

Randa stepped closer to him, and Justin tensed up. The smell of her perfume drifted up his nostrils.

"I'm sorry, Justin. Your ex-wife sounds like an awful woman." She rubbed his arm in a comforting manner.

"Randa, it's okay that I have memories of her. We were married a lot longer than you and Gareth. When I start crying in my beer, shoot me," he said, not wanting her pity.

She winked at him. "With pleasure."

Randa felt a movement on her bed through her sleep-induced haze. She heard a bark and realized it was Zack demanding her attention.

"Okay, honey, just thirty minutes more," she whined, closing her eyes and turning over. Zack watched as Randa shifted to a new position and got comfortable. He barked again, indicating he was ready to go out. "Okay, pooch. I'm awake." She sat up and looked for her robe. "I'll take a shower and meet you at the front door."

She stood and wrapped her robe around her body and walked to the bathroom. Justin had certainly surprised her last night, she thought as she turned on the shower. Randa wouldn't have expected him to let a woman send him to the poorhouse. Maybe that was why he was so angry and distant all the time. He thought all women were looking for a meal ticket and was afraid of being used.

When Randa appeared downstairs, dressed in a T-shirt, shorts, and tennis shoes, Zack was waiting for her. After she put her hair up in a ponytail, they were on their way to the park. Once they got there, she unleashed Zack and let him run free.

Usually when they came to the park, Zack would run for thirty minutes, do his business, and return, but when he hadn't returned after an hour, Randa began to get a little nervous. *He's still just a puppy,* she thought, trying not to panic. He couldn't really defend himself against the larger dogs. She began to run through the park, looking for her canine friend. Finally, she spotted him playing with a group of children. "What were kids doing at the park at this hour of the morning?" she muttered. When she called his name, his little ears perked up. He ran full speed toward her, and to Randa's horror, so did the children.

After answering a ton of questions about the puppy, she and Zack finally made their getaway. At home, Zack ran directly to his bowl and began gulping water. Randa ate breakfast and decided to go back to bed. This would be the last Saturday she would be able to lounge around, since she would start volunteering at the shelter next week.

The phone rang as she entered the bedroom.

"I hear you and Justin had to work late last night," Beatrice said in lieu of good morning. "Darius is worried that Justin is forcing you to work long hours."

"No, actually we finished kind of early. We actually had a real conversation. We talked about exes, of all things."

"You told him about Gareth? You hardly ever talk about him to strangers."

"Yes. He was quite shocked. You should have seen the look on his face when he found out that Gareth is white. I didn't tell him everything, just that we're divorced and he was gay."

"Well, Darius will be relieved. You know, he told me you remind him of his sister before she and Curry started dating. He may be a little overprotective of you since he knows what you went through at Fuentes."

"I thought so. He told me if Justin got out of line while we were working late to let him know."

"So what was Justin's ex like?" Bea asked, dying to know.

"She sounded horrible, like a siddity, material girl. But you know how men always try to make it sound like it is the woman's fault. I'm sure she was like that when he met her."

FOUR

Joe's Pizza sales had increased by twenty percent shortly after the new ad campaigns started. Darius praised both Justin and Randa's efforts at the weekly meeting. "Jose is very pleased," he said. "He's impressed with the radio ads and would like the print ads to reflect the same light-hearted comedy. Did the stations come up with that, or was it an outside company?"

"No, it was Randa." Justin nodded to his assistant as she sat next to him. Slowly, he was getting over his insecurities about his performance at work and was learning to accept both that Randa was brilliant and that there was nothing he could do to change that. "She wrote the scripts reflecting the different demographics for each station. You know, hip-hop, alternative, and classical."

Darius smiled. "Excellent job, Randa. Do you think you could do that printwise? We want to start at the local level, then gradually work our way up to some of the trade papers."

Randa nodded at Darius. Her mind had already been heading in that direction. "Labor Day is approaching. Isn't there some arts festival in Arlington?"

"Yes, it's the weekend before Labor Day. My wife has talked of nothing else," Curry commented.

"I was thinking Jose could have a booth at the festival and sell pizzas," Randa offered. "Maybe print the menus and the Dallas-Fort Worth locations on the box."

"That sounds good, Randa," Darius complimented. "You've really been using your brain on this. I'll run these by Jose this weekend. I'm having lunch with him Sunday to give him an update. Oh, and Randa, he wanted me to tell you how happy he is with your idea." Darius placed an envelope in front of her. "It's from Jose, personally."

"Thank you, Darius." She didn't know how this would bode with Justin. He'd probably think she was trying to outshine him or something. "Justin has helped me a lot with the implementation of the ideas," Randa told her boss's boss.

"I appreciate *everyone's* efforts," Darius amended.

After lunch with Beatrice, Randa returned to her desk and noticed a note from Justin. When she opened the note, she swore under her breath. "I knew it!" she blurted. She had to work late to get a storyboard ready for next week's presentation. Randa had taken a job as an assistant to get more free time, but it looked like she was working the same number of hours and getting half the pay. Sighing, Randa crumbled up the paper and threw it in the wastebasket. She had planned to look for a new dress for the opening of Jose's restaurant after work instead. The envelope Darius had given her contained an invite asking her to be Jose's escort for the evening.

Later, Randa rushed back from dinner and into the conference room, hoping to beat Justin there. He was already sitting at the large table, with his jacket hanging on the back of a chair, when she walked in. His tie was carelessly thrown on another chair. As he was hunkered over a large board, she admired the width of his shoulders. He had a good, strong back, which probably meant he had a good, strong chest, she rationalized. She placed her purse and packages on the table.

"Have you been waiting long, Justin?"

Justin turned around with an angry scowl on his face. "No, I had an idea and wanted to work it out before *you* got here."

"Sorry I'm a few minutes late. I had to run out and buy an outfit for tomorrow," she explained as she took off her jacket. She knew by Justin's foul mood that it was going to be a long night.

Justin turned and faced her again, his expression grim and his voice harsh. "I noticed you shop a lot. Lisa loved to shop. She would always come home with five or six bags filled to the top with clothes."

Randa silently counted to ten before responding. She was appalled that he would compare her to his ex. "For your information, Justin Brewster, I have investments, mutual funds, and bonds. The reason I took this job was for more free time, not the income."

"I'm sorry, Randa. I just thought—"

"I know exactly what you thought. I'm not your ex," she said firmly. "I had to get something special to wear since I am Jose's date for the party."

"You're Jose's date?" Justin shouted at her.

Randa didn't know why he was yelling. "Yes, his wife is in Spain, visiting relatives. I'm just going to introduce him around to other people in the firm, that's all." Randa took a deep breath. "You know what? This work night is over. I can finish my part of the project from home." Randa grabbed her things and left the conference room with Justin at her heels.

"Randa, wait. I'll walk you downstairs," he yelled after her.

"Oh, no. I don't want you doing anything for me. You'll say it was my fault you didn't get any work done. I'm not that opportunist that you foolishly married." She chastised herself for letting him get under her skin. "Good night!"

She grabbed her bags and her purse and walked down the hall.

As Randa exited the elevator for the parking garage, she realized she had left her mace upstairs. Any other time, she would have gone back to get it, but it was only just after seven and she didn't want to risk another confrontation with Justin. Surely, no one would be out there.

As she took short, angry strides to her car, she thought she heard the sounds of steps behind her. She assumed it was Justin following her and walked faster. She noticed his Ford Explorer was parked a few spaces from her car. The steps behind her sped up, and she added more speed to her walk as well.

When she felt him behind her, she immediately tensed. "What is it now, Justin? Am I walking too slowly? Maybe your ex walked a different way."

"Give me your keys and your money, lady," a deep, raspy voice demanded.

She turned around, expecting to see Justin's stoic face, but she was quite surprised. Randa stared at a masked man as his eyes pierced through her. "Keys? You must be crazy." She turned around to run. "I'm not giving you my keys."

He grabbed her and pressed a gun against her temple. She jumped at the feel of the cold metal against her skin. He spoke slowly and carefully. "Give me your damn money and your keys now!" He put his finger on the trigger and squeezed.

Randa exhaled when she heard the click of an empty barrel. She tried to think of a way to get out of the situation. She could kick him in the groin, but would she be able to get help in time? The car-jacker's voice alerted her, making her blood chill as he pressed his body against hers. The faint smell of burnt rubber filled her nostrils.

"The next chamber isn't empty—"

"Randa!" Justin's voice roared through the parking lot.

Startled, the thief ran, and Randa fell to the concrete.

The next thing she felt was a large hand gently tapping her face. She tried to swat it away, but the tapping continued.

"Randa, are you all right? Did he hurt you?" Justin placed his hands on each of her cheeks.

Slowly, Randa opened her eyes and screamed. Realizing it was Justin who held her, she stopped and hugged him before bursting into tears. He comforted her as much as his stiff movements would allow.

"It's okay. Did he hurt you?" Justin was furious with himself for not insisting to Randa that he follow her to her car. He took out his cell phone from his pocket and called the police, then continued to hold her as she cried uncontrollably. "The police should be here any second. Are you okay?"

Randa didn't answer; she hung on to Justin for dear life. The more she cried, the tighter she clung to him. "Randa, did he hurt you?" Justin asked through clenched teeth. The thought of anyone laying a hand on her infuriated him.

Finally, she spoke in a broken whisper. "He was going to kill me! He was going to take my car!"

"Shh!" Justin comforted her by rubbing her back. "He's gone now. It's okay." He held and rocked her until she calmed down, but he didn't release his hold on her. As they heard sounds of the sirens and saw blinding red and blue lights, Justin exhaled. "Good, the police are here," he noted. "It'll be fine, Randa."

After Randa gave the police a detailed description of the attacker, she watched the officers get into their squad car and leave. Randa and Justin exchanged glances. Knowing that Justin probably wanted to leave as much as she did, Randa started for her car, but her weak, rubbery legs wouldn't carry her to it. Justin slipped an arm around her waist to steady her.

"Why don't I drive you home?" he offered.

"How will I get my car?" The tears Randa tried to hold back fell at their own leisure.

"You can have it towed to your house," Justin said, guiding her to his truck. "Or I can pick you up tomorrow when you're feeling better and you can get it then."

Randa stopped walking. She felt bad that she had been so mean to Justin earlier, and now he was going out of his way to make sure she was alright.

"What is it?" Justin asked, tightening his grip on her narrow waist.

She took a deep breath. "Nothing, I was just thinking how right you are."

Justin placed Randa in the passenger seat of his truck, then went back to retrieve her packages. After he buckled her in and closed the door, they left the parking garage.

As he exited onto Commerce Street, he realized he didn't know the way to her home. "Randa, where do you live?" he asked.

She mumbled something incoherent and fumbled

through her purse, finally handing him her driver's license.

Justin looked at the plastic card. "I don't have a city map in the truck, Randa," he said softly.

She took the license out of his hand, turned it over, and returned it to him. "I've never been good at directions. When I first started, I got lost a lot."

Directions from her house to work were typed neatly on the back. *Very Randa, very anal*, Justin thought as he made his way to her home.

As he drove, Justin contemplated what he was supposed to do once he got to Randa's house. Would she be afraid to be alone? Would she even want him to stay? At best their relationship could be described as civil.

Justin helped Randa into her house and had to contend with Zack. The dog constantly jumped and barked as he settled her on the couch. Justin had figured he'd stay until Randa was calm and then he'd leave, but after an hour, she still hadn't spoken a word and continued to tremble in his arms.

Finally he said, "Randa, it's late. I'd better go."

She nodded, but didn't release his hand from her iron grip. "Please stay. I don't want to be alone right now," she pleaded.

Something in her soft voice made Justin forget his determination to leave. He kissed Randa's forehead and smothered kisses in her long hair. She snuggled into him again and he put his arm around her, enjoying the feel of her against him. He held her close for several more minutes until she announced that she was ready for bed.

Justin stopped her as she headed upstairs. "Randa, I'll stay. But I'll sleep on the couch. I'm not going to take advantage of you."

"I'm not offering sex, Justin. I just need company."

She focused those hazel eyes on him, and he knew he was a goner. "Please stay until I fall asleep." She turned again and headed upstairs, and he reluctantly followed.

"I have pajamas that should fit you in the closet," she told him when he entered the bedroom. "You don't have to get under the covers either."

She walked to the bathroom and closed the door.

With a sigh, Justin changed into the pajamas, knowing what they were doing was a disaster waiting to happen. He was her boss and there was no reason for him to be in her bedroom, much less her bed. Tying the drawstring on the pants, he wondered whose silk pajamas he was wearing. He heard the bathroom door opening and stretched out on top of the covers, watching as Randa walked out in a long nightshirt that reached her knees.

"I could ask," he said, indicating the pajamas he wore.

"You could. But you might not like the answer," she countered. She eased under the covers and turned away from him. "They were for my brother. I bought them for Christmas, but I saw something else I wanted him to have instead, so I kept them," she said, flipping over to face him. "Thank you for staying, Justin."

Justin nodded. "Do you need to take something to sleep or relax?" He remembered Lisa kept tranquilizers by the bed.

Randa snuggled under the covers. "No, just talk to me until I fall asleep."

"What could I possibly talk to you about?" He looked over and saw her hair fanned out across the silk pillow, giving her a soft, sexy, and very vulnerable look.

"Your family, hobbies, job, something. I just can't handle the quiet."

Justin watched as giant tears filled her eyes. He wanted to wipe them away, take her into his arms, and whisper that everything would be alright. He loved the way Randa could change from fiery and determined to sweet and demure.

"All right," he said, launching into a series of stories about the changes in his life since he had moved to Arlington. He finished his story with, "I'm glad I moved here, and believe it or not, I'm beginning to think of you as a friend." He couldn't believe he had just confessed his feelings to Randa and looked over to see her reaction.

He saw she had fallen asleep. Justin smiled as he lay down on the pillow next to her, noticing how relaxed her smooth, beautiful features were as she slept. He thought she looked nice without makeup and wondered why she wore so much of it at work. He leaned closer to her, knowing touching those lips with his would cost him. He kissed her anyway.

FIVE

Justin, just go to sleep, he told himself. He closed his eyes but found sleep wouldn't come. He knew it was a mistake to climb under the covers with Miranda Stone, but he'd done it anyway. Now her body was snuggled tightly against his. As soon as she'd grabbed him, his eyes had snapped wide open as the lower part of his body became fully awake. He held his breath as Randa's slender fingers traveled under his pajama top and pulled him closer.

Justin wanted to stop her roaming hands, but he couldn't. They felt too good. He hadn't been in bed with a woman since his divorce, and his ex-wife was never as amorous as Randa was in bed. Randa threw a bare leg over his and his mind traveled back to the present at a thundering speed. He would have to wake her, or tomorrow they would both be sorry.

"Randa," Justin spoke softly, shaking her gently. "Randa, wake up."

She moaned and withdrew her hand, but left her leg in place. Justin had finally relaxed when, five minutes later, she turned away from him. *Good thing tomorrow is Saturday*, he mused. At least he could sleep all day without any distractions.

By some miracle, Justin finally fell asleep but was stirred awake by a movement on the bed. Reluctantly, he opened his eyes and found himself face to face with Zack. The pooch sniffed at him, then at Randa. Satisfied with his investigation, the dog exited the room.

Sensuous sounds from Randa's side of the bed alerted Justin to her presence. She turned and snuggled closer to him, and he wrapped his arms around her. Realizing he was touching Randa in an intimate fashion, Justin stopped immediately. He didn't want her to accuse him of taking advantage of her in her vulnerable state. He tried to scoot away from her, but she only snuggled closer. Too tired to fight a losing battle, he let her use his body as a pillow.

When he thought she was finally comfortable against him and couldn't move any closer, she did. He didn't know if he had enough resolve to untangle her limbs from his, but he had to if he wanted his erection to go down. He moved her leg, which was now between his legs, then pushed her upper body off him. As he turned her over to face the other direction, she let out an ear-piercing yell.

"Please, don't hurt me!" she begged.

"Randa, it's okay," Justin said, taking her into his arms to comfort her. "No one will hurt you as long as I'm here. You're safe with me." He gently rubbed her back as he spoke.

Suddenly, she wrapped him in an embrace that would have tested the best of men, pressing her full bosom against his chest. The only thing separating Justin from paradise was a layer of silk.

He couldn't fight both his erection and Randa at the same time and tried to put some space between them. Defeat lingered in the room. When he didn't think the situation could get any worse, Randa kissed him. It was a small kiss, but a kiss just the same.

"Justin, don't let him get me!" Randa yelled, grabbing him closer to her. He put his head back on the pillow and prayed for strength. Randa's nightshirt had twisted around her body and now revealed her thong underwear and a flat stomach. He closed his eyes again and fought against the wishes of the lower part of his body, but those red thong panties invaded his thoughts. He gritted his teeth and began to count.

Randa's hand worked its way to his chest and began to unbutton his pajama top. Justin grabbed her hand to stop her. He was about to voice his objection to what was taking place when he realized Randa's mouth was centimeters from his lips. He'd been so busy concentrating on her breasts pushing against his chest that he hadn't noticed she was so close.

He'd used more willpower than any other man would have, and he could no longer hold out. Justin gave into the urge to kiss Randa's full lips, and to his surprise, she kissed him back. Slowly, his hands slid into her hair as she eased herself on top of him. She parted her lips and naturally, he slipped his tongue inside her mouth. His lower body had taken over. Only when she moaned did Justin realize what he was doing. His assistant was scared and hurting, and there he was, taking advantage of her.

Justin immediately broke the kiss and pulled his face as far away from hers as possible. He wanted Randa, but he didn't want her to regret her actions in the morning. "I'm sorry, Randa," he said sincerely. "I lost control."

Randa sat up, straddling him and staring him in the eyes as she caught her breath. "Justin, I need you. I want the contact." She leaned down to kiss him and rotated her hips against the bulge in his pants as she did.

She began to unbutton his top once again and this time he did not stop her. When she'd removed his shirt, Justin pulled her to him and pleasured her with a deep kiss that left her wanting. When his hands moved to her bottom, Randa sat upright and began to pull her nightshirt over her head. Justin rose to help her and enjoyed the creamy feel of Randa's soft honey-toned skin beneath his fingers.

Randa gently pushed him back when she was clad in only her panties and allowed him to admire her. He stared at her beautiful body for several long seconds before he reached out to touch her. It had been too long since he had enjoyed physical intimacy with a woman, and he eagerly anticipated giving Randa all the pleasure and comfort she desired. He would worry about the repercussions on Saturday morning.

"Randa, do you have any condoms?" he asked.

He watched the smooth contours of her backside as she reached over him and opened a drawer in her nightstand. With the foil packet in hand, she smiled weakly and said, "If you don't want to have sex, I understand." She climbed off of Justin and lay on her back beside him, waiting for his answer.

Justin got out of the bed and took off his pajama bottoms before sliding next to her again. She tore the packet open and pulled back the covers to reveal Justin's body in all its glory. Every muscle of his perfect physique was swollen in anticipation of the act they were about to share.

Without further hesitation, he drew her into his arms and kissed her, savoring her full C cup breasts and neck. He left a trail of hot kisses, beginning at her earlobe and stopping somewhere in the nether regions of her stomach. Randa moaned his name and blissfully writhed her body under his. He peeled the thong panties from her slender frame with a smile on his face as he threw them on the floor.

Easing himself back on top of her, he gazed at how

beautiful she looked, basking in the dim moonlight that stole into the room. He leaned down and kissed her, softly at first, then much harder as passion consumed him. Weeks of being turned on by those short skirts had taken their toll. His tongue played with hers as his hands roamed her body, giving pleasure to each place he touched.

When he knew she was ready to receive him, he entered her body, watching her face for a reaction. His kisses became more intense as he surged further inside her body. She wrapped her legs around him, driving him deeper. He loved her passionately until her body began to quiver. When she moaned against his mouth, igniting him further, Justin slowly eased down her neck, leaving kisses along her chin. "Are you okay?" he asked as he nuzzled against her.

Randa nodded as he kissed her mouth again, arching her back as he pushed against her one last time. Together they fell over the edge of their orgasms, leaving gasps of pleasure to fill the air.

Saturday morning, Randa woke up alone, but the rumpled sheets, the other pillow on the floor, and the fact that she was tired and sore indicated Justin had been in her bedroom. She was happy to know that she had not merely dreamed her fantasy.

She wondered why Justin had left without leaving so much as a note. *He's still Justin, the cold, sad man I encounter every day at work,* she reminded herself. Did she actually think he was going to walk into the room with a breakfast tray? Randa shook those thoughts from her head as she got up to take a shower.

After she dressed and fed Zack, they headed for the park. As she watched him run and torment the children, she took out her cell phone and called Beatrice. She needed some advice about the previous night.

"Well," Beatrice said when Randa told her what had taken place, "I'm shocked, but I'm glad you got some. Even if it was from Justin," she added as an afterthought. "I can understand you not wanting to be alone last night. What did he say this morning? I can just imagine his stiff face over breakfast."

"That's just it, Bea. He was gone when I woke this morning. I'm sure he thought I threw myself at him last night," she said with regret.

"Well, you did, Randa. I still can't believe he left, though."

"I bet he's thinking that I'm going to file sexual harassment charges or something," Randa said, looking around for Zack.

"I say if he does think something that stupid, he deserves to be divorced. You guys are both adults. He could have said no or gone home if he didn't want to have sex. Don't worry, Randa. Besides, it's been ages since you slept with a man," Beatrice added in her motherly tone. "I'll see you tonight. I bet he won't be there."

"Oh my gosh!" Randa slapped her hand to her forehead as Beatrice ended the call. "I forgot all about the opening."

Randa sighed as she turned off her phone. Zack soon joined her. "Well, there you are. You didn't bite anyone, did you?" She leaned down and attached the leash to her hyperactive dog. Zack's bark was his answer.

"Okay, sorry. Let's go home." Randa was glad the park was within walking distance of her house. As she led Zack back to their house, she told him of the plans for the evening. "Well, Zack, you'll be on your own tonight. Mommy has to go to an opening. No women in the house while I'm gone. I can only deal with one dog at a time."

The opening of Jose's newest venture, The Sea Shell, was very elegant. Randa arrived at the seafood restaurant in a limo, courtesy of Jose. Although the wrecker service returned her car that morning, she wasn't quite ready to sit behind the wheel. Once Jose heard about her unfortunate encounter, he insisted she be picked up anyway.

Now, she was seated at a table, chatting with Beatrice.

"Randa, you look lovely. You can pick out all my clothes from now on," Beatrice beamed.

Randa's slender hand glided gently over her form-fitting dress. The sleeveless lilac formal gown tailored her body perfectly. "This dress makes me feel 25 again. I'm glad I splurged on it."

Beatrice laughed. "By the way, I told Darius about the attempted carjacking."

"Why Bea? That's all I need."

"After you called this morning, he called. He had been trying to contact Justin Friday night. He asked me for Justin's home number, since he knows I keep everyone's contact information for emergencies. I had to explain why you guys weren't at the office and the reason Justin had to drive you home. Darius is sweet, but when he's protective of you, watch out!"

A horrible thought entered Randa's mind. "You didn't tell him that Justin and I—" She couldn't bring herself to say the words. Randa thought she could just dismiss sex with Justin as just another experience, but she was deeply hurt and embarrassed that he'd left without saying good-bye. As usual, Beatrice could read her thoughts.

"That two lonely people reached out to each other in a moment of lust?" Beatrice grinned at Randa's shocked expression. "No, of course not."

As the guests filtered in, Randa's eyes roamed the crowd for Justin. She doubted he'd attend, but she still looked for him.

"Are you looking for me?" Jose asked, taking a seat beside Randa.

"Yes, I was. Jose, this is Beatrice." Randa hurried through the introductions. She smiled as Jose's charming personality dazzled Beatrice.

"You are very beautiful, Señora." He kissed Beatrice's hand before releasing it. "Too beautiful to be alone. Where is your husband?"

Entranced by Jose's charm, Beatrice momentarily forgot she was married. "W-Who?" She looked down at her hand and noticed her wedding ring. "Oh, him. I think he's talking to Darius." Her brown eyes never left Jose's.

"If you were my wife, I would not leave you for one second in fear of someone stealing you away."

Beatrice groaned and smoothed the edge of her graying hair. "Where were you ten years ago?"

Randa whispered into Beatrice's ear. "He's been married over thirty years."

"Damn!" Beatrice sighed and withdrew her hand from Jose's. "Well, it was a short-lived dream, but it was damn good."

Beatrice's husband soon joined the trio, and once again introductions were made before Randa and Jose left the table. As she introduced him to other members of the firm, Jose asked her the dreaded question feared by every single person in the world.

"Why aren't you married? You're too beautiful to be alone," he said, voicing his concern.

"I don't know, Jose. Before it was because of my job, but now I can actually say that I'm going to give the dating game an honest shot."

"That's my girl."

They both watched as Darius approached them. Randa guessed the woman accompanying him had to be his wife. They complemented each other, reminding Randa of those couples that were eternally happy. He looked very handsome, and his wife looked beautiful. Randa also noticed the flashy diamond wedding ring she wore.

"Hello, Darius," Randa said, greeting him.

"Hello, Randa, Jose. This is my wife, Cherish."

The group exchanged further pleasantries and began chatting. Then Randa and Jose continued to make their way around the brightly decorated room. She noticed another familiar face approaching her. *This has got to be the sign of the damned,* she thought. She excused herself from Jose's side and went to greet Gareth. "Hello, Randa." He smiled and his blue eyes twinkled.

"Hi, Gareth, it's nice to see you." She hugged her ex-husband. "Where's Josh?" she asked of his lover.

"He's around here somewhere. You know, playing the dutiful wife," he said, surveying Randa's dress. "You look nice. Very relaxed. You know, like the old days."

Randa watched the man she loved so long ago. He looked like an ad from a fashion magazine. "Oh, I wanted to thank you for the flowers at my mother's funeral and at my new house. I won't even ask how you knew." She winked at him. One thing she could never figure out was how Gareth knew so many things about her life even though they were no longer husband and wife.

"Contacts, baby, contacts. I know every move you make."

"Why?"

Gareth picked up Randa's hand and kissed it. "You helped me come out of the closet. The least I can do is keep track of you."

"Gareth!" she chastised playfully.

"So how do you like your new job?"

"I like it. I'm not as stressed out as I was at F&G. Thank goodness."

"I hear they want you back."

"They shouldn't have fired me in the first place. Why would they want me back?"

"Because they've lost so much of their business."

Randa laughed, remembering back when she and Gareth married. Her former employers had told her she couldn't work on his account any more so Gareth had moved his account to another agency. Now he owned a string of upscale eateries all over the U.S. "I'll never go back to that life again."

Gareth tugged her arm and led her to the bar. "What would you like?"

"Champagne."

"Of course. Still your favorite."

As she spoke with Gareth, Darius approached her. Her ex-husband made his exit, mumbling something about finding his wife.

Darius watched the blond man leave Randa's side. "I hope I didn't interrupt anything. Wasn't that Gareth Cornworthy of Worthy's Eateries?"

"Yes, he's also my ex-husband," Randa said before she realized she had omitted that fact in her interview.

"I heard he was gay," Darius said, coughing at his indiscretion.

"He is. Long story."

Darius coughed again as he changed the subject.

"Randa, Bea told me about last night. I'm really sorry that Justin didn't escort you to your car."

"It's not his fault, Darius. I always walk to my car alone." She knew Justin would blame her for any repercussions he would receive for not walking with her.

"I know. If you ever work late again, make sure someone, either Justin, Curry, or myself, escorts you to your car."

"Yes, Darius."

"Why don't you take Monday off?"

"I'm fine, Darius."

"Take Monday. I've cleared it with Justin. You need some time to recuperate."

"Thank you, Darius." She knew it was pointless to explain to her boss's boss that she was fine.

"Did you drive here? Someone should drive you home."

"No, actually Jose sent a limo for me."

"Good." Darius waved at Jose. "I think he's looking for you."

"Yes, he's probably thinking I deserted him. Excuse me." Randa walked toward Jose only to be stopped again. Someone tapped her on the shoulder. She turned around to find herself face to face with Justin. He didn't wear a smile, and he didn't say hello.

"I'm told you're taking Monday off," he said coolly. He wasn't sure what, if anything, the previous night had meant to Randa, and he didn't want to show his hand just yet. Randa's low-cut dress wasn't making his attempt to look uninterested any easier. Justin tried to train his eyes on her face, but somehow they kept drifting to her cleavage. When he realized she had coughed to get his attention, he continued speaking. "What did you do, run to Darius and tell him I attacked you last night?"

"What? No, Justin." The tender man who had pleasured her last night was gone. Evidently, Justin had morphed back to asshole demeanor. "Monday was Darius's idea. If you have a problem with it, you need to speak with him," she whispered curtly. "He knows only of the attempted carjacking, nothing else."

"Good. Because last night was last night." She hadn't shown any emotion toward him, so he wouldn't express any either. The look on her face told him he had gone too far.

Randa silently counted to ten, then to twenty, then to thirty before she retorted. "Look, Justin. I'm an adult; you're an adult, too, I hope. I don't expect anything to come out of last night. It was good sex and I'm over it." She stalked away from him as fast as she could before her tears began to fall.

SIX

Monday, Justin sulked in his office. He watched as a parade of managers and directors came by his desk, looking for his assistant. Once they realized that Randa wasn't there, they didn't linger. He realized he was behaving like a spoiled brat. He had been a jerk to most of the assistants in his short time at the firm. No wonder no one spoke to him unless absolutely necessary. He had judged each woman with the preconceived notion that they were like his ex, and now they were punishing him for it.

Why couldn't he just let go? He'd all but ruined a potential relationship with the first woman that had made him happy since he'd met Lisa in college twenty years ago. Randa was independent and smart, and she wasn't after his bank account. She didn't even take money from her husband when she divorced him. He smiled as he thought of Randa, still not believing they had made love.

He also couldn't believe how beautiful she looked in that dress at the opening. But instead of telling her how lovely she looked, he'd said the most obnoxious thing that came to his mind. Why couldn't he just ask her if she felt the way he did? The worst she could answer was no. Maybe he couldn't handle the rejection. A knock interrupted his daydreaming, and he saw Darius at his door.

"Hi, Darius, what can I do for you?" Justin sat ramrod straight in his chair.

Darius walked inside, closed the door, and sat in the chair that Randa always used. "I wanted to talk to you about Randa."

Justin could only think one thing: she told. He kept his poker face and waited for Darius to continue.

"If you have to have her work late again, make sure either you or the security guard escorts her to her car," Darius said. "I don't mean see her to the elevator. You should make sure she drives away in the car safely. I don't want a replay of Friday night."

You and me both, Justin thought, *but for different reasons.*

Darius continued. "Do you anticipate any more late nights? I know we've got some big projects coming up. I'd like to see most of them handled within business hours."

"Most can be," Justin said. He wondered what Darius was leading up to. In the short time he had worked at Sloane, he knew Darius didn't go to see anyone. On the rare occasions he did, it was serious. A familiar knot of tension grew in Justin's stomach. It was the same pain he felt during his divorce proceedings. "A few things can't," he amended. "You know, like the Art Festival meeting, it's on a Saturday. Then there's the board meeting about the budget, but she doesn't have to attend that." Why did he feel like Darius was asking his intentions toward Randa?

Darius studied him for so long, Justin became nervous. "Justin, are you and Randa getting along? I mean, I know she used to be the advertising director at F&G, so she's used to doing more than she's doing right now. How are things between you two?"

"Well there have been a few bumps, but we're getting along." Justin played with the gold pen on his desk. "I have given her more duties, and somehow she still finishes early. Plus, she's been helping with the pizza account."

"That's fine. I've looked at her ideas, and she has great insight. I noticed you two arguing at the opening," Darius added. Justin stopped fiddling with the pen, waiting for Darius's final blow. "It doesn't look good when the woman who helped land the pizza account and one of the managers of that same account are fighting like two kids over a toy."

"It was just a misunderstanding, that's all, Darius. Nothing to worry about."

"I hope not, Justin." Darius rose from his chair. "I'll need the updated numbers on Joe's Pizza by Friday," he said, leaving the office.

Justin couldn't believe it. Was Darius warning him that his own job was in jeopardy if Randa wasn't happy? He'd clearly upset her at the party, and he knew working together would be hell now. But he would have to get back on Randa's good side if he wanted to stay employed.

Justin leaned back in his chair, replaying the conversation in his head. He'd answered all of Darius's questions correctly, and he hoped his boss appreciated the effort he was putting forth.

"You look like you could use a break!" Curry stood smiling in Justin's doorway. "Want to grab some lunch?"

Justin almost looked behind him to see if someone else was standing there.

"Justin?"

"Sorry, Curry. I was preoccupied," he lied. "Lunch sounds great."

The men walked across the street to the local diner in silence. Justin wondered why Curry wanted to have lunch with him. He must be in more trouble than he realized.

As they reached the restaurant and got their meal, Justin decided to just relax and began to laugh.

"What's wrong, Justin?" Curry asked, not understanding the outburst.

Justin shook his head. "Nothing, man. I'm just noticing how many women are checking you out. You don't even seem to notice."

Curry smiled as he sliced his roast beef. "I know. Before I was married that would have given me such an ego boost, but now it doesn't do a thing for me."

Justin knew something of Curry's checkered past, but didn't mention it. "Yeah, I remember those early days of marriage," he recalled wistfully.

"I don't know if you know this about me or not, but this is my third."

"Wow, man."

"I know. Darius was less than pleased when Darbi and I first started dating." He took a gulp of his tea. "I think he was harder to convince of my feelings toward Darbi than she was."

Justin liked Curry. He was the poster boy for a happy marriage. He laughed as a woman stopped by the table and put her business card down before walking away. "Man, I know you love your wife, but that's a lot of temptation."

"Not really. My wife is beautiful and I love coming home to her and my son. There are just as many men willing to hit on a married woman. Last week, Darbi came by to have lunch with me and I went to the men's room. I'm walking back to the table and there's a guy sitting in my seat chatting with my wife."

"I would have been kicking some ass!" Justin interjected, taking a bite of his sandwich.

Curry shook his head. "Well it would have been hard, since he was a member of the Dallas Cowboys." He smiled as his cell phone rang. "That's probably her," he said, wiping his hands on a napkin and reaching into his suit pocket for his phone.

Justin listened to the one-sided conversation. He almost felt guilty. But oddly enough, it gave him a microscopic thread of hope that one day he would have that type of connection to someone again.

Curry nodded. "Oh, baby, that's great. If you really want to. I don't mind cooking. Okay. I love you. Bye." He closed his phone and took a deep breath. "I don't know what it is about her, but just talking to her makes my day."

Justin knew that feeling, and he envied it. Suddenly, he couldn't stand the smile on Curry's face or the giddiness in his voice. "You guys are great together. I hope I can find that one day," he blurted, attempting to disguise his envy.

"Personally, I think you have. I noticed you and Randa exchanging some heated words at the dinner Saturday night. Actually, Darbi noticed it. She said it looked like some kind of lovers' quarrel."

So that's what this was all about, Justin mused. "Yeah, we were having a quarrel, not a lovers' one, I'm afraid. We're like oil and water."

Curry grinned at him, silently letting him know that he didn't buy one load of his crap. "Sometimes getting that oil and water to mix is half the fun. Who knows, you might start a little fire?"

"I don't know if I am ready to go up in flames just yet," Justin countered.

* * *

Randa enjoyed her day off. She slept late, watched *Home & Garden Television*, and relaxed by spending time in her new home and reflecting on Friday night. Maybe she should have sent Justin home. *Well, too late now,* she mused, as she sat in front of her computer.

Randa knew it was just a moment of weakness and that she should move on. Evidently, Justin already had. But she couldn't forget how good it felt to be in his arms or to hear him snoring in her ear. Quickly, she shook those lusty thoughts from her mind and resumed shopping on the Internet.

An hour later, the phone rang. Randa walked to the nearest one and answered. She was nothing short of shocked when she recognized the caller. Justin's baritone voice sounded curt as usual. No tenderness. Not even the customary greeting; he just started speaking. "We need to talk. Could I come by after work, say about seven?"

He didn't give her chance to answer before he hung up on her. Randa stared at the phone, then returned it to its cradle. What the hell was wrong with him? He was so bitter over that bitch he was married to that he'd started to hate all women, it seemed.

Justin watched Randa lounge comfortably on the couch. He had refused her offer to take a seat or have a drink. He had to take care of business. It was a simple plan: explain about Friday night, tell her it was more than just sex he wanted from her, and get out of there fast. But somewhere between entering her house and watching her recline in that seductive pose on the sofa, he had lost his nerve.

"Randa, I just wanted to get Friday night straight." He spoke with an attempt at determination, but when he saw the bored look on her face, he couldn't tell her what was growing in his heart. Instead, he said, "I think we were both feeling the effects of the prior events of that night."

She rolled her eyes at him. How many times or different ways was he going to tell her it meant nothing? She sighed heavily. "That's okay, Justin. I take full responsibility for my actions and don't blame you for anything. So don't worry. I won't go running to Darius, playing the victim like your ex would, if that's what you're afraid of."

"I just wanted things between us understood."

"They are." Randa stood to show him to the door. She couldn't believe she'd ever thought there was any potential between them. "If that's all, good night."

Justin let out a tired breath. Again his words had come out twisted. Knowing their working relationship and his job were at risk, he tried to make it better. "Randa, I didn't drive over here to get into an argument about Friday. I just want to set the record straight."

She faced Justin and took a deep breath. "Why are you such a jerk all the time? It's very straight, Justin. As far as I'm concerned, it was a one-time thing and won't happen again." She watched as Zack trotted into the kitchen. "It's Zack's dinnertime, so if there's nothing else, I'll see you in the morning." Randa stared into his eyes as if daring a response from him. "That is, if I am still employed."

"Why wouldn't you be?" he asked. Did she really think he was cruel enough to fire her?

"I just thought—never mind."

Justin watched her as she walked in front of him, escorting him to the front door. He knew if he walked out then, things would never be right between them. The palms of his hands were sweaty and his pulse was racing. If he had more hair, he would've run his fingers through it. He kept thinking about the woman he made love to and the sounds she made, and how good she made him feel inside and out. She still made his blood boil.

"Something smells good," he commented as they reached the door.

"Spaghetti," she offered. "Do you always switch gears like that?" Randa wiped her palms on her sweatpants. "I mean, one minute you're ranting and raving I took advantage of you, the next you're talking about food."

Justin ignored her question. "Spaghetti is my favorite. When I was married, Lisa refused to cook it. She claimed it was peasant food." He hoped she'd invite him to stay.

Her good manners took over. "Well there's plenty if you would like to join Zack and me for dinner."

Justin offered her a genuine smile. "I'd like that."

They enjoyed a peaceful meal of spaghetti, salad, garlic bread, and wine. There were no raised voices and no damning words, just two people having dinner and conversation.

"I didn't realize you're 38," Justin said after Randa revealed her birthdate. He helped himself to another portion of spaghetti and salad. "This is excellent."

"Does my being 38 cause a problem for you? I think my job performance speaks for itself." She was still bitter over his previous statements, and she swallowed her wine in one gulp.

"No, no, Randa. I think you look great. I thought you were in your early thirties. I was just surprised, that's all."

"You weaseled out of that one pretty good." She grinned that glorious smile at him, and it ignited his passion for her. Justin concentrated as she spoke.

"Most men usually think I'm 28 or so."

"Which men?" Justin finished the contents of his second glass of wine in one gulp and poured a third. He didn't like to think of other men being interested in Randa. "I mean, are they strangers or men you know?"

Randa baited him. "Just men," she said vaguely. "Actually, one of Jose's general managers asked me out. I turned him down, of course. He was only twenty-five." She knew Justin was getting riled up and she wanted to see him sweat. Maybe he did care, just a little.

"Was that the blond guy I saw you hugging?"

She looked pensive as she answered. "No, that was Gareth."

Justin choked on his wine. "That was Gareth? He looked like a model. You know, like one of those guys you see on the cover of those romance books, not wearing any clothes."

Randa watched as he put another liberal helping of salad on the plate, then topped it with dressing. He ate like a man who had been starved. "Yes, most people think he's too good-looking to be gay. But he's happy."

"So, who asked you out?" Justin persisted.

"He was from the Atlanta office. Did you see the broad-shouldered black guy? He said he had played college football for TCU."

Justin immediately knew whom she meant. The guy looked like a walking building, and he'd overheard women commenting on his physique. "Why did you turn him down? You won't get many chances like that at your age." Justin smiled as he raised the glass to his lips, daring her to respond.

Randa laughed. "See, Justin. That's what I mean. I start to think you're human, and then you mess it up." She dabbed her mouth with the linen napkin and placed it on the table. What did she ever see in him? "Would you like dessert? I have cheesecake," she said, ignoring his irritation as she walked to the refrigerator.

"That sounds great." Justin watched her with male satisfaction. Randa was probably like most women, he mused. She'd have a sliver, then say she was full. He was amazed when she plopped a huge slice of cheesecake in front of him. He was even more surprised when she placed another huge piece on the table for herself. "Are you sure you can eat that much?" he asked, picking up his fork.

"Yes, I'm sure. I love cheesecake." Randa picked up a spoon and began to eat the whole slice.

When dessert was finished, Randa watched Justin as he prepared to leave. It was past eleven P.M., and he'd consumed the better part of a bottle of wine. "Justin, you can stay here," she offered, seeing the glassy look in his eyes. He turned to face her with an inquisitive look. She stopped him before he said something stupid. "Before you get your motor running, you're sleeping in the spare room." She rose from the table and began walking toward the stairs. "It's down the hall from my room. The first door on your left."

The next morning Randa awoke, stretching her body as Zack hopped on the bed. "Good morning, honey," she said, rubbing his fur. "Did you wake our guest?" She got out of bed, put on her robe, and tiptoed down the hall to the spare room. Justin slept soundly. Not wanting to wake him, she closed the door. "I'll wake him after my shower," she told Zack as he followed her back to her bedroom.

Randa sat at her kitchen table eating breakfast when Justin walked into her kitchen. With neither one being used to company that early, they only muttered good morning to each other.

Quietly, he sat beside her at the table and looked at her. She didn't falter under his gaze.

"Your skin is pretty. Why do you wear the war paint?" he asked.

Randa sliced through the insult and smiled at the compliment. "War paint? I haven't heard that expression in years. You don't like makeup, do you? Fallout from the ex?" Randa smiled at him in pity. "At F&G, they thought women should wear makeup. So I guess it's fallout from my old job. Old habits die hard."

"Why don't you try not wearing makeup some time? I mean, I think you look fine without it."

It was a compliment Justin-style. "Maybe I will," she conceded. Randa continued to sip her coffee as she watched the enigmatic man next to her.

It had been two weeks since their dinner, the last time Justin had seen Randa outside of work. He caught himself watching her all the time—as she worked, as she walked down the hall to the copier, when she talked on the phone. His communication skills seemed to have taken a nosedive. Every time he was ready to ask her to lunch or dinner, he became tongue-tied. He didn't quite know how to start with her.

A commotion in the lobby stopped his daydreaming. He walked to his office door and noticed some of the other assistants circled around Randa's desk. "Ladies, is there a problem?" he asked.

The women scattered as he neared Randa's desk, and then he saw the reason for the commotion. Two dozen red roses sat in an elegant vase on her desk, and a small white envelope with her name etched in calligraphy stared at him from the bouquet. He wondered who sent them and why.

"Justin, what are you doing?" Randa asked as she neared her desk.

Justin stared at her. She was carrying a large bouquet of birthday balloons in her arms. The balloons, however, were not nearly as distracting as the clingy suit she wore. She caught him watching her hips as he scrambled for an answer.

"I-I was admiring your flowers. What's the occasion?"

"My birthday. I'm 39 today." She sat the balloons next to the roses. "The balloons are from my brother, and the roses are from Gareth."

Justin felt awful. Not only had he not acknowledged her birthday, he hadn't noticed the birthday banner on the front of her desk. This was a chance to make up for all his wrongdoings or at least get a good start on a better relationship with Randa, and he'd missed it. "Randa, since it's your birthday, how about I take you to lunch?"

"That's great, we can all go," Beatrice said as she neared the desk. "We were just coming to get Randa."

Justin nodded. He had intended lunch to be the springboard to a new beginning, but that would prove difficult with Beatrice and the other assistants along. He resigned himself to the inevitable. "Lead the way, ladies," he said.

Beatrice observed Justin's expression. "Darius and Curry will join us at the restaurant. Curry's son had to have his shots today, and they both had to go. Curry's a mess whenever his son has to go to the doctor," Beatrice explained.

Justin noticed the other assistants nodding in

agreement. Curry's weakness for his son was known companywide.

Beatrice looked at her watch and nudged him. "Darius called and said they are on the way to the restaurant and that they'd meet us there."

The group headed for the elevator. Counting the other assistants and secretaries, Justin found himself on the elevator with seven women. They chatted the entire way to the restaurant. Lucky for Justin, it was only a block away.

After they were seated, Justin saw Darius and Curry walking toward the table. Relief flooded through his veins. *No more talk about menopause, husbands, and diapers,* he thought. It would be nice to just talk about sports. To Justin's dismay, the conversation never headed in that direction. The subject turned to Curry's infant son, Christian. Justin gave up and listened as the women questioned Curry.

"How's Chris doing?" one asked.

Curry wiped his eyes. "He's doing better than his father. Every time he has to get a shot, I have to leave the room."

Darius laughed at his brother-in-law. "Today was no different. I stayed in the room with Chris while Curry cried like a baby in the waiting room."

The women all laughed and then shared their doctor's office stories. Finally Darius took the reins and moved the conversation back to the birthday woman.

Darius presented Randa with a small box. "It's from Jose," he told her, raising his eyebrows. He also gave her an envelope. "This is from the directors."

Randa opened the small box first. The women shouted when they saw what was inside. She held up the slim gold bracelet for the other assistants to admire. Justin's heart plummeted as she pulled another card from the bottom on the box. *Like Jose had to get another gift,* he fumed.

"It's a membership to the gym," Randa laughed. Then she reached into the box, picked up yet one more item, and laughed boisterously. "This is good for one table dance at Zorro's Pipe Shop." Zorro's was the hottest male strip club in Fort Worth. Randa looked at the women at the table. "Can we go Friday night?"

When they all agreed, Darius and Curry exchanged amused glances and started laughing.

Randa was puzzled at their expressions. "Is it a bad club?"

Darius grinned. "No, last year our wives went there for girls' night, and they had a good time." His eyes met Curry's. "They got plastered and we had to go get them."

"Oh, then we definitely have to go," Beatrice concluded.

SEVEN

Justin sat in the weekly directors' meeting, not hearing anything Darius said. His boss could have told him he was fired, and he would have never known. His mind was on the night ahead.

Randa and some of the women from the office were going to the strip club and that was all they had talked about for the last three days. It was getting the best of him. Justin kept imagining Randa jumping up on stage and grinding with a stripper. When Beatrice produced two bundles of one-dollar bills and Randa did the same, he knew they were going to act like fools. Darius attracted his attention, bringing him back to the meeting.

"Justin, how are Jose's numbers?" he asked.

Justin shuffled the papers before him. Luckily, Randa had made a spreadsheet, so he wouldn't look like a complete idiot. "His same-store sales are up about thirty percent from the same time last year," he answered. "Since we've been doing so well, can't we ease back on doing the TV ads?"

Darius pondered his question. "That's just what I was thinking, Jose wants to hold off, too. He says there is so much junk on TV, he doesn't want to add to it. Great work, Justin."

Justin nodded. *Finally*, he thought, *some recognition*. With that little boost of confidence, he started making more suggestions in the meeting, all of which were met with approval from Darius and the partners.

Justin knew he was doing a good job. Smiling to himself smugly, he got lost in the whirlwind of ideas circling through his mind.

He heard Darius calling his name and answered, "Yes, Darius?"

"Are you planning on staying in the meeting all afternoon?" Darius smiled as he had caught Justin daydreaming. He'd noticed his new employee had been doing that a lot lately.

Justin looked around the room again. As he feared, everyone had gone. He blushed as he spoke. "Sorry, I was just brainstorming. I guess I got distracted."

"Is everything all right?"

"Yes, everything is fine. I was just thinking about the campaign."

Darius nodded and left the room.

Justin watched him make his exit and he reprimanded himself for getting caught daydreaming—by his boss, no less.

Randa smiled as her coworkers waved at her. She started walking toward them, fighting her way through a herd of drunken women. "This is why I quit coming to clubs years ago," she muttered as she weaved her way to the table. Randa arrived to find ten women seated at the table with as many bottles of champagne.

"Hey guys, sorry I'm late. Justin made me stay late, tonight of all nights." She took a seat after giving the waitress her drink order.

Beatrice laughed at her. "Aw, Randa, don't give us

that. You know he didn't want you coming here, anyway. I heard him telling Curry how he thought it was silly for women to go watch naked men dance."

She laughed as Bea grabbed the waiter by his exposed derriere. "Bea, what will James think?" Randa asked of Bea's third husband.

"He loves it when I come home horny."

Randa shook her head and burst into a fit of giggles. "Beatrice! I should be shocked by your frankness, but I've known you too long."

Soon the first dancer came onto the stage, and Randa watched as the reserved assistants and secretaries became wild, loose drunks with the rest of the club. As the spirit of the night hit her, she found herself dancing along. When the assistants chipped in and got her a lap dance, she gave in to the urge to reach inside the man's G-string and put a five-dollar bill inside. She laughed as the women chanted her name.

Saturday morning, Randa woke with a slight hangover. Luckily, she hadn't drunk as much as the other women. As she recounted the night before, she calculated she'd probably had six glasses of champagne. It was a lot easier to drink than Scotch or bourbon, she reasoned, yawning.

After breakfast, she took Zack out for his run and returned home to change. She was supposed to start her volunteer work several weeks ago, but so much had happened that she'd never had a chance. She felt bad for telling the attendant she was reliable and then standing him up.

Randa dressed comfortably in jeans and a T-shirt, and then headed for the shelter. Determined not to adopt any more pets, she got out of the car.

After listening to a quick sermon on the dos and don'ts of volunteering, Randa was led to her station. Her job was to feed and water the cats and to change the litter boxes. She figured she was safe until she walked to the first cage and saw five kittens—three calicos and two tabbies. They meowed as she fed them, and Randa petted each one. "Where's your mother?" she asked the kittens as she changed the litter box.

She moved to the next cage and saw more cute cats. Randa felt her resolve not to adopt one slipping away bit by bit. "I cannot have a dog and a cat," she muttered to herself, moving to the next cage.

After two hours of feeding, watering and cleaning, she had finished her duties, but decided to stay longer to play with the animals.

"Careful. You'll end up with a house full of pets," a male voice warned.

Randa looked up into the face of a very attractive man in his mid-twenties. "I know. I have talked myself out of a kitten already. I already have a dog. I just love animals." She brushed a few strands of loose hair from her face and hoped her ponytail looked presentable.

"Me, too. I had to move to a bigger house to accommodate them all. I have five cats and four dogs."

"My goodness!" she exclaimed.

"I know. Luckily, I'm a vet."

Randa watched the slender man as he spoke of his animals with passion. She could tell he loved his work.

"I'm Dr. Bryan Andrews. I'm the Saturday vet," he said, extending his hand. "I haven't seen you around." His gaze lingered on her face.

She knew he was trying to guess how old she was. "I'm Randa Stone. I adopted my puppy a few months ago, and I just started volunteering today."

She watched his brown eyes on hers and blushed under his gaze.

"That's good. Volunteers are always needed. I'm glad to see you here. If you have any questions, don't hesitate to ask me."

As she digested his statement, she wondered if the doctor was trying to pick her up. No way, she was too old for him, she thought. He looked to be twenty-five, tops. "Thank you, Dr. Andrews. My shift was over an hour ago. I was just visiting with the animals before I left." Randa took off her smock, revealing her "I volunteer and I'm proud of it" T-shirt.

"Please call me Bryan. I was getting ready to leave myself. How about coffee or something?"

Randa's stomach growled. "How about lunch? I'm starving."

"There's a deli about three blocks from here if you'd like to join me."

"I'll follow you in my car," Randa prompted. Animal lover or not, Bryan was still a stranger. She dug into her purse for her keys, making sure he saw her can of mace.

After two hours with Bryan, Randa noticed it was past three in the afternoon. She'd enjoyed his company, but it was time for her to go. "Bryan, it was great talking to you. Zack is going to kill me, though," she explained. Randa stood, grabbed her purse, and prepared to leave.

"Will you be at the shelter next Saturday?" he asked, standing as well.

"Here. Let me give you my number." She scribbled the seven digits on a napkin and handed it to him. "Just leave a message if I don't answer. Zack will enjoy the noise on the machine."

"I'll give you a call this week," Bryan said, folding up the napkin and placing it in his wallet. "Strictly as a friend, of course." He winked at her.

"Of course. Friends." Randa smiled at him as she left the deli. Wasn't there one single, sane man left in his late thirties? Would she have to marry someone nearly fifteen years her junior just to have a decent husband?

After another lonely weekend, Justin sucked up all his apprehensions about telling Randa the truth about his feelings and decided that he needed to talk to her on a more intimate level. He knew they had jumped into bed too fast and that she would think he was just trying to have sex again. He wouldn't have minded the diversion, but he wanted to start slow and become friends with her before they made love a second time.

Monday morning, he walked into the office determined to take her to lunch and get acquainted, but he didn't get a chance to. Curry stopped him before he made it to his office.

"Justin, we're having an emergency meeting in the conference room."

"I'll be right there," he said. Justin walked into his office, wondering what was going on. His last report had been flawless, and the feedback for the pizza campaign was exceptionally positive. He had no idea what the meeting could be about. Justin deposited his briefcase on his desk and headed to the conference room. When he entered, he noticed that Darius and all the partners were waiting for him. He spoke to everyone and took his seat. As Justin settled in his chair, Darius began speaking.

"This morning I received a courtesy call from

Javier Fuentes, Randa's former boss. He said it was a friendly call, but it wasn't really. He claims that the ideas Randa is using on Jose's campaign don't belong to her."

Justin's heart sank when he realized Randa was in trouble. He listened as Darius continued.

"I've talked with Randa this morning and she assures me that these are her ideas that F&G had originally turned down. She has shown me proof that she had submitted them and they were rejected. They lost about 80% of their business when they let her go, and I've learned that they are trying to coerce her into returning. I was told that they are filing an injunction against Jose's campaign, since he left them for us. Legal is filing a countersuit against them for slander. They have assured me that since she has copyrights to all the ideas she submitted and F&G rejected them, she's done nothing wrong." He looked around the room at the solemn faces.

Justin coughed, showing his uneasiness. "What does legal think will be the outcome?"

"Well, they think that F&G is doing this mainly to force her to go back to them. They also think we'll want to avoid a lawsuit or bad press and fire her. My question to the five of you is what do you think we should do as a company?"

Randa, fired? If he'd been offered this opportunity when he first arrived, she would have been as good as gone. But now, there was no way he could get rid of her. He'd fallen for her. Hard. The thought of not seeing her five days a week, even if she wasn't speaking to him, caused his stomach to turn. Sure, she drove him up a wall, but all of their arguments had been his fault. Randa had been nothing but patient, and he'd continued to make a jerk of himself. He had to support her. "I think there's an obvious answer. Of course we have to stand behind Randa. She's responsible for landing our biggest, most recent client and she's an amazing employee. Instead of talking about firing her, we should be wondering what we can do to keep her. She'd be an asset to any agency. Randa knows that, and we should recognize it."

Five astonished faces watched Justin defend his assistant. All this time, they'd assumed he couldn't stand her, and now they wondered what had brought on his change of heart. Darius grinned at him. "We had agreed on that earlier, but it had to be unanimous. Glad to see your thinking is in sync with ours."

It was a win-win all the way around. After the directors discussed the matter further, they moved on to other issues. After about two hours, Justin was finally dismissed. He walked back to his office, planning to ask Randa to lunch if she hadn't already left. He figured he could always say it was to discuss F&G and it wouldn't look like a date. As he neared her desk, he noticed a tall man waiting for her. She was nowhere to be seen. "Can I help you?" Justin asked, sizing up the competition.

"I'm waiting for Randa," the younger man said. "Are you Justin? She said she had to go the copier. She'll be right back."

"Thanks," Justin said, wondering who the hell this *boy* was waiting for his woman. He walked into his office with a scowl on his face.

When Randa reappeared, Justin decided he would ask her out for dinner instead. They could go somewhere more intimate after work. She appeared at his door, disrupting his thought process.

"Justin, I'm going to lunch," she said, tugging at a string on her suit. She walked inside of his office and spoke in a hushed tone. "By the way, I want to thank you for your vote of confidence. I figured you would have used your chance to get rid of me," she said sheepishly.

She was right. If that had happened a few weeks ago, he wondered what his answer would have been. "Randa, you're gifted," he told her. "Sure we've had some bumps, but I think we're improving, don't you think so?" There was so much more he wanted to say, but as she stood before him in her customary short skirt and heels, he couldn't find the words.

Randa nodded. "I appreciate that." She turned to leave, then remembered why she had gone to his office. "My friend Bryan surprised me for lunch today," she said, turning to face Justin. "Do you mind if I take a little longer than the usual hour?"

"That's fine," Justin said, swallowing his anger. "New friend?" He hoped she didn't detect the malice in his voice. "Actually, yes," she said, letting the vagueness of her response hang in the air.

EIGHT

After their lunch date, Bryan escorted Randa to her desk. Justin noticed the small bag she was carrying from a very chic restaurant and fumed. It was from the Italian place that he'd taken her to for dinner after she landed the Gutierrez account. As Bryan stood at her desk saying his good-byes, Justin strained to hear their conversation, but was unsuccessful. They were whispering, and unless he wanted to be very obvious and stand by the door, he could not make out their words.

After he saw Bryan leave, Justin called Randa into his office. He watched as she took her chair, crossing her legs in a way that drove him mad. "Well, now that your friend has finally left, can we concentrate on the Art Fest? Does he think you can't walk to your desk alone, that someone might attack you on the way from the elevator to your desk?" Justin's jealousy was in full view.

Randa raised her hand to her mouth to stifle her laughter. "If you're referring to Bryan, he's just a friend." She leaned back in the chair, enjoying the moment. "Do you know him?"

"No, I don't know him." Justin picked up his pen and began tapping it against the desk as he always did when he was nervous. "How are the plans for the Art Fest coming?"

Randa pointed to his pen before she spoke. "Are you through tapping out the Top 40, or should I wait?"

Justin's gaze followed the direction of her finger, and he realized he was banging his favorite writing utensil very loudly and quite rapidly against the wood desk. He set it down and waited for Randa to continue.

She opened her notepad and said, "Everything looks like it's on schedule. I have the booth reservations confirmed, and Bea and Mica have volunteered to hand out fliers."

"Why fliers? People will see the pizza stand," he pointed out.

"Because research shows that if you hand out fliers to hungry customers, there is an 80% chance they will take the advice of the flyer. I was thinking we'd do something on brightly colored paper that announces Joe's Pizza. Jose wanted me to wear something skimpy and stand out in front of the stand. I talked him out of that, thank goodness."

Pity, Justin thought. He could easily imagine her in very short shorts with a T-shirt tied in a knot.

Randa coughed, attracting his attention. He was blatantly staring at her with a stupid grin on his face. Quickly, he thought of business. "Any other things going on with Jose?"

"No, everything has been done. Jose's son, Enrique, will be working with me on Saturday," she offered with a smile.

Justin didn't like the look on her face. Something about the way her lips curved upward piqued his curiosity. "Is Jose's son old enough to help? You know, he has to be eighteen to work around those ovens. State law, I checked." Justin thought about volunteering to help her.

"I'm glad you're looking out for Jose. Ricky is 28 and a lot of fun." Randa left out that he'd been married for six years and that she knew his wife personally. She liked getting under Justin's skin since it was so easy to do.

I just bet. Justin stared at her for a long minute. *Just say it,* he pleaded with himself. *Tell her how you feel. Ask her to dinner.* He wanted to, but again his words failed him. He'd messed up with Randa so many times before, and he was afraid to broach the subject with her. He figured she would turn him down for sure.

Justin had to say something. He was just staring at those hazel eyes, and the silence had become unbearable. Somehow he found his nerve. "Randa," he began, clearing his throat to give himself more time to compose his thoughts.

"Yes, Justin?"

He shuffled the papers on his desk. "Never mind." He imagined how disappointed his brother would be if he knew he couldn't talk to a woman. Justin was undeniably attractive, but he'd always been nervous when it came to the ladies. He took a deep breath and tried one more time. "Randa?"

"Yes, again, Justin." A smug grin tugged at her lips.

"W-would you like to go to dinner tonight?" He held his breath as he awaited her answer.

"Depends on who's going."

Justin couldn't hide his look of confusion. "What do you mean?"

She answered him with a straight face. "If it's Justin, my boss, then no. If it's Justin, the man, yes. They're two different people."

"I'm sorry, I'm not following you, Randa."

"Let me put it this way. When we're here, you're detached and cold. Every woman is not your ex," she reminded him. "But when we had dinner at my house, you were human, almost likable," she teased. She stood and straightened her short skirt. "When you decide which Justin will show up, let me know; then I'll give you my answer." Brushing a piece of lint from her suit jacket, Randa rose from her chair and left his office.

Randa sat at her desk, willing her heartbeat to settle down. She could not believe he'd asked her out, and she was proud of her reaction. She definitely wanted to go out with him again, but he had to understand that his rudeness would not be tolerated.

Randa only waited a few moments before Justin buzzed the intercom on her phone.

"Could you come into my office?" he asked for the sake of anyone listening.

She walked into the office and sat in the chair, waiting for his answer.

Justin closed his office door. Observing Randa as he walked back to his seat, he spit out his answer. "I thought about what you said earlier. I know I'm unbearable around the office sometimes, but I'd like to show you the nicer side of me. If you'd let me take you to dinner again, I can promise I'll behave."

"Then I'll meet you at the elevator after work," Randa said cheerfully.

Later that evening, Randa waited for Justin at their customary meeting place: the elevator. They were going on an official date. He didn't tell her where they were going or if they needed reservations. She decided not to worry and to let him handle it. Justin soon appeared, pushing the down button and ushering her inside with his hand on the small of her back when their ride came.

"Where are we going, Justin?" Randa asked as

she opened her purse. She smiled as she saw the canister of mace looking back at her.

"Well, I thought we could take your car to your house and then go to the Chateau for dinner."

The elevator doors opened and they walked to their vehicles. Randa thought a little conversation was needed. "Well, it seems that we're two unattached people going on a date."

"It seems that way, doesn't it?" Justin countered. He slipped his hand into hers and held it all the way to her car.

After depositing her car at her house and checking on Zack, they were on their way to the restaurant. Randa wasn't used to the Justin who sat in the driver's seat. He played classic jazz on the radio and caressed her hand as he drove. After they arrived at the restaurant, he parked the truck and opened her door for her. She inhaled his cologne as he put his arm around her and led her into the restaurant.

"I like this Justin," Randa stated as they were seated at the table. "This is a kinder, gentler man. One I'd like to see more often," she hinted.

"Thanks, I guess."

Justin stared at her over the lighted candles and explained his erratic behavior to her. "Sometimes I feel like I don't know who I am anymore. For so long, I was trying to be someone else. I think I lost the real Justin somewhere along the way."

"I know what you mean," Randa said empathetically. "I think I'm in the same boat. When I was at F&G, I had to play with the big boys. So that meant drinking Scotch by the liter and learning how to smoke a stogie. Since being blessed with getting fired, I've rediscovered myself. So it's possible. You just have to get in touch again."

"How?" Justin watched as a waiter approached the

table to take their drink orders. He ordered a bottle of wine, and the waiter left.

"Start with hobbies. Take some time to remember what you used to like. I always loved animals but didn't have the time to dedicate to one. Now I have Zack. I wouldn't trade him for anything," Randa said.

"I know. Your eyes light up when you talk about him. You treat him like he's a member of the family. I don't think I would have checked on an animal before I went to dinner." He took a deep breath. "I just don't remember much before Lisa. I know I used to love art, but then I think that was because of Lisa, too."

Randa smiled across the table at her date. "Well, looks like you have a lot of discovering to do," she said, taking his hand in hers. A warm feeling came over him and he remembered the way he felt when she had made that same gesture on one of their earlier outings. "You probably just have to start small. You know, go to an exhibit or something. Too bad you missed the first art festival. It was the small one, but the big one is coming up. That's the one we're doing the pizza booth at."

"Well, maybe I'll stop by then. Come show my support for you." He took her hand and brought it to his lips, giving it a short peck.

"I'd like that very much." The waiter returned with their wine bottle. He filled their glasses and took their dinner orders. As he departed, Randa leaned in closer to Justin and asked, "What did you do in college for fun?"

He was almost too embarrassed to answer. "Lisa."

Randa opened her mouth, then closed it, choosing her words carefully. She knew his ex-wife was a sensitive subject. "Well, since Lisa isn't part of the equation anymore, I think there's a Justin inside screaming to get out."

"Maybe a certain person could help," he urged. "You know, she could show me around town." He winked at her as he took a sip of his wine.

Randa nodded. He seemed harmless tonight, she thought. Knowing that somehow her random act of goodwill would come back to haunt her, she offered anyway. "I'll bet she would, if you asked her properly."

He enjoyed the word play, but now he was against the wall. He would have to ask her out again. "How about Saturday?"

"It would have to be the afternoon. I volunteer at the animal shelter in the mornings." She picked up her fork and began eating the salad the waiter had just placed in front of her.

"Saturday afternoon it is." Justin clinked his glass to hers, sealing their plans.

NINE

Justin waited patiently at Randa's house Saturday afternoon. He looked in his rearview mirror for any sign of her car. He was a little early, but he was also really excited about their date. They were going to the art museum in Dallas, then dinner, he hoped. He glanced at his watch and smiled. She would be home soon.

Thirty minutes later, Justin saw Randa's black Infiniti approaching the house. He glanced in his mirror, making sure his face was free of telltale signs of toothpaste, aftershave, or drool. After giving himself a pep talk, he stepped out of the truck as she turned into her driveway and entered the garage. He met her as she closed her car door.

"I'm sorry, Justin," she began. "I didn't mean to leave you waiting."

Justin smiled, not wanting anything to go wrong. He had been looking forward to this moment all day and hoped his anxiety didn't show. "It's okay. I'm early." He noticed Randa's T-shirt and jeans and told her, "You look nice." She thought he was being sarcastic until she noticed the way he was admiring her tight jeans. They were her favorite pair and hugged her curves perfectly.

She fanned herself, smiling as she stepped back

from him. "Whew! I smell like cats and dogs! I need to take a shower and walk Zack; then I'll be ready."

"Why don't I take Zack for his walk while you're showering?" Justin volunteered. He would have done anything to get their date started.

Randa stared at him for a moment. "Are you sure? You don't strike me as an animal person."

"I like animals. I just choose not to have one." He wanted to laugh at her concern for her dog, but didn't think it would go over well with her.

Finally she gave him the nod of approval. "Okay, you can walk him. The park is about two blocks down the street that way." She pointed north. "Zack will lead you to it."

Justin nodded as they walked inside her house. Zack was happy to see his owner and smothered her with puppy kisses when she picked him up.

Randa put him down and went to the hall closet to get his leash and dog collar. Initially, Zack was a little resistant to Justin walking him, but slowly warmed up. After Randa gave her pup a final pat on the head, the two men in her life were gone.

Justin sighed at his actions as he walked to the park. Was he really so anxious to go on a date that he'd volunteered to walk a dog? As they entered the park, he decided that he was that anxious. All he could think about as he bent down to unleash Zack was Randa and not saying anything to offend her. Watching as the dog took off like a bullet, he sat on a bench and waited for him to return.

By the time Justin and Zack made it back to the house, Randa was dressed and ready to go. She kneeled and patted her puppy again as he gulped his water, instructing him to behave while she was out. She stood and faced Justin, leading him from the kitchen.

"I know I've already said this, but you look really nice," Justin commented as she locked her front door. He gazed at her sweater and slacks ensemble with appreciation.

"Thank you. You look very nice as well. Linen trousers look good on you." She wanted to add that they accented his high, muscular behind perfectly, but thought better of it. They walked to the truck in silence. When Randa reached for the door handle, Justin stopped her.

"I'll get that for you, Randa." He opened the door, and she slid inside the truck. He closed the door and walked to the other side. Randa watched him as he started the engine. *What kind of date will this be,* she wondered. She hoped she wouldn't regret saying yes.

The drive to Dallas was quiet, and Randa was grateful. After listening to kittens and puppies howl at her all morning, the silence was like heaven. She could devote her time to wondering about Justin and how good he looked. Halfway there, she noticed he hadn't said a word since they'd left her house. She relaxed against the leather seat, choosing not to complain, and watched as the scenery sped by.

After they parked and entered the expansive museum, Randa and Justin realized that they would not be able to look at everything in one day. While they were perusing the exhibition floor plan, Randa's stomach made a loud grumbling noise. She thought Justin hadn't heard it, but just when she thought she was in the clear, he chuckled.

"What's so funny?" Randa asked nervously.

"Well, at first, I couldn't tell whose stomach was rumbling. But I think it's you. How about a snack first? I realize you didn't get to have lunch today."

Randa laughed freely. "I'm starving. I didn't think

my stomach would betray me so quickly." She pointed to the deli. "How about there?"

He nodded and they went inside the busy restaurant. After finding a table and giving their orders, they decided on which exhibits to see.

"How about Jean Michel Basquiat?" Justin suggested. Since I saw that movie on cable, I'm really curious about his work." He noticed the frown on her face. "I take it you don't like Basquiat."

"Too modern. How about Monet?"

"Too commercial. I'll bet that's the first exhibit people visit, and the gift shop is undoubtedly full of Monet posters, Monet mouse pads, and Monet cups," he teased.

"Of course. It's Monet," Randa countered. "I prefer the classics like Monet, Picasso, Renoir, and Matisse. Impressionists are my favorite, in case you couldn't tell."

The waiter approached their table with their orders. Justin watched Randa as she opened her sandwich and took off some of the lettuce and all of the onions.

"Why didn't you just say no lettuce or onions? I'm sure they wouldn't have minded taking them off."

"I wanted a little for the flavor. How about a compromise?"

Justin waited to take a bite of his sandwich. "Okay. What?"

"We could go to both. Which one first?" Randa sipped her soda. "Since this outing is for you, we can see Mr. Modern before Monet."

Randa sat back in her seat and saw Justin's smile. When he was relaxed, he was quite good-looking. She watched two women behind him, talking loudly, trying to get his attention. He ignored them and Randa silently gave him ten cool points.

"It's a deal then," he said, then began to eat his lunch.

As they walked out of the Monet exhibit, Justin grabbed Randa's hand. "How about a trip to the museum gift store, just to prove my theory?" he taunted.

Randa played along with his little game. "What theory would that be, Justin?"

"My theory of how commercial Monet is. Care to wager a little bet?" He stopped at the gift shop's entrance, silently challenging her.

"What will I get if I win?"

"You can take me to lunch on Monday," he said as they entered the busy shop. "If I win, you can fix me breakfast one morning." He winked at her.

"Well, looks like it's a win-win for you, huh? How can I refuse?" Randa noticed something and smiled. She saw the Monet posters on the wall in the back of the shop and saw a Basquiat poster as well. "Looks like Monet isn't the only commercial artist here," she said.

Justin followed her gaze. "I have no idea what you're talking about, Randa," he lied, egging her on.

"You know you see Jean Michel what's-his-name on display right next to Monet." She stood directly in front of him, daring him to deny it, and poked him playfully in the chest. Her hand met the firm wall of muscle beneath his shirt, and she quickly became flustered. Catching herself, she said, "So I think I'll call that a draw."

"All right, you caught me. Because of the draw, how about dinner?"

She dragged him to the Monet section of the shop. "Right after I look at some of his work."

* * *

After they left the gift shop, Randa and Justin walked toward his truck.

"Are you sure about dinner?" Randa asked as they neared his truck.

"Yes, I'm sure. We've had fun, haven't we?" He had enjoyed her company that afternoon. She never expected anything more than he could give, and that made him feel good. "What would you like to eat?"

"How about seafood?"

"Sounds great." Justin opened her door and she got in the truck.

She watched him as he drove, admiring his chiseled features. "What did you think of the exhibits?"

"I like them. I didn't think I would like something so commercial as Monet or Picasso, but I did. Thanks for forcing them on me." He glanced over at her after his playful remark.

"Any time. If you really like the Impressionists, there is another exhibit at Maza's in Dallas. They specialize in Monet-like paintings." She paused. "Here's a question for you. What kind of sports do you like? Don't tell me, do you play golf?"

"Actually, no. I watch it on TV sometimes. Why do you ask?"

"It just seems like golf would be your sport. You know, the whole corporate management image. I know Curry plays, and Darius is learning."

"Actually, the ex wanted me to learn so I could network more. But I was so busy at work; I just never had the time. But I like most sports, especially tennis."

"Can you play, or do you just watch it for the women?"

"I can play, but a little babe watching never hurt." He watched her shocked expression. Did he strike a chord of jealousy? He hoped so. "I'm wounded, not dead. I'm told I play pretty well."

"I love to play. I never had time before, but now that that's changed, we should play sometime. There are some courts close to work. We could play when you're not forcing me to work late."

"Yes, we should." A feeling of contentment ran through Justin's body as he listened to Randa. She was so self-assured, so confident, so not like Lisa. He couldn't imagine spending an afternoon at a museum with her or ever hearing her volunteer to sweat for anything. Even sex.

As they arrived at the restaurant, Randa decided Justin was quite charming and very personable when he wanted to be. She felt sorry for the lives they had both lost—his to a shrew of a wife, hers to a high-pressure career. Surely, there was a way they could both find what they were looking for. If they were lucky they could find it in each other, she thought.

After Justin parked, he opened the door and helped Randa out of the truck. As her feet touched the ground, Justin stepped closer to her and kissed her gently. "Thanks for this afternoon."

Randa licked her lips, enjoying the taste of him as he grabbed her hand and proceeded into the restaurant. She looked at the brightly painted interior as they were led to their table.

She didn't speak until the waiter took their drink order and retreated from the booth. "This is very nice, Justin. How did you hear about this place?"

"Curry told me about it. He says the food is awesome and not to pay attention to the décor. His wife loves to eat here." Justin watched her as she searched the menu for a choice. "Have you met his wife?"

"Yes, she's very nice. They seem really happy together."

Justin nodded. "You're right. Sometimes just listening to him talk about his wife and kid makes me realize happiness is still possible, no matter what you have to go through to get there." He took a deep breath, almost wistful. "Have you decided what you're having for dinner?"

Randa shrugged her shoulders. "I don't know. Everything looks good. What are you having?"

"The grilled salmon fillet with dill. I love salmon." Justin set the menu on the table. "In Oregon, eating seafood was like eating a burger or steak here."

"I can imagine what a shock it is living in Texas for you, foodwise. A couple of years ago, I was stuck in Maine on business for a few months and I discovered seafood. It was delicious and fresh. I almost dreaded coming back to Texas."

As the waiter returned with their drink orders, Justin marveled at the woman sitting across from him. She had so much experience, so much personality. She was beautiful and smart, and he loved listening to the soothing sound of her voice. A feeling came over him that he'd never known before.

After an enjoyable dinner, Randa invited Justin inside for coffee. She hoped he didn't misread her invitation. The entire evening, he had been talkative and nice—two words she would have never used to describe Justin Brewster previously.

Zack met her at the door, barking nonstop. He was mad she had left him for so long. Randa immediately kneeled down next to him and massaged his back until he quieted down. "I'm sorry, honey. We'll go out in a little bit," she comforted, laughing as the dog bolted away.

Justin watched the interaction. He tried to envision Lisa being that loving or unselfish. "Randa, I should go with you and Zack," he offered. "It's late and I wouldn't want you to get attacked again or something."

She looked up at Justin from her position on the floor. "Justin, that's not necessary. I've taken him out late before."

He only shook his head. "No, we can go right now. I don't mind, and I don't want anything to happen to you."

Randa sighed in defeat. He was being a typical man, trying to keep his damsel from distress. She wasn't used to being watched over, but it was a nice feeling to know he cared.

"All right, I'll just get his stuff." She walked to a nearby closet.

Justin waited patiently until she returned with the leash and collar. They walked in silence to the park, Zack's breathing being the only noise. As they reached their destination, Randa released the dog. She and Justin laughed as they both watched the dog run full speed to a wooded area.

"He didn't do that earlier," Justin commented as he watched him.

"Maybe because you're a stranger," she teased with a giggle.

"I am not! I've seen him four times. We're like old friends." Justin turned toward Randa and pulled her close to him. "I hope I'm your friend, too. Not just your boss." He leaned down and kissed her passionately on the mouth, smiling inwardly when a moan escaped her throat. "This evening was wonderful, Randa, I've had a good time," he said when he felt she was thoroughly satisfied.

"Me too, Justin." Randa took a deep breath and looked into his eyes as if she knew what was on his lust-filled mind.

Justin's hand found hers and they started to walk. "What are you doing tomorrow?" he asked, pulling her closer to get a whiff of her perfume.

"I'm busy all day." Her face lit up, and he thought she looked even more beautiful. "Tomorrow is my niece's eighth birthday. My brother is a single parent, so I'm helping him with the party. He fears being in a house full of girls."

"Is he divorced?"

"No, his wife passed away about three years ago, just after the birth of my nephew. I try to help with the kids as much as I can, but I haven't seen them much lately with all the overtime I've been doing."

He heard the thread of regret in her voice. "I'm sorry, Randa. I didn't mean to bring up bad memories." He drew her to him for a comforting hug.

"I know. It was a shock at first, but we've adjusted. It hit my brother the hardest, of course. The kids started calling me Mom Number Two and that got shortened to Mom Two." She smiled at the thought of her niece and nephew. "Those months after my mom died, the kids were a great comfort to me. I was so worried about them, I didn't focus on my own grief."

Justin nodded, but said nothing else. He thought about his own family. His parents were still alive and healthy. His brother, Jason, had been happily married for over twenty years, and had two sons. Justin's marriage was the first relationship casualty in the family. He watched Randa, who was obviously deep in thought; she had had so much loss in her life.

"I'm sure there's something I could do to help you set up for the party," he offered. Was that his voice volunteering to attend a birthday party for an eight-year-old girl?

Randa stopped walking and stood in front of him. "Oh, Justin, that's not necessary. There will be *ten* eight-year-olds there. Girls. You'd go mad."

"It could be fun. I could meet your brother and your niece and nephew." He kissed her again, putting his arms around her waist, wanting to feel her body against his. His tongue dipped deeper into her mouth this time as he felt her quiver in his embrace. Justin stifled his own moan as he felt her arms hugging him, bringing him even closer to her body and slowly ending the kiss.

"Well?" he asked with his lips on her neck, smothering the slender column with kisses.

"Yes." Randa tried to untangle herself from Justin before she jumped on him right there in the park. "What were we talking about?"

Justin held her tighter and planted a smooch on her forehead. "Birthday party. What time shall I pick you up?" His hands lingered around her waist.

Randa smiled as she noticed Zack's return. "How about noon?" She pulled his head down for another kiss.

Justin nodded, then took the leash from her hand and reattached it to Zack.

TEN

As Randa unlocked her front door, Zack bolted to the kitchen for his water bowl. She shook her head as she watched him from the living room, then glanced at Justin as he closed the front door. "Would you like something to drink?"

Justin grinned. "How about some juice?"

Randa nodded and started to walk to the kitchen, but Justin grabbed her hand, pulling her body to his. He covered her mouth with his again. He'd never been the kissing type, but for some reason, he couldn't get enough of Randa's soft, full lips. "Later," he mumbled against her lips.

She knew she had two choices. One, she could ignore the feel of his erection against her stomach, or two, she could give in. As he thrust his tongue deeper inside her mouth and pressed her tighter against his growing need, she decided to go with the latter option.

"Justin." She moaned his name. Her only answer was a pair of hands roaming down her back and cupping her round bottom in a gentle squeeze. His hungry kisses swept down her neck, and she felt a familiar ache in her core. It had been months since they'd made love and she wanted, no needed, to feel him inside her. The events of the afternoon had been gently nudging them in this direction. She disentangled herself from his embrace and led him up the stairs to her bedroom.

As she closed the door, she turned to face Justin and was surprised to see his eyes brimming with love. It had been a long time since a man had looked at her that way.

"Randa, you do something to me," he said. His voice was low and husky with desire. "I just can't figure out what." He pulled her sweater over her head, careful not to disturb her hairstyle, and began to unsnap the front clasps of her bra with one hand. After releasing her breasts from their confines, he grazed her nipples with his fingers, then his mouth. He was pleased when he felt them harden in anticipation.

She felt electrical sparks every time he touched her. Quickly she led him over to the bed, unbuttoning his shirt and easing it off his broad, chiseled shoulders until he stopped her.

"I'll take care of that," he told Randa, kneeling before her. His hands caressed her waist and his lips showered horizontal kisses across her narrow waistline. Slowly, he unbuckled her belt, unzipped her slacks, and slid them down her legs. His hands caressed every inch of her and she cried out his name with want.

Stepping out of her slacks as they pooled at her feet, she took a deep breath as he undid his pants and let them fall to the floor. He was clad in only a pair of blue silk boxers, and his brown muscles were rippling perfection.

Randa couldn't wait any longer. Pulling him to her, she kneeled to kiss his stomach and ran her tongue across his six-pack abdomen. She smiled as the muscles tensed under her touch. "You're gorgeous," she told him, pushing his boxers down his muscular legs. "Absolutely gorgeous."

Justin didn't answer. Instead, he picked her up and wrapped her legs around his waist as he moved to the center of the king-size bed and stretched his long body beside hers. Randa was paralyzed with pleasure as he eased his hands under her body and began to massage her bottom. Arching her back, she unwittingly thrust her breasts into his waiting mouth. "Now that's better," he said, moistening his lips with his tongue before drawing one of her erect nipples into his mouth.

After several minutes, Justin couldn't tease her any longer. He reached down on the floor, and, grasping for his trousers, he fumbled through the pockets and retrieved a condom. He slipped it on and looked down at Randa's flushed body. She was the epitome of beauty as she waited expectantly for him to return to her arms.

Randa looked up at him, her hazel eyes filled with passion and desire. Their lovemaking had been satisfying the first time and she'd had no complaints, but it couldn't compare to what she'd just experienced, and she hadn't even welcomed him into her body yet. This Justin had her breathing hard and on the brink of an orgasm, with just a little foreplay! He slid her panties down her legs, then joined his body to hers once again. She eased her hands down his broad shoulders as he kissed her wildly, sending her near the brink of ecstasy.

"Baby, please," she begged. He kissed her slowly from her neck to her navel.

"Should I continue?" he asked, pleased that she had trouble catching her breath. She only nodded.

He licked and suckled her like a man with a purpose. When she began to cry out, indicating to him that she was near the peak of pleasure, he entered her and thrust his tongue in her mouth to stifle her cries. He stroked her quickly and deeply until her body quivered and calmed. She thrust her hips up, begging him to seek his own end and he hung on to her for dear life as he felt his own orgasm nearing. Randa cradled him between her legs as she continued to undulate her hips, bringing her man wave upon wave of release.

Randa awoke the next morning to discover Justin was gone. "I should have known he'd run," she said, feeling the tears welling in her eyes. She hated herself for being so stupid and believing the fairytale of love was possible. Although she was alone, she wrapped her sheet around her body, covering her physical vulnerability. As she looked around the room, Randa wondered if Justin even had the decency to leave a note this time. "Probably not," she mused as she got out of bed and walked to the bathroom.

After she finished her shower, she wondered why Zack wasn't barking for his morning walk—usually, that's what she awoke to on the weekends. She called his name, and when he didn't run to her, she became nervous. Clad in only her towel, she ran down the stairs to look for her dog.

Walking into the kitchen, she saw Justin at the stove, cooking her breakfast. Zack was munching away at his meal in the corner. Her teary eyes met Justin's as she walked toward him.

He kissed her gently on the lips as she sniffed back tears. She didn't want to seem like one of those weepy women who believed in a Prince Charming, but she thought Justin might be close. She reprimanded herself for thinking he'd left her again. "Okay, where's my boss?" she asked playfully. "What did you do with him?" Randa giggled as Justin wrapped her in a bear hug and slipped his hand beneath her towel. She kissed him and felt him stiffen beneath the thin layer of terrycloth.

"You know, I could take offense at that statement," he said, winking at her. "But I won't." He released her and led her to the table. "This is for that asshole that slept with you and ran the other time. I'm sorry about that, Randa. I was so overwhelmed that night and I didn't react like a real man should have."

"Justin," she started, but he held a finger to her lips to silence her.

"I know, Randa. Last night was intense and I wasn't expecting to turn into a horny teenager, but I'm glad I did. Did you enjoy yourself?" He pulled out a chair for her. "Sit down, your breakfast of champions is almost ready."

Randa did as she was told. Justin placed a mug of coffee in front of her. When she stood up to get the flavored cream from the refrigerator, he appeared at the table with the container of it before she could get out of her seat. "Woman, do you ever do what you are told?" he teased, favoring her with a kiss on the forehead.

"No," Randa countered, smiling as he poured the cream in her cup. "Most of today's independent women don't. It makes life fun."

Justin put two plates on the table. Randa looked at her plate in awe. She couldn't remember the last time someone made breakfast for her outside of McDonald's or Burger King. Justin obviously thought she ate like a horse, judging by the pile of food on her plate. She grinned, biting her bottom lip. He was right! "This looks delicious, Justin. What is it?"

"Huevos rancheros, with a little something extra." He watched her take a heaping forkful of the eggs and put them in her mouth. He laughed as she closed her eyes and moaned.

"These are delicious. I think I found another thing you're good at." She quickly ate the eggs, bacon, and toast. She raised her plate and pushed it toward him, silently requesting more.

He took her plate and refilled it before putting it back in front of her. "What do you mean, what am I good at?" He took his seat across from her.

Randa almost choked on her toast. "I meant cooking. Do you cook often?" She took a sip of coffee and watched him over the rim of the cup.

"Not really. It's no fun when you're alone. You know, cooking for one just reminds me that I'm single again."

Randa watched him as he ate. She didn't mean to bring up the past, but since she had, a little prodding was in order. "Who cooked when you were married?"

Justin stared at Randa and tried to remember. "Well, on the weekends, we usually ate brunch at one of Lisa's friends' houses. It was more of a social event than a meal. They served bird food like those tiny sandwiches you can pick up with two fingers. We never had meals like this. She detested spicy food. She said it would give her high blood pressure."

Randa was silent. If she ever met Lisa, Randa would knock her out on general principle, she thought. She changed the conversation to a happier topic. "My niece's birthday party is at three. I promised Karl I'd be there by noon, which is about two hours from now. Do you want to stay here while I get ready, or do you want to meet me there?" Randa hoped he would agree to stay. She usually liked having her house to herself, but she loved having Justin share her space with her.

He paused with his fork in the air. Justin enjoyed being wanted just as much as Randa enjoyed having him. He nodded his head. "I'd like to stay," he told her, then ate his eggs.

After they finished breakfast, Justin waited for Randa to get dressed, then helped her gather the supplies for the party and put them in his truck. Then they headed to his town house so that he could change. As they drove, Randa began to feel a little nervous. This would be the first time she would see his home, even though she'd already slept with him.

While Justin hurried upstairs to change, Randa explored his house. His interior walls were blank, devoid of any pictures or decorations. The fireplace mantle stood bare and lonely in the corner. His house was just that: a house, certainly not a home. The room gave her a little chill.

As she thought of a housewarming gift for him, something that would add some character to his house, the phone rang, startling her. She wasn't going to answer it, but Justin shouted down the stairs, asking her to pick up. She was comforted that he had nothing to hide from her.

"Hello?" she answered confidently.

Dead silence met her on the other end of the phone, but she could tell the caller didn't hang up. Randa could hear very faint breathing and whispering.

"Hang up. It's must be a wrong number," a masculine voice said.

Finally, a female voice came across the line. "I definitely have the wrong number," she said.

Randa shook her head, hanging up the phone. They sounded too old to be kids, she thought.

"Who was it?" Justin asked as he walked down the stairs. He was dressed casually in a polo shirt that emphasized his muscles and blue jeans that showed off his spectacular backside.

"They said they had the wrong number," Randa explained, taking a seat on his sofa.

Justin froze. "W-was it a woman?"

"Actually, it was a woman and a man. They were whispering." Randa noticed Justin's stoic face. "Justin, are you all right?"

"Yeah, just some reminders of a horrible life. It was probably a wrong number. Are you ready?"

As they drove up to her brother's large house, Justin saw the evidence of the party. A giant moon walk sat in the corner of the perfectly manicured lawn and balloons were everywhere—on the door, on the columns that supported the house, even on the Jaguar that occupied the driveway. A large banner that read "Happy Birthday, Princess" hung over the front door, marking the occasion.

Justin was overwhelmed. He had expected a small, intimate birthday party, not a salute to Walt Disney. Two children ran to greet Randa as he walked up the driveway beside her. They stopped dead in their tracks when they noticed Justin.

Randa squatted down to the level of the children and held out her arms, and they proceeded once again. "Mom Two! We missed you!" her niece yelled. Randa hugged and kissed them and then picked up the little boy. "Justin, this is my niece, Jessica, and my nephew, Preston. Say hello to Mr. Brewster, guys."

The children mumbled hellos but remained close to Randa. Justin knew he had his work cut out for him. These kids were very protective of her. He kneeled down in front of Jessica, extending his large hand to her. "Happy birthday, Jessica. I'm Randa's boss."

Jessica looked at the man and then at Randa.

"Mom Two, he doesn't have two heads!" Turning to Justin, she said, "Mom Two said you were an alien."

Randa gasped at her admission, but Justin laughed. "Well, I'm sure that was her early impression of me. I'm quite normal, right, Randa?"

"Y-yes, Justin." She turned her attention to her niece, making a mental note to remind her that she was not to repeat what she heard grown folks say. "Jessie, why don't you go find your dad for me?" She let Preston down and watched as the children scampered away.

"Sorry, Justin, she must have overheard me talking to her dad," Randa offered.

Justin noticed she didn't deny she said it, only that she hadn't meant for her niece to hear her. She was honest, he thought. He added that to the long list of things he liked about Randa. As they approached the side door, a tall African-American man met them. Justin guessed him to be in his late forties.

"Randa, I've been calling your house," the man said, his frustration evident. "Major disaster ahead."

"What is it, Karl?" Randa was immediately at her brother's side. "I planned the party down to the last detail."

"Jessica informed me that one of her friends is going to have a clown at her party next week. Do you think I should try to find one at the last minute?"

Randa patted her brother's back as she wrapped her arm around him, leading him back into the house. Justin followed them silently. "Karl, she doesn't have to have everything that her friends have. It teaches her individuality. Face painting and the moon walk are quite enough." She noticed the men sizing each other up as they entered the large kitchen. "Oh, I'm sorry, Karl. This is Justin Brewster, my boss."

Karl looked at his sister with mischievous eyes. "I'm not going to ask. Nice to meet you, Justin."

"Likewise. We are also friends. Don't believe everything that you've heard," he said.

"Randa never embellishes," Karl countered.

"True, but I'm trying to change."

"You better," her brother challenged.

ELEVEN

Soon the children claimed Randa's attention and led her away from the men. The guys remained, talking by the pool. Justin realized that Karl Stone adored his family. He also realized Randa's brother was *the* Karl Stone, an attorney to the superwealthy. He was very protective of Randa and made that fact known clearly to Justin.

"Miranda has been through many changes lately," he told Justin. "She's a blessing to the kids and me. I don't want her getting hurt over something fleeting. Although Gareth is gay, he was the best thing for her at the time."

Justin knew in an instant that whatever he had hoped to establish with Randa, he would have the shadow of Gareth to contend with. "I understand. I'm recently divorced myself, so we're both discovering freedom from our former lives."

Karl nodded. "Randa is smart, but sometimes she doesn't see what's in front of her. Gareth showed all the signs of being gay, but we never noticed them. We were all shocked."

"She told me."

The men walked back inside the house, following the noise of the TV, and found Randa sitting on the floor with the kids. Preston was sitting in her lap, and

Jessica sat beside her with her arm looped through her aunt's. Justin watched silently from the doorway.

After Karl called the children to lunch, Justin seized the opportunity to talk to Randa alone. He walked into the room and sat beside her on the floor, taking the spot Jessica had vacated. "You are great with those kids, and they adore you."

Randa nodded as Justin's hand found hers. "They are very special to me. I enjoy being a surrogate Mom."

"I think you would make a terrific real mom," Justin told her. He saw the surprised look on her face and his heart started beating rapidly. He needed to get off the subject of babies, and fast. It could only lead to trouble. "Karl mentioned that you guys have relatives in Oregon and Washington."

"Why do you do that? You say something controversial that's on your mind, then you change the subject like I'm not going to notice what you're doing." Randa laughed at his shocked expression. "Justin, don't worry. I know you want no part of a relationship. At this point in my life, I don't either. I'm still sorting things out. To answer your question, yes, we have family in Salem, Oregon and in the Seattle area. My mom was originally from Seattle and she moved here when she married our Dad. He was in the Air Force."

His heart sunk when Randa said she didn't want to be part of a relationship, but he didn't show it. "You never mentioned your dad." It was just another part of the Randa puzzle he hadn't solved yet. "Is he still living?"

"No, he died about ten years ago."

Justin was silent as he watched her eyes brim with tears. He swallowed the question that stuck in his throat—why didn't she want a relationship with him?

"When my father passed away, I was out of the country on business. I missed the funeral." Randa wiped at her eyes. "It wasn't because I couldn't get back in time. It was because I was in the middle of a project and didn't want to lose the momentum. Needless to say, my mother was furious at me. That's one thing I really wish I could change."

"Did you and your mother ever make up before she passed away?" Justin couldn't understand how she could have picked a job over her father's funeral.

"Yes, it took years of me taking her to the cemetery every Sunday after church, but we did make up. I learned a valuable lesson. Family first, job second, but she died before I could really put that philosophy into action."

He better understood her reasoning on some things, like when she refused to work late because it was Jessica's playdate. He didn't know if he had the dedication to say no to work. He already knew he couldn't say no to Randa.

By the time the party ended, Randa wore a tired smile. All her hard work and planning had paid off, and several parents were shocked to discover she'd put together the party all by herself.

Justin had thoroughly enjoyed himself and was glad he came until Gareth showed up at the party at the last minute. He was followed by Josh, who carried several large boxes, making the other gifts pale in comparison. Randa sent him an apologetic look when she saw him grimace as he overhead Jessica referring to her ex-husband as Uncle Gareth.

As she and Justin enjoyed the quiet of the ride back to her house, Randa dreamed of a hot bath, a glass of wine, and lots of rest. She glanced at Justin as he drove. The party should have been awkward for him since he didn't have any children, but it wasn't. He'd joined the other fathers and talked like he had a house full of children. Too bad he doesn't want any, she thought. He'd make a good dad. She saw his lips moving, but couldn't comprehend the words.

"What'd you say?"

"I was saying the party wiped you out. Why don't you take tomorrow off?"

"No, I'll be fine," she insisted. "A hot bath, lots of sleep, and I'll be as good as new."

Those plans changed the minute she opened her front door. Zack was waiting for her, anxious to go out, and Randa didn't think she could move another step, let alone take him out for his run. "Oh, baby, I'm sorry. Mom is tired. The backyard will have to do." She walked toward the couch and sat down.

"I'll take him, Randa," Justin volunteered. He'd hated walking Zack at first, but now he enjoyed the task. It made him feel needed and useful. "I don't mind, really."

Randa nodded her thanks as she curled up on the couch.

The next morning Justin walked to his office and saw Randa at Beatrice's desk. He liked the back view of a short skirt he hadn't seen before, and she was wearing his favorite pair of stilettos, too. He stood in the doorway of his office as she walked to her desk. "Good morning, Randa. How did you sleep?"

Randa blushed and immediately looked around to see if anyone had heard his improper question.

"Justin, that's private," she whispered harshly, chastising him like a teenager. "We're at work." She sat at her desk and tried to look busy, effectively ignoring him.

That only infuriated him. He thought she would be a little less frigid after what they shared Saturday night. "Well, I can't turn my emotions on and off like a faucet," he said, standing over her desk.

"Justin, I didn't turn off my feelings. This is our workplace, and there are rules," she reminded him.

"That's not an official rule, Randa. You know that as well as I do." He folded his arms across his chest, giving him the appearance of a pouting child.

"Well, the unwritten rules are clear. No hanky-panky. My sleeping arrangements are off-limits from eight to five, Monday through Friday."

Justin shoved his hands in his pockets. He hadn't thought she actually took that rule seriously since she'd slept with him, but evidently, she did. "So I can ask you at lunchtime then? Technically, you're off the clock."

She smiled, not looking away from her computer screen, when she realized he wasn't giving up easily. "Yes, you can," Randa said.

"How about lunch today then?" He planned to kiss her as soon as he got the chance to since he hadn't done so the night before. By the time he'd returned with Zack, Randa had fallen asleep on the couch. After carrying her to bed, he'd left.

"Bea already asked me. Sorry." She turned around and faced him with a triumphant grin on her face.

"You baited me. Okay, how about dinner?"

"You have a dinner meeting with Darius, Curry, and Jose." She turned around and resumed working.

"What about after dinner? I could come by and

have dessert," he whispered in her ear, nipping its lobe with his tongue.

Randa's face flushed and she turned to glare at him in surprise. When she saw the determined look in his eye, she gave in. "Dessert will be fine, Mr. Brewster."

He gave her a playful peck on the cheek and told her, "That's what I like about you, Randa. Lisa never met me halfway on anything." Justin smiled at her and walked into his office.

Randa's face fell at his last comment. She'd thought several times that Lisa might still be in his heart, and now she knew for sure that she was.

The following Monday, Justin was in a foul mood. The Arlington Art Fest was four weeks away, and he had barely seen Randa, at work or otherwise. He was supposed to go visit with her at home last week, but she'd cancelled their plans at the last minute, saying she was too tired. Whenever he wanted to see her, she said she was busy off-site with the last-minute details of the pizza booth or that she was helping Karl with the kids.

On top of that, Lisa had left a multitude of messages on his answering machine at home. He wondered about her sanity sometimes. He'd noticed Curry talking with Randa in a hushed tone the few times she was in the office, blocking his chance to speak with her. He'd overhead some of their conversation earlier and knew they were going to lunch that day. Even though Curry was married and Justin considered him a friend, it didn't stop him from feeling jealous. Justin's blood boiled every time any man came within walking distance of Randa, and he wondered what was going on between her and Curry.

Sitting at his computer, Justin was putting together

some figures for a new spreadsheet to keep his mind off of her when Darius knocked on his door.

"Do you have a second, Justin?" Darius asked.

Justin nodded. Was there any way for an employee to tell his boss he didn't have time?

Darius walked into the office and pulled the door behind him. "There may be a few shake-ups in the company soon and I just wanted you to know that your job is secure."

Justin looked at him quizzically. "Is this about Randa?" He hoped they hadn't changed their minds and decided to fire her anyway.

"Yes and no. She is a factor in our decisions, though. I just wanted to give you a heads-up. When the partners give me the okay, I'll fill you in on the information I have."

Justin wasn't sure exactly what he was getting at, but he didn't get the feeling Randa would be let go. While Darius was in his office, he wondered if he should ask him if he'd noticed any odd behavior between Randa and Curry. Curry was Darius's best friend, and surely he'd know if they were dating.

Just as he fixed his mouth to compose his question, Darius's phone rang.

"Hold that thought," he said, reaching for his phone. "Darius Crawford." His voice was strong and authoritative.

"Hi, Darbi. No, Curry's not in my office. I think he went out for lunch. You want to hide what at my house?" He laughed. "Yes, I know it's your first anniversary, but does he really need a titanium golf putter? I know that's the one Tiger Woods uses, but that's still not going to help Curry's golf score." Darius listened as his sister continued talking. "Okay, you can hide it at the house. Just let the nurse know or she'll blab to him." He hung up the phone. "I'm sorry, Justin. You wanted to talk to me about something?"

"Yes, I did." A knock at Justin's door interrupted the conversation again. Curry burst in with a folder in his hand. "Oh, sorry," he said excitedly. "Justin, this will only take a second." Curry thrust an envelope forward for Darius to review. "You have to see this. Randa has been helping me get this together for Darbi for our first anniversary. I'm taking her to Ireland for two weeks!"

So that was why Curry was always hovering around Randa's desk, Justin thought. He should have known a man like Curry wouldn't do anything to jeopardize his friendship with Darius or his relationship with his wife.

Curry placed the envelope in Darius's lap. "Darius, you know I couldn't tell you before or you'd blab to Darbi, ruining the surprise. I'm telling her tonight over dinner."

Darius nodded and smiled at his brother-in-law's enthusiasm as he spread the brochures across the desk. Justin looked at the brochures as well.

"Randa is amazing," Curry bragged. "She has a friend that runs a travel agency and got me a great deal. We're flying in to London for a few days, then on to Dublin. Two weeks almost doesn't seem like enough time."

Justin waited patiently as the men wrapped up and left his office. He was thankful that Darius was so enthused over the trip that he'd forgotten to ask Justin to tell him what was on his mind. If Curry hadn't barged in, Justin would have humiliated himself, his boss, and Randa. She would never want to be in a relationship with him then.

He realized he was going to have to trust Randa more. So far she'd done nothing to make him feel he should doubt her and each time he judged her, he was incorrect. *She's not Lisa*, he kept telling himself. He repeated it over and over, as if he were trying to make it sink in.

TWELVE

The following evening, Randa volunteered to baby-sit the kids while Karl was interviewing witnesses for an upcoming case. She loved spending time with them, but her body was telling her she needed to spend a little grown-up time with Justin, even if she was mad at him. The last time they'd had a real conversation, he had compared her to Lisa, and she wasn't over it. He'd been less than understanding about not seeing her over the last few weeks and seemed to have no idea that she was upset or that he'd done anything wrong.

After feeding and bathing Jessica and Preston, she settled with them on the couch to watch *Finding Nemo* before she put them to bed. Preston, as usual, was in her lap. She inhaled the smell of the freshly washed toddler and relaxed. That comforting scent did wonders for her jangled nerves.

When the doorbell rang, Randa laughed as Jessica quickly jumped off the couch. "Can I get it, Mom Two?" she begged.

"You can see who it is, but don't open the door."

Jessica ran in the direction of the front door. "It's the man from my party that didn't bring me a present," she shouted.

Randa was puzzled by Jessica's description. Then she started to smile. Jessica reminded her constantly that she'd never received a gift from Justin. Surely, he wouldn't bring his sourpuss around here. She walked to the door and got her answer. He was dressed casually in jeans and a snug-fitting T-shirt that showcased his upper body. His mouth was firmly set.

Randa braced herself for the fight she was about to have as she opened the glass storm door. "What are you doing here, Mr. Brewster?"

Justin stiffened at her tone, but he wasn't deterred. "I need to see you, Randa. It's been two weeks."

As he stepped inside the entryway, he looked down at Jessica as she stood between him and Randa, acting as her guardswoman. "If we could speak privately, I'm sure we could rectify the situation."

Randa watched Justin as he squirmed in front of Jessica. "Justin, we're watching a movie. You're welcome to join us." She grabbed Jessica's hand and walked back to the living room, leaving Justin to make up his own mind.

Justin followed them and plopped down on the love seat. As he watched Randa and the kids, he picked up a pillow. "Randa," he started, but Jessica interrupted him by telling him to be quiet.

"This is Mom Two's favorite part. She likes the music," Jessica informed him.

Justin nodded and waited for the movie to end.

Randa wanted to laugh at Justin's sad face. She knew he probably had other ideas for the evening that she would have no doubt enjoyed, but too bad. That's what he deserved for showing up unexpectedly.

Since he was still a relative stranger to the children, they were hesitant to follow their normal bedtime routine. Gradually, they relaxed, and Preston finally fell asleep. Randa stood with the toddler in her arms and grabbed Jessica's hand. "I'm going to put the kids to bed," she announced. She didn't offer Justin any options.

Justin was frustrated beyond belief. Not only did he miss Randa terribly, he wanted to talk with her about Lisa's messages on his machine. He knew his ex-wife would show up on his doorstep any day now, and he wanted to talk to Randa about that possibility before it happened. Justin also wanted to tell Randa about his feelings for her before Lisa arrived. He didn't know what that nutty woman was up to, but undoubtedly it would wreak havoc on his life. He wondered how Randa would react to the news.

As she descended the stairs, Justin got a lovely view of her long legs and felt his groin tighten. He felt like a horny sixteen-year-old whenever he was around her.

"Justin, why are you here?" she asked, sitting on the sofa.

He patted the space beside him on the love seat, hoping that she would be just a little cooperative. As usual, she was not. He shook his head in defeat. "I'm sorry if I interrupted your time with the kids," he said softly. "I wanted to talk to you about something that's important to me. I thought if we sat together, we could speak in a more civilized tone."

She stared at him as if he spoke Swedish to her. Finally, she got up and walked over to him, standing in front of him, but refusing to sit. "Okay, talk, Justin."

Justin took a deep breath. If she wanted to be difficult, he would be difficult, too. He slipped both his hands under her nightshirt and ran them up the back of her legs, squeezing firmly when he reached her soft bottom. "You still want to be hard-headed, huh?"

She squealed softly and swatted at him, but he didn't move. "Preston and Jessica are upstairs," she whispered harshly. "They are barely asleep."

Justin nodded and squeezed again. This time he

leaned forward in his seat and buried his head against the space just below her lower abdomen as he did. "Does that mean you want me to stop?" He looked into her hazel eyes and saw her face was flushed with desire.

Randa exhaled deeply and ran her fingers through his hair. He kissed her body softly through the thin nightgown and sent shivers down her spine.

She squealed in delight again, but stepped back from him. "I can't, Justin. I'm too paranoid they'll wake up and catch us," she pleaded.

"It's your doing. If you'd sat next to me as I asked, we wouldn't be doing this." He favored her with a cocky smile and sat back on the love seat, patting the space next to him again. "Ready to sit?"

Dutifully, she took a seat and smoothed her night-shirt down so that Justin couldn't peek at her legs.

He sighed and began with the easiest of his thoughts. "Randa, I want to know what you're feeling for me. I know it hasn't been a long time, but I feel a connection with you. I know I don't have any rights to all your free time, but I need to see you more than once every two weeks. You won't acknowledge me at work, but you're chummy with everyone else, and after hours you're always busy."

Randa stopped herself from rolling her eyes. He was clueless. "Justin, you know we have to be careful around the office. I don't want to lose my job by breaking the rule, unwritten or not."

"I have just as much to lose as you do, but I happen to think we have something worth exploring. I'm tired of hiding my feelings."

Randa gazed at him, her eyes brimming with tears. "Why do you feel such a connection? Is it because of the sex?"

Justin's temper exploded. "I'm not dignifying that with a response. How could you think that?"

"You know my niece and nephew are upstairs and that didn't stop you from feeling me up, did it?" she shot back. She knew she wasn't addressing the real issue, but she couldn't bring herself to say that she knew he was still in love with Lisa.

"You didn't tell me to stop either, Randa!"

She pointed toward the stairs and put a finger over her mouth, indicating he should keep his voice down.

"You know what, you can remain on your icy throne and add a notch for my name," Justin ranted, heading for the front door, but Randa was faster. She planted herself between him and the exit.

"Justin, that's not what I meant." She stared up at him. "I don't know what I'm feeling. You, of all people, should appreciate someone saying the wrong thing at the wrong time. Can we talk about this?"

He looked at her, still determined to walk out the door, but the sight of her full lips quivering made him want to stay. Instinct told him to kiss her, but he couldn't, not after she'd accused him of using her for sex. "Why do you want me to stay? You just said you don't know what you're feeling and that I'm using you for sex. I thought your words were quite clear."

Randa didn't relinquish her position against the door. "I said that because I know how you feel about Lisa. You can't feel connected to me if you're still in love with your ex-wife." She moved out of his way and went back to the living room, regretting the words that had come from her mouth.

Justin followed her, wanting to set the record straight. "How could you think that?"

"Because your marriage has scarred you, and you need closure before you will be able to move on. I can say that because you are constantly comparing me to Lisa. Even when you don't say her name, I feel like she's always in the room with us."

Justin sat beside Randa. Now there was no way he could tell her that Lisa had been calling and would likely be coming to Texas. Randa would never understand. He tried to explain his position to her as best he could. "Randa, I spent fifteen years of my life with her. It's natural that I would still care about her," he pleaded.

Randa stared at him with angry determination. If he wasn't willing to accept what she knew, there was no sense in dating him anymore. "It's time for you to go, Justin."

Justin tried again to explain his feelings to Randa, but she had shut him out. Knowing nothing he could say would get her to listen, he walked out of her house a defeated man.

A few days later Randa entered the office to find Darius waiting at her desk. She immediately became antsy but calmed down after she counted to ten. "Did you want to talk to me, Darius?" she asked, walking up to him and throwing her coat over her chair.

"Yes, I did. Let's talk in my office." Darius stood and walked down the hall.

Randa followed him quietly. She entered his office, realizing this was the first time since the interview that she'd been in there. Once again, she noticed the pictures on his desk of a curly-haired baby with a chubby, honey-beige face. Curry's bright face dazzled her from another photo. Her gaze rested on a wedding photo of Darius and his wife.

Darius noticed her observing his pictures. "I know my family isn't what you had expected, but for all the twists and turns it's endured, it was well worth it." He sighed and leaned back in his leather chair.

"The only thing that matters is that happiness is the end result," she said. Now that her last prospect at happiness had fallen through, she had accepted that she would never have her own family.

Again, he nodded. "Very true."

Randa felt smothered by all the happiness in that room. It was a life she would never know. "What was it that you wanted to see me about, Darius?" she asked, hoping to get her mind off her loneliness.

He nodded. "Of course, I didn't mean to keep you waiting. Randa, I know F&G is going to offer you your old job back. Javier gave me a courtesy call this morning. We want you to stay at Sloane because we know you have great potential. I am offering you a promotion to assistant director of marketing. And a raise."

Randa was shocked. "I appreciate the offer, Darius, but no."

"You're going to F&G?"

"No, I'm staying here. For sixteen years, I let that job dictate my life. I rarely dated after my divorce, had no hobbies, and I certainly couldn't have had my dog. I have more time for my niece and nephew now, and I like the work and the hours. So thanks, but no thanks," she said firmly, leaving no room for negotiation.

Darius relaxed. "Well, I'm glad you're staying. You still get the raise."

"Thank you, Darius." Randa stood as his phone rang, and quietly left his office. As she walked down the hall back to her own desk, she laughed. The old Randa would have grabbed that promotion and all the work that went along with it and asked for more.

* * *

After eating alone at the diner across the street, Justin walked into his office and sat down behind his desk. He could see Randa happily gabbing with Bea, and he wished she would pay him the same attention. As far as he could tell, she hadn't so much as looked in his direction, much less spoken to him, since their argument at her house earlier in the week.

He released a ragged sigh and slumped back in his chair, wondering what to do about Randa. The blinking red light on Justin's phone attracted his attention. He checked his messages, and his blood began to boil when he recognized the voice of his caller.

"Justin, it's Lisa," she purred. "I'll try to call you later."

Now she knows where I work! Justin had known this day was coming every since Randa told him about the prank call at his house, but he was still caught off-guard. He shook his head and buried his head in his hands. This was all he needed. Randa was already angry with him and believed he wasn't over his ex. He'd never be able to convince her that he was over Lisa once his ex-wife inevitably showed up. He just hoped she wouldn't come to his job.

Justin was sure she wanted money, but he was determined not to give her any. She'd caused so much grief in his life that he thought she should be paying him. He picked up the phone and called his brother for some advice.

"Hello?" Jason answered. He'd just left a meeting and had walked into the office on the last ring of the phone.

"Hey, Bro."

"What's going on? You don't usually call me at work. Everything okay?"

Justin filled him in on the message he'd just received and explained his fears about Lisa showing up in Texas. "Jason, do you really think she would show up here?" he asked, his worry evident. "She has to have realized by now that I would get over her eventually."

"But have you?" Jason remembered that even after fifteen years of an unhappy marriage and the discovery that Lisa's reckless spending had left them in the poorhouse, Jason still had to talk Justin into getting a divorce.

"I was married to her for a long time. There will always be a part of me that loves her because she was in my life for so long." He knew his brother didn't understand his logic, but he wanted to explain his point of view anyway. "The Lisa that I divorced was not the Lisa that I married. She was a very insecure woman, and I thought I could give her the security that she needed to be happy. All that spending and competition with her friends was just to make her feel better about herself. I wasn't able to give her what she needed. It's my fault that Lisa started to behave like that. In a way, I feel like I failed her."

Jason was silent for several seconds as the impact of what Justin had just revealed sank in. His brother had never revealed these thoughts to him, and he was taken aback. "Justin, there is nothing you could have done to change Lisa. You say she wasn't like that in the beginning, but she was. Everyone saw it but you. Mom, Dad, me—we all knew she wasn't what she seemed, but you were so happy and in love, you never would have believed us."

"So you sat by and did nothing?" Justin bellowed.

"You were happy, Justin. Who are we to tell you

whom to fall in love with? Would you have listened if we had told you?"

Justin was angry, but he knew his brother was right. He'd fallen in love with Lisa the first time he saw her, and no one could have convinced him they weren't meant to be.

"You're right, I wouldn't have listened. And I know you don't think I am, but I am over her now." He paused for effect before he said the next sentence. "I met someone here." "That's great, Justin. What's she like?" Jason was happy for his brother.

"Her name is Randa. She's my assistant and she's very independent and pretty. She's got the most beautiful hazel eyes." Justin stopped when he realized he sounded like a lovesick teenager.

Jason laughed. "Well, I don't think I've ever heard you refer to Lisa like that. I'd love to meet her whenever I can come down for a visit."

"Definitely." He failed to mention that Randa currently wasn't speaking to him. Justin was still trying to figure out a way to get back in her good graces.

"I'm glad you opened your heart to someone," Jason said.

"Whoa! I never said I opened my heart." Clearly, Justin was still in denial. "I just said I met someone, that's all."

"Just keep your guard up, Justin," his brother reminded him.

Justin wondered at his brother's serious tone. "Where'd that come from?"

Jason exhaled a deep breath. "Well, remember when you separated, and Lisa immediately moved in with that guy? I found out they'd been together before you were legally separated." He hadn't planned to tell his brother that, but now that Lisa was on Justin's trail, Jason didn't want her to be able to sweet-talk her way back into Justin's life. She was an awful woman, Jason thought, but his brother had had it bad for her at one point.

"I figured she was sleeping with somebody," Justin said. He felt a pang in his heart at his brother's words. He'd been devoted to Lisa throughout their marriage, even though he wasn't happy. He had been a good, no, a great husband. Jason was right, there was nothing he could have done to change her. "I can't believe I lost so many good years of my life to her. I feel like I was in prison and was just recently released."

"You can't dwell on that," Jason said optimistically. "Just focus on the future and this new woman in your life. And remember the pain Lisa's caused you when you face her."

After saying good-bye, Justin hung up the phone with his brother and began working on another report.

Randa stepped away from the door just by his office. She'd been on her way to drop off a bundle of papers from Darius when she'd overheard him talking about his marriage. She had no idea that he blamed himself for its failure and Lisa's behavior, too. She felt awful for blowing up at him when he told her he still cared about his ex-wife. Randa figured she of all people should have been more understanding, especially since she still loved her ex-husband. *But I'm not in love with Gareth,* she thought. Randa didn't know what to make of that situation. But, walking back to her desk, she wondered what she could do to make things better between her and Justin.

Later that night, Justin went to Randa's house determined to talk to her. It had been too long since they'd spoken, and he was miserable. *Where is she?* he wondered as he rang the doorbell repeatedly. Zack answered him with several barks. "No, I'm not your mom," he yelled through the door.

Justin walked back to his truck and drove home. Pulling up to his town house, he was surprised to find Randa's car parked in front of it. She hadn't spoken to him all week. He exited his truck and waited as she walked toward him.

"I was beginning to think you weren't coming home," Randa blurted. "I know I should have called first, but I wanted to surprise you."

"What are you doing here?" Justin asked, clearly surprised. He saw Randa's reaction and amended his question. "Not that I'm not glad to see you."

"You don't want me here?" she said with a wounded voice. Randa knew there was a chance he might not want to see her. They hadn't spoken in forever. She turned to walk back to her car, her ponytail bouncing as she did. "I knew this was a bad idea," she muttered.

Justin caught her arm and gently pulled her toward him. "No, don't ever think that." He wrapped his arm around her shoulder and led her back toward the house. "I was surprised because I was just at your house waiting for you. How about dinner?"

Randa sat at the small dining-room table and waited for Justin to seduce her with food. He prepared grilled salmon seasoned with dill and lemon juice, steamed vegetables, and a green salad. She quickly ate her portion and leaned back in the wood dining-room chair. "That was delicious, Justin," she complimented. "You'll have to show me how to do that."

He shook his head, walking around to her chair and helping her up. "It's a family secret. Why don't we have our wine in the living room?"

She nodded, grabbed her glass, and walked toward

the open area. As she entered the room, that chill she felt the first time she entered the house returned. "Why don't you have anything on the walls?" she asked Justin softly. "They look so bare and lonely."

"I know. I've been meaning to buy some pictures and decorations, but I'm not very good in that department." He motioned for her to sit on the couch.

She took a seat beside him and nestled into his body. Randa would never admit it, but she had missed him very much. "You have family and friends; you should have pictures of them up." She scooted closer to Justin and looked up at him with her hazel eyes. "A few pictures might make you feel better. Since the Art Fest is coming up soon, how about I get you a house-warming present?" She leaned against his chest, inhaling his cologne.

Justin leaned down and kissed her forehead. "You're my housewarming present. Can you stay tonight?" The house seemed less empty with her in it.

"I can't. I have to walk Zack, or he'll pee on everything." She paused. "I don't have to walk him this minute, though." She grinned at him and batted her eyelashes innocently. Randa knew they hadn't talked through any of their problems, and she hadn't apologized for making a scene at her home. They were having a perfect evening, and she didn't want to disrupt it with memories of their argument. Plus, she had other needs that were taking precedence at the moment.

Smiling as he caught the hint, Justin stood, offering Randa his hand. "We'll finish this conversation upstairs," he said nuzzling his lips against her neck.

Justin smiled as Randa tossed in her sleep. It was well after midnight, and she was still snoring. He had every intention of waking her two hours ago, but after making love, they were both exhausted and had slept peacefully. As she clung to his body in her sleep, Justin thought about the past and his future. He needed to tell Randa about Lisa, but he didn't know if she thought he was still in love with his ex. Randa had come by his house and they'd made love, but she hadn't said a word about their last fight. Did that mean she was over it? He wanted to wake her and tell her what was going on his life, but Justin didn't want to spoil their wonderful night together.

He let his hand slide gently over her body, caressing her curves. She felt so alive and so not ashamed of her feminine attributes. Pulling her closer to his muscular chest, he held her to him and inhaled the clean scent of her hair. Randa made him feel complete and at that moment, he knew he'd found real love.

When Randa got to work the next morning, Justin wasn't in his office yet. *Thank goodness,* she thought. He was supposed to wake her at ten P.M. so she could go home to walk Zack, but he'd fallen asleep beside her and she hadn't awakened until the middle of the night when she'd heard him crying out Lisa's name. She'd slipped out of the bed without waking him and had gone home to let Zack into the backyard. She hoped Justin had that same empty and alone feeling he'd given her when he'd abruptly left after the first time they made love.

She walked toward the copy room, then stood in the doorway and watched Bea give the copier a swift kick in defeat.

"Bea, why don't you just call the service man?" she asked. She watched as her friend reared back to give the ancient copier another good hit, but miraculously, it began to purr like one of the kittens at the shelter.

"Because Darius told me to order a new one, but this one is like an old friend. We fight. I get it fixed. I know I have to let go," she said, looking up at Randa. "Don't you just glow this morning? How are you and your formidable mate?"

Randa stepped back to look down the empty hall and breathed a sigh of relief. "Bea, remember that subject is off-limits here," she whispered. "Anyway, that's where I was last night. When I got home this morning, Zack had peed on the floor to show me how upset he was. I had a heck of a time getting the smell out." She neglected to tell her how she'd practically run from the house with tears streaming down her face.

"I thought I smelled Lysol. Did you take a bath in it?" Bea laughed as Randa began sniffing her blouse. "I'm kidding, girl. I can't even smell it that much. Spray on a little cologne. Better yet, go downstairs to the gym and take a shower."

"Bea, I couldn't."

"Miranda Stone, I've known you for ten years, and you always have extra clothes in your car. I'll cover for you. If Mr. Jerk has to have something done, I can do it."

Am I really that predictable, Miranda wondered, stopping by her desk to retrieve her keys and mace. She always carried an extra outfit in her car, complete with underwear. Maybe she was that anal, she thought, pressing the down key on the elevator.

Justin approached his desk with apprehension, dreading Randa. He didn't like paybacks, and the sting of waking up alone was still fresh in his mind.

After the great evening they shared, he hadn't expected her to sneak out like that. Maybe she was now using him for sex, or perhaps this was her way of getting back at him for comparing her to Lisa.

He was all set to walk past her like she hadn't hurt his feelings, but he saw her chair was empty. Except for her first day of work, she had always been on time. Inspecting her tidy area, he saw her computer was on. He figured she was already at the office but assumed she was somewhere gabbing with Bea.

Justin walked into his office and took a seat. Remembering an upcoming meeting, he started to compile his notes, but was interrupted when his phone rang. Justin sent a silent heaven-bound prayer, hoping it wasn't his ex-wife. He relaxed as he recognized Bea's voice.

"Justin, Randa had an errand. If you need anything, I'll be happy to help you in her absence."

He knew Bea wasn't crazy about him. Why would she volunteer to cover for Randa? "Thank you." Justin replaced the phone to its cradle and resumed studying his notes.

About thirty minutes later, he noticed Randa walking to her desk. He pushed the intercom button just as she took her seat. "Ms. Stone, if you could step into my office."

She stood and walked the few feet to his office. When she appeared in the doorway, he asked her to come in and close the door. Randa composed herself as she sat. "You wanted to see me, Justin, or Mr. Brewster, or whatever you're calling yourself today?" she asked curtly.

He was in no mood for her childish games. "Why did you leave like that?" he barked.

"Like what?"

"Like a thief in the night?" he blurted.

Randa avoided eye contact. "You called me Lisa in your sleep, and I had to feed Zack." She stood and walked to the door. "If that's all, I have to meet with Ricky and Jose for the final plans for the Art Fest." She walked out of his office.

Justin sat dumbfounded. How could he have called her Lisa? Maybe because he had been thinking about what to do about Lisa when he was falling asleep. He knew it wasn't out of love, but how could he make Randa understand that? The situation was spinning more and more out of control, and Lisa hadn't even appeared yet. He just wondered how bad things would get when she did show up. He slumped back in his chair and tried to figure out how, or if, he could save his relationship.

THIRTEEN

Randa sat in her car, looking blankly into space, not giving any thought to whoever might venture past and catch her in a vulnerable moment. Tears tumbled down her face as her fingers caressed her steering wheel. She gave herself ten points for not losing her cool in front of Justin. After all, she didn't want him having the upper hand in their relationship. Was this even a relationship anyway, or just well-timed sleeping together? She knew he had had a horrible marriage and needed closure to move on. But did he want to move on? She'd heard him excitedly tell his brother he'd met someone, but then amend that to say he hadn't opened his heart.

With a sigh, Randa caught a glimpse of her face in the rearview mirror. Reaching into the console, she retrieved a box of Kleenex and wiped at her streaked makeup. As she did, she noticed her skin as if for the first time. She did have a nice complexion. Why did she still wear all that makeup when it wasn't necessary anymore? She didn't want to admit Justin was right about the war paint, as he'd called it.

She decided that she would treat Justin like any other business deal from then on. Seeing the relationship in terms of debits and credits would help her put whatever it was they had into perspective. If it didn't look profitable, she would sever her ties and move on. With a resigned sigh, she started her car, exited the parking garage, and headed toward Joe's Pizza's headquarters.

Later that afternoon, she sat in the corporate office of Joe's Pizza, located in the ritzy area of West Fort Worth. Gazing out of the conference room window, she watched the busy Interstate 20 traffic. Fifteen years ago, Joe's Pizza was the first corporate office in this desolate area. Now it contained more than fifty major corporations. Randa smiled with pride. She had talked Jose into moving into the building.

She waited for Jose and Ricky to join her. When they entered, each took a seat beside her. Jose's assistant followed them in, but the elder Gutierrez shook his head and told her to leave.

"If I need to write something down, Ricky can do it. Go," he ordered.

Randa laughed as the woman retreated. "Jose, you could be nicer," she admonished.

"Only to you, Randa. Now how are you coming with the Festival?" He looked at the large box of samples Randa had brought with her. "Next time, you get one of these men walking around here in those expensive suits to carry that for you. I will not have you straining your muscles when I have able-bodied directors walking around."

Randa reached into the box. Jose was in a mood. "Well, Mr. Gutierrez," she began. The r's rolled off her tongue, making him smile like she knew he would. "I have brought a proof of the flyers and some sample menu boxes, and I await your approval." She laughed as she passed the paper to both of the men.

Jose studied the paper carefully. Randa knew he was looking for any flaw he could find. He was a perfectionist, much like she was.

"I like this," he said. "I also like the fact that it is in

three languages on one sheet of paper." He inspected the first pizza box as well. He held it up in the air and then he kissed it. "Bueno, Randa, bueno. This is spectacular!" He nodded to Ricky.

Randa smiled at both the men. "Great! I'll put in the print order on Monday, and they'll be ready by Wednesday. I can bring them over after work. Or would you like me to keep them until the festival?"

"No, my strong son will pick them up for me." Jose pulled an envelope out of his breast pocket and presented it to Randa. "This is for you."

She glanced at Jose, then at Ricky, and opened it. Inside was a Disney World Cruise for two. "Jose, I'm flattered, but this is too much. This is for a week on the Mickey Mouse cruise! You know he's my favorite."

Jose beamed. "It was Ricky's idea. You know, Randa, you and I have been together longer than some marriages. You've been with me since the beginning and helped me expand from a one-oven pizzeria to the national chain it is now. I probably owe you more than I could ever possibly pay you. Consider this as a down payment on how much you have helped me." He kissed her on the cheek. "Who knows, maybe you'll get to take it for your honeymoon?"

"I don't know about that. I don't even have a fiancé," she said, slightly embarrassed.

He shook his head. "Is that why you came in here with puffy eyes? Come on, Randa, Mr. Right was probably the one you were fighting with."

Randa stared at Jose in disbelief. Maybe she shouldn't stop wearing makeup just yet. How could he have known she was crying earlier? She had to change the subject before she started blubbering like some silly schoolgirl with her first case of puppy love. "Let's go over the pizza schedule for the festival, shall we?"

* * *

Justin paced his townhouse like a caged tiger. After a few well-placed calls, he still hadn't located Randa. He checked with Jose's office and discovered she'd left there hours ago. He tried her at home but got the answering machine. Arlington was too large a city for him to find her by chance. His phone rang, interrupting his pacing. He picked it up, hoping it was Randa. His blood chilled as he recognized the voice.

For fifteen years he had lived in misery and not known it. Now that he had a glimpse of what life should be, saying no to Lisa would be easy. As he listened to her try to use her feminine wiles through the phone line, he smiled, thinking of Randa. She would never pull a pathetic stunt like this.

"Justin, I need money. You make more than enough to support yourself. Are you going to let your ex-wife starve?" she whined.

"Yes."

Lisa was shocked by his answer. "This is because of that woman who answered your phone that morning I called, isn't it?"

Justin remembered that call. It was the day of Jessica's party. "What are you talking about?"

"Justin, we were married for fifteen years. I'm only asking you for ten grand. That's not so much. What about all those good times we shared?" Lisa pleaded.

"When? Before or after you started sleeping with another man?" he shouted. Justin had tried to hold his temper, but too many thoughts of hurt and disillusion flittered through his mind. "No, Lisa. You should be paying me for all the misery you've caused in my life," he yelled again before hanging up the phone on her.

Justin stomped to the kitchen and grabbed a beer

to calm his nerves. As the cold liquid slid down his throat, he thought of Randa. He loved her, but was he ready to tell her? She was angrier at him than she had ever been before, and rightfully so. If she'd called out Gareth's name in her sleep, he would have left too. Perhaps telling her he loved her now would only be a disaster waiting to happen. She would think he was saying it just so she wouldn't be mad at him. He could, however, sort out the night before with her. He walked to the wall phone in the kitchen and angrily punched her number.

He smiled as he heard Zack's barking when the answering machine kicked on. Justin decided to leave a message. "Randa, this is Justin. . . ." He wanted to say more, but what he could possibly say on the phone to right the situation?

Justin hung up the phone and drove to Randa's house. As he entered her neighborhood, he saw her turning into her driveway. He hoped no children would emerge from her car.

By the time he reached her house, she had already closed the garage door. Justin would be forced to ring the bell.

Randa opened the door, surprised to see him. She held Zack back as she let Justin inside the house. After he was in, she let the dog go and he immediately went to Justin and sniffed his hand. Satisfied he was safe, Zack trotted off to another section of the house.

Justin stared at Randa as she waved him to the living room. After they were both seated, he spoke. "Randa, I'm sorry for the other night. Lisa's been on my mind a lot lately."

She shook her head and averted his gaze. He was telling her what she already knew. "Justin, apologies aren't necessary. Sometimes your subconscious speaks volumes."

He didn't like the look in her eyes. She was disappointed in him. "Let me explain, Lisa's—"

"There's no need, Justin. You were married a long time. You can't shut off your feelings for her, I understand. I still love Gareth, not in the way you love Lisa, but I care for him and his happiness."

Justin didn't realize how badly he'd hurt her until that moment. He knew she was upset, but until she actually spoke, he had no idea to what extent. He had hurt her unintentionally, but he had hurt her just the same. "You can call me Gareth in your sleep, and we'll call it even," he joked, trying to lighten her mood.

It brought a tiny smile to her face. "That wouldn't make it right, Justin. But I appreciate the offer."

He picked up her hand, wishing he had the soul of Langston Hughes or the words of William Shakespeare, but he didn't. He would just have to settle for being honest. "Randa, I don't care for Lisa. I care for you, though. Very much." He scooted closer to her and said, "There are some things concerning her that I have to deal with, but I need you to trust me."

"I'm too tired and too hungry to think about any of this, Justin," she said, confusion evident in her voice. She knew he cared, but she wanted more. For the moment, he made her happy, though, and she decided to enjoy the feeling. She'd worry about all the drama with Lisa later. It was starting to seem like Justin had more debits than credits.

He glanced over her features and noticed the lines of fatigue around her eyes. "I bet the festival is taking all your energy," he diagnosed. "Why don't you go take a shower, and I'll order some food. It's the least I can do." He expected her to tell him no, that she could provide for herself, but she stood and walked toward her bedroom. He walked to the kitchen in search of a take-out menu.

After a few calls and finding out that it would take at least an hour for a delivery, he rummaged through her refrigerator for some kind of food. It seemed everyone in Arlington was ordering in on the same night. He smiled as he spotted pork chops just the way he liked them: center cut and thick. Figuring he could cook them in under the amount of time it would take to have a pizza delivered that night, he decided that they would do for dinner. He spotted Randa's electric grill and went to work.

When Randa returned to the kitchen dressed in lounging clothes, Justin was grilling the last pork chop. He smiled as she paused in the doorway, watching him.

"I thought you were going to order pizza or something?" she asked, taking a seat at the table.

"It was going to take just as long for them to deliver as it would for me to cook." He placed a plate in front of her, then sat across from her. Randa took a bite of the pork chop and moaned. "What's wrong? They aren't too spicy, are they?" Justin asked.

She shook her head and chewed slowly. "These are good. Usually, I fry them, but these are delicious."

Justin smiled as she praised his food. Zack appeared and Randa fed him little bites.

"I thought real food was bad for him," he reminded her.

"I know. He's spoiled. I'll pay for this," she said, offering Zack another bit of meat.

Justin watched her eat. He didn't want to risk saying anything more that might upset her, so he kept his mouth shut. The last thing he wanted was another fight. He just wanted a quiet evening so he could show her how important she was to him.

FOURTEEN

As Randa entered the lobby of her office, she was on cloud nine. She and Justin had spent a glorious weekend together, making love multiple times. He'd cooked every meal they ate and had been a perfect companion. He hadn't mentioned Lisa even once. She was beaming with joy until she saw Darius was waiting for her at her desk again. She hated it when he did that. She glanced at her watch, but it was only 7:50. *I'm not late. What could he want?* she wondered. Randa calmed down as she neared her desk. "Good morning, Darius. Is there something I can do for you?"

Darius smiled at her worried expression. "Don't worry, Randa, it's not that drastic. I wanted to talk to you privately. Perhaps over lunch?"

"Sure, Darius." She watched as he stood and reached inside his blazer pocket, retrieving his computer organizer.

"I'll meet you upstairs at noon." He walked down the hall to his office.

Randa settled at her desk. *Upstairs?* The top floor of their building had a French bistro, Cartisan, where all of the city's bigwigs ate. This must be big news, she guessed. One more thing she didn't need. After a few minutes of deliberation, Randa realized there was nothing she could do but wait until noon and see what Darius wanted. She sat at her desk and continued to work on the final plans for Art Fest.

After she was satisfied that everything had been done, she met Bea in the break room for a cup of coffee.

"You look very satisfied," Bea teased her. "Is it because you have finally stopped wearing all that makeup, or is it the fact that Justin's truck was at your house all weekend? Has he said he's in love yet?"

Randa touched her face as if feeling it for the first time. This morning she had taken Justin's advice and didn't wear any cosmetics. Her skin felt clean and smooth. She stirred her coffee and sighed. Their weekend together had sealed her feelings for him, and while Justin had admitted he cared for her, he hadn't said anything about love.

"You know, Bea, we spent the entire weekend in bed, but not once did he say anything committal. I think I would have felt better if he had said, 'Slam-bam, thank you, ma'am!'"

Bea laughed. "Randa, you know Justin's not going to put his feelings into words. Especially with the marriage he had. He's like a war veteran. Justin's not ready to go into battle yet. Just be thankful he's showing up for a tour of duty."

Randa giggled at her crazy friend. "Thanks." Bea always had a knack for putting things in their proper perspective. "Bea, I know you can't give me details, but Darius asked me to lunch upstairs. Do you know anything about that?" Bea avoided looking at Randa. "I just want to know if it's good news or bad, that's all. I hope they didn't change their minds about firing me because of the F&G case," Randa worried.

Bea shook her head. "I can't tell you what it is, but

it's good news. You don't have anything to worry about."

"Thanks, Bea," she said, hugging her friend.

As the women walked back to their respective offices, Randa noticed Justin talking to Curry in the hallway. She sat at her desk, checked her e-mail, and then looked at Justin's appointments for the day. She saw he would be in meetings most of the morning.

Randa tried to concentrate on her work, but memories of their weekend together kept running through her mind. When Justin walked into his office, dressed in a black suit that accented the broadness of his back, her heartbeat accelerated, and Randa thought her heart would pop out of her chest.

Justin smiled as he took a seat behind his desk. After two days and two nights with Randa, he was tired, but in a good way. He'd more than enjoyed himself that weekend, but he wanted more from her than her body. He remembered when she told him a while back that she wasn't looking for a relationship, but a lot had happened between them since then. He wondered if she'd changed her mind.

With all that doubt, Randa still found a place in his heart. As she entered his office, Justin looked up from a small pile of paperwork that he hadn't finished over the weekend, silently approving of her formfitting blue suit. Did she have every color of stilettos ever made? he thought when his eyes reached her feet. Looking at her, he saw her face was free of makeup, except for lipstick. To him, she had never looked more beautiful. She smiled, and his heart instantly melted.

"Justin," she said lightly. "Justin?"

He blinked, coming out of his daydream. "I'm sorry, Randa. What is it?"

"You have a meeting in ten minutes in the conference room."

He nodded, and she left the room. His gaze was riveted on her body, watching the muscles in her legs move as she walked.

He walked to the meeting and took a seat at the large table. As usual, Darius was the facilitator.

"I have a favor to ask all of you," Darius started. "I would like to offer Randa Stone the job of tech manager. Before you decide, I would like to offer my reasons. She almost single-handedly worked on the Art Fest project for Joe's Pizza, donating much of her spare time to it. She has a flair for writing copy and gave a fresh slant to some old campaigns. I also think she could breathe new life into the annual investors' report. Are there any objections?"

The partners turned to look at Justin, and he couldn't understand why. Surely they didn't expect him to object after he'd previously supported her. "I think that's a great idea, but I do have a concern," Justin said.

Darius smiled. "Yes, Justin," he said, urging him to continue.

"Who will replace Randa? She's only been with the firm a few months. What will the other assistants think about her leapfrogging?"

"Good point. Randa, if she takes the promotion, wouldn't leave her current position until a suitable replacement is found. I think this move will show the other assistants that when we see an employee excelling in a certain area, we'll guide them to the top as best we can."

Justin nodded in agreement. As he listened to the partners speak on Randa's behalf, he wondered if this would mean he'd have even less time to spend

with her. He wasn't so sure this was even what she
wanted. After all, he'd heard she turned down the
offer to be his assistant director. Randa liked having limited hours and more free time. She was
already complaining she was bogged down in overtime preparing for Art Fest and had too little time to
do the things she enjoyed. He couldn't even remember the last time she'd been to the shelter.
When Darius dismissed the meeting, Justin walked
back to his office wondering what Randa would do.

Randa met Darius in the Cartisan restaurant as
arranged. To her surprise, Darius sat alone at the
table. She smiled as he rose from his seat as she entered the room. He pulled out a chair for her, and
she thanked him.

"You're welcome," Darius said, taking his seat
again and launching into an explanation of why he
wanted to see her. "Randa, I feel that you're a valuable asset to the firm, and I'm glad you gave us the
chance to stretch your potential. You seem to excel
at writing assignments. I want to offer you the job of
tech manager."

Randa was floored. She was expecting a pat on the
back for her work on the Joe's Pizza campaign, not
a promotion. "Darius, I couldn't," she said. "I told
you when you offered the last—"

He raised his hand to stop her refusal. "Hear me
out before you say no to this one. You could set your
own hours and work from home if you wanted to.
You'd be overseeing the writing of brochures and
manuals. You have a flair for it, Randa," he persisted.
"I think you should pursue it. It's a forty-hour-a-week
job. You've already told me how important Zack and
your family are to you."

Randa considered the option. She did love the writing aspect of it, but then she wouldn't see Justin or Bea or any of her other friends at work. Then again, she could buy another Mercedes. "Could I think about it, Darius?"

Darius continued listing all the perks of the job. "You'd have your own office and assistant. You'd be in charge of five people. And no, you can't have Beatrice as your assistant, she's mine!"

They both laughed at the idea. Randa began to think about the job. She liked being an assistant and being near Justin, but if it was a position she would love, why not? "I'd like to think about it if I could. I don't want this turning into my former job, where I worked seventy-plus hours a week and still took a ton of work home. I like the life I have now."

Darius held up his hands. "Okay, Randa. Take a few days and think about it. I think you would be perfect for the job."

Randa didn't want to let Darius down. He'd hired her after those idiots at F&G let her go just because she wasn't Hispanic. She knew she owed him. "I'll definitely think about it."

"Great, let's order lunch." He raised his hand to summon the waitress.

Soon a woman dressed in a short, black skirt and white cotton blouse came to the table with two menus and a tray with crystal goblets of water on it. She smiled as she spoke to Darius. "Mr. Crawford, may I take a drink order for you and your guest?" the pretty woman asked, handing each of them a menu.

He opened his menu and quickly made a selection before he closed it, glancing at Randa. "Are you ready?"

She hadn't looked at very many of the choices but didn't want to seem like she couldn't make a decision on something as simple as lunch. "Of course, Darius," she said, stalling as she continued to read.

"Ladies, first."

Randa chose the first thing she saw. "I'll have an iced tea and the filet mignon with baked potato and salad." She handed the menu back to the waitress, hoping she hadn't ordered too much.

As usual, Darius always made her feel at ease. "Let me get a Coke, a T-bone steak, and a salad." He smiled at the woman as he handed her the menu. After she had retreated from the table, Darius spoke. "If I eat too much today, I will have two women mad at me— Darbi and Cherish. Darbi's cooking tonight."

Randa plotted the hazards of being too nosy with her boss after he had just offered her a promotion. Curiosity got the best of her. "Why is it so special that your sister is cooking?"

Darius snickered. "Well, Darbi just started cooking after my nephew was born. Usually Curry cooks, or they eat at my house. This is her first attempt. We're going over for dinner tonight." He shook his head and smiled.

Randa felt a pang of envy in her stomach as Darius talked about his wonderful family life. "That sounds great, Darius," she said with false enthusiasm.

As she added several packets of sugar to the iced tea the waitress had just put on the table, she wondered if her turn at happiness would ever come.

Randa walked back to her desk after her meeting with Darius, surprised that Justin wasn't at his desk. She'd forgotten to tell him about her lunch meeting and knew he'd been wondering where she'd disappeared to for two hours. She couldn't wait to tell him the good news.

Justin didn't return to his office until almost five.

Randa was shutting down her computer when he appeared at her desk.

"You think I could take you to dinner tonight?" he asked.

"I'd like that, but I have to walk Zack first." She turned off her computer and gathered her belongings. She'd tell him about Darius's offer over dinner. Then they could celebrate afterward in the bedroom.

He looked at her, his lips a thin line of frustration. Justin wondered why she wasn't telling him about the promotion. "Sounds good. How about eight?"

"See you then."

Randa nodded and left. After she got on the elevator, she exhaled. Visions of their weekend together had flashed through her mind and she came very near to breaking with decorum and smothering Justin with kisses in their place of work. He wouldn't have minded, but she didn't want to break her own rule.

As Randa prepared for her date, she wondered if Justin would be spending the night. She wanted him to stay, but she had too much on her plate this week to entertain all evening. She slipped on a black sheath dress and black pumps and was about to put on her diamond earrings when the doorbell rang. Randa grabbed them and headed to the foyer.

"Hi, Justin," she said, picking up her purse from the console table and pulling the door behind her.

As he drove, Randa knew he had something on his mind because he was too quiet. Was it Lisa? He'd said there were some things to take care of concerning her, but what? She would have asked, but she wanted to keep her head buried in the sand for at least the night. She had a feeling doom was waiting for her around the corner.

Over dinner, Justin waited for Randa to tell him about the promotion. He wanted to talk to her about it, but he refused to introduce the subject. If the position made her happy, he would encourage her to take it, even though he would miss interacting with her all day. As he drove back to her house, he couldn't wait any longer.

"So, are you taking the job?" he asked, straining to keep his eyes on the road.

"How did you know?" she said in a surprised voice. "I was going to tell you over dessert." She reached across the armrest and massaged his leg.

Justin moved her hand. He wondered if there was a reason she hadn't said anything. Maybe she'd already taken it and not said anything. He wondered if he was being paranoid. "I have my sources," he said curtly. "Were you going to tell me, or was there going to be a stranger sitting at your desk one morning?"

"Justin, I didn't mention it because Darius told me I had some time to think about it." *What is he so mad about?* she wondered.

He listened as she shifted in the seat and began fiddling with her purse. She was getting angry. "So what's your decision?" he blurted.

"I haven't thought about it, as I just said a few moments ago," she fired back.

Justin fumed at the game of chase she was playing. "Surely you have an idea. It would mean a lot to your career and it would be a lot more money if you took the job."

"Money isn't everything, Justin. Your ex really did a number on you, didn't she?" she said, her irritation clear. "The creative aspect of the job intrigued me."

"I knew it! I knew you were going to take it."

An Important Message From The ARABESQUE Publisher

Dear Arabesque Reader,

Arabesque is celebrating 10 years of award-winning African-American romance. This year look for our specially marked 10th Anniversary titles.

Why not be a part of the celebration and **let us send you four specially selected books FREE!** These exceptional romances will be sent right to your front door!

Please enjoy them with our compliments, and thank you for continuing to enjoy Arabesque.... the soul of romance bringing you ten years of love, passion and extraordinary romance.

Linda Gill
PUBLISHER, ARABESQUE ROMANCE NOVELS

P.S. Watch out for our upcoming Holiday titles including *Merry Little Christmas* by Melanie Schuster, *Making Promises* by Michelle Monkou, *Finding Love Again* by AlTonya Washington and the special release of *Winter Nights* by Francis Ray, Donna Hill and Shirley Hailstock—*Available wherever fine books are sold!*

New Holiday Titles

ARABESQUE

★BET BOOKS

www.BET.com

SPECIAL OFFER!
4 BOOKS
FREE!

A SPECIAL "THANK YOU" FROM ARABESQUE JUST FOR YOU!

Send this card back and you'll receive 4 FREE Arabesque Novels—a $25.96 value—absolutely FREE!

The introductory 4 Arabesque Romance books are yours FREE (plus $1.99 shipping & handling). If you wish to continue to receive 4 books every month, do nothing. Each month, we will send you 4 New Arabesque Romance Novels for your free examination. If you wish to keep them, pay just $18* (plus, $1.99 shipping & handling). If you decide not to continue, you owe nothing!

- Send no money now.
- Never an obligation.
- Books delivered to your door!

We hope that after receiving your FREE books you'll want to remain an Arabesque subscriber, but the choice is yours! So why not take advantage of this Arabesque offer, with no risk of any kind. You'll be glad you did!

In fact, we're so sure you will love your Arabesque novels, that we will send you an Arabesque Tote Bag FREE with your first paid shipment.

* PRICES SUBJECT TO CHANGE.

YOU'LL GET 4 SELECT ROMANCES PLUS THIS FABULOUS TOTE BAG!

ARABESQUE

**Visit us at:
www.BET.com**

"What are you saying, Justin?"

"You always talk about how you want more time to yourself, but money drives you just like every other woman."

It was a thinly veiled comparison between her and Lisa. Randa had enough.

"Stop the truck." She opened the door before he could come to a complete stop.

Justin watched in shock as she got out of his vehicle, slammed the passenger door, and started walking.

"I'll walk the rest of the way, Mr. Brewster."

He knew it was only a half a mile to her house, but it was night and she had on stilettos. He pushed the button, letting the passenger window down and yelled, "Don't be silly, Randa. Get in the truck."

"Not if you were the last fool on earth!" she shouted. Randa continued walking.

"Randa, I'm sorry, please get in the truck." His voice was softer this time, but equally as firm. He kept his foot on the accelerator, easing along beside her like he was Morgan Freeman and she was Miss Daisy.

Finally, she stopped and turned to face him. "I am Randa, not Lisa," she screamed. "When you understand that, then we can have something. Until then, stay the hell away from me." Randa was in love with Justin, but she couldn't play second fiddle to any woman to keep him.

Justin cursed himself for implicitly referring to Lisa and starting another war. He just couldn't get it right with Randa, no matter how hard he tried. They'd spent a perfect weekend together and now, he'd ruined whatever was between them.

Randa continued to march toward her house and Justin followed. He made sure she got inside safely and when he saw her turn on the light in her foyer, he sped off, screeching his tires as he left.

Justin was in the conference room for the weekly meeting two days later. Randa was back to ignoring him, and she hadn't spoken to him since their last date. He'd let his paranoia and trust issues get in the way and had blown up at Randa for no good reason. He blocked out most of the meeting and zoned back in just as Darius said, "Randa has decided to take the tech manager position. She's working out at the Art Fest for the rest of the week. If anyone needs assistance, please contact Mica or Beatrice."

He thought Darius would have elaborated on her decision, but he didn't.

"Justin, you and Randa can start interviewing in the next few weeks," Darius continued. "Is that okay?"

"Yes, Darius, that's fine." What else could he say?

"Good."

When the meeting ended, Justin walked back to his office in a trance. In a few weeks a stranger would be sitting in Randa's chair. He wouldn't be able to watch her walk to the copier or laugh with other assistants anymore. God, how he liked the sound of her laugh; it was so full and rich. Every time he heard it, he wanted to join in. He wondered where her new office would be.

He sat down at his desk, mapping out a strategy. Not for an upcoming meeting or an ad campaign, but for how to get back in Randa's good graces.

He stared at the blank computer screen, angry that he had put himself in this predicament again. What could he do to make it up to her this time? Take Zack to the vet? Take her on a trip? Neither one had time to take off from work. Especially now that she was going to take the job. He knew she wasn't the type for jewelry as a peace offering. Justin didn't know what to do, but he had to do something.

FIFTEEN

Saturday morning, Justin dressed for the Art Fest. At the end of the weekly meeting, Darius had requested that all management make an appearance to show support for Randa and Jose. It gave Justin the opportunity he needed to be there and not look like the begging man he was sure he would turn into when he saw Randa.

Justin missed her the previous week. Several times he'd called to apologize, but each time he'd talked to her answering machine, and she'd never returned any of his calls. He hoped he could pull her aside at the festival and tell her he was sorry for comparing her to his ex again.

When he arrived at the festival, he wasn't prepared for the Randa he saw. She was dressed in short denim shorts and a T-shirt advertising Joe's Pizza, like in his daydream. The cotton shirt was tied in a knot in the front, exposing her flat stomach to the Texas weather. She wore a baseball cap with her hair in a ponytail that was pulled through the open end in the back. She was in total control, directing the cooks and servers with the precision of a drill sergeant.

Justin also saw both Mica and Beatrice handing out fliers to passersby. As he glanced around the festival, he noticed some of his coworkers were milling around, but he didn't feel like hobnobbing just then.

Since Randa was busy, he decided to browse through the booths. Maybe he could take Randa's suggestion and get some art for his house.

As Justin walked, nothing caught his eye. He turned down another aisle, and a tall man behind a counter called out to him.

"Brother, you look like a man in search of a 'Baby, I'm sorry' gift."

Justin laughed. "Dead on."

"Well, let me show you some of my creations. Is the lady into the art of our people?"

"She likes all art." Justin looked through the artwork, and while it was good, it wasn't what Randa liked. It was too modern, and she preferred classics. One painting that mirrored Basquiat's style caught his eye, and he could easily imagine it in his living room. Randa would be proud.

As he paid for the artwork, he finally noticed a painting that Randa would like. Since he needed all the points in the world to get back in her good graces, he bought it for her. He took both pieces of art to his truck, then returned to the festival and headed for the pizza booth.

To his dismay, he noticed Gareth standing next to Randa with his arm around her waist. If he didn't know better, he'd swear that Gareth was straight.

"Why don't you take a picture? It will last longer," Bea teased, handing him a flier as he stood in line. "Doesn't Randa look nice today? Guys have been hitting on her all morning; they all think she's 28. If I had been a jerk to her earlier in the week, I would really be feeling like a fool right now," she said before walking toward Randa.

"Well, Justin, you asked for it. And now you're

getting it," he muttered. He stood in the long line
of pizza customers. As he surveyed the area for
more competitors for Randa's attention, he noticed her brother and his two kids. He watched
as Randa picked up Preston and hugged him, easily imagining her being a mother to their children.
Justin shook his head to clear the thought from
his mind.

The line started to move, and Justin was soon at
the counter. "Supreme and a Coke," he told the
teenager behind the counter. He handed over his
coupons and received his food. Just as he turned
around with his purchase, Preston ran into him,
knocking the food out of his hands and onto the
ground. Immediately, Justin stooped to see if the little boy was okay.

"Oh, Justin, I'm sorry. He was chasing his sister,"
Randa pleaded, picking up her nephew. "What were
you having? I'll get you another." She grabbed a
handful of napkins from the counter and began wiping his shirt.

He took the napkins from her hand. "Please, I can
do it myself," he said, wiping the front of his clothing.
Every time she touched him, a fire started in his loins.

"Justin, what did you have?" Randa persisted.

"Supreme and a Coke." He watched her lean over
the counter and retrieve the order for him. His gaze
lingered on her bottom.

"Here you go." She handed the tray to him and
disposed of the empty one. "I'm really sorry Preston
ran into you."

"That's okay, Randa. Can you take a break? I'd really like to talk."

"Really, I think you stated your position quite
clearly the other day."

Justin sighed. "I'd like to apologize, if you could spare a few minutes?"

Randa watched him for an agonizing moment, wondering if it was even worth hearing him out. She handed Preston to his father and then walked to the booth to whisper to one of the workers. She returned to Justin with two slices of pepperoni and a Coke. "Okay, Justin. Lead the way."

He quickly led her to a table under the tent. Justin wanted to get it over with as quickly as possible. "Randa, I would just like to say I'm sorry about the other night. I was selfish and upset, and I took my frustration out on you."

Randa bit into her pizza, nodding her head. "Yes, Justin, you did. I can't see why you were so upset about Darius asking me to take the tech manager position."

"Because I didn't want to lose a good assistant."

"Is that all I am to you?" She shook her head. This man was unbelievable. "I do a good job, and we occasionally sleep together, so I guess I'd be hard to replace." She sipped her soda and stared at him, her hazel eyes unwavering.

"No, that's not what I meant. You're the one who didn't want any play at work, remember?"

"Justin, you know the rules just as well as I do. I just think we should follow them, especially with us being in plain view of the rest of the company." She sighed, tired of repeating herself to him. "Look, I'll make sure I find you a capable assistant to take care of all my duties, okay?"

"I don't want another assistant, I want you!" Justin raised his voice. "Can't you see that? I wanted to object when Darius brought the job up, but what was I supposed to say? 'Oh no, Darius, we're sleeping together.'"

"I'm not even angry about you wanting me not to

take the job. Before we argued, I wasn't even going to take it. I only said yes so I could get away from you."

Justin was hurt by her statement, but he knew it was his own fault. He chugged his drink to buy some time. "Why?"

"We need some distance. Maybe we're too close and too convenient to each other," she said thoughtfully.

"You've got to be kidding."

Randa wiped her mouth and placed the napkin gently across her plate. "Look, I'm fond of you, Justin, but your ex has your mind so messed up, you can't see straight. You need space to figure out what you want to do and who you want to be with. I won't live in the shadow of your ex-wife. Every time things aren't perfect between us, you start to treat me like I'm her, Justin, and I'm not her. I'm tired of it."

He sighed heavily. This wasn't how he was expecting this conversation to go. "I'm much closer to getting her out of my head thanks to you, Randa." He reached across the table and grasped her hand. "Congratulations on your new position. I just hope there's still room for me once you start." He took a gamble putting all his feelings on the table. No pain, no gain.

"Of course, there is." She felt the sincerity in his voice and wiped her eyes with her free hand. Randa could tell he felt about her the way she felt about him, even if he hadn't said it.

"Are you working all day?" Justin asked.

"Just until three. Jose is coming for the evening shift. It's the Gutierrez men tonight."

"How about we look at some art after you get off?"

"Oh, no. I've been here since five this morning. I just want to go home." Randa checked her watch. "I'd better get back. Those kids have probably had a party in my absence." She picked up her tray of uneaten food and threw it in the trash can.

Justin did the same, walked her back to the pizza booth, and said good-bye. He waved to Bea, then left the Art Fest. Feeling defeated, he dragged his feet all the way to his truck.

Later that night, Justin's phone rang during the news. He was happy to hear Randa's voice, even if things were still left up in the air between them.

"I think I'm just exhausted. I stayed until after six. Every bone I have aches, and my feet are swollen."

He grew concerned. "Are you okay?" he asked. Randa's voice was just above a whisper, and he could barely make out the words.

"Have you eaten?"

"No, I'll eat later. I'm going to lie down." She hung up the phone, and Justin grabbed his keys and wallet.

Randa sounded awful, and he wasn't convinced she was okay. Plus, this was a good way for him to make up for the ass he'd been last week. He headed out the door straight to Randa's.

He knocked on her door and waited. It took her awhile to get the door, but she finally made it. Justin watched her walk in slow motion back to the couch. Randa plopped down and let out a tired breath. Zack watched her from a safe distance.

"Why don't you soak in a tub?" Justin suggested. "The hot water might soothe your tired muscles." He stood over her with a worried look on his face.

"Too much energy," she squeaked. Randa leaned against the couch and yawned. "I just want to lie here and sleep."

Without another thought, Justin picked her up and carried her to the bathroom. He thought of the hazards of leaving her alone in a tub of water. When he looked over at her vanity while he prepared her bubble bath, he saw she was falling asleep.

Justin finished with her bathwater, then undressed her and helped her into the tub. He was surprised she wasn't voicing her apprehension and complaining that she could do it herself. She sighed as he began washing her gently and kept perfectly still as he massaged her aches in slow, circular motions. As she relaxed in his arms, Justin smiled. *So this was what being in love meant.*

When she had called earlier, all he thought of was getting to her and relieving the tired sound in her voice any way he could. If that meant he had to be a nursemaid, then so be it.

After he helped her out of the bathtub and dressed her in a nightshirt, he placed her across the bed and went to the kitchen to prepare dinner. By the time he'd returned with a tray of food, Randa was sound asleep. He tucked her under the covers and went to the room down the hall.

Randa awoke Sunday morning to the aroma of breakfast—eggs, bacon, and orange juice. *Maybe I'm delirious from starvation,* she thought.

Soon Justin, who was shirtless, entered the room with a tray. "I thought you might be hungry, so I prepared a little something for you." He sat it on the bed in front of her.

"T-Thank you, Justin." Randa looked down at her bedclothes. "Especially for last night." She vaguely remembered him bathing and dressing her.

"It was nothing. Maybe you could repay me the favor one day." Justin handed the loaded plate to her. "How do you feel?"

"Exhausted. Remind me never to volunteer for anything again." She took a bite of eggs and quickly reached for the orange juice. After gulping down half of the contents of the glass, she gasped, "I should have known!"

"Sorry. Force of habit." He handed her a napkin to wipe the water that had welled in her eyes.

"Justin, I'm going to start hiding the spice rack when you come over." She smiled at him as she finished her orange juice. "Is this the only way you cook eggs?"

"In the last year, yes. I can make you some plain eggs, if you like." He watched her with puppy-dog eyes.

If she said yes, she'd hurt his feelings. "No, Justin. These are fine." Randa coughed, trying to rid the last bit of pepper from her throat.

Justin stood and took the tray. "I'll make some medium ones," he said and started to walk out of the room.

"Justin," Randa called. He stopped and faced her. His big brown eyes played havoc with her heart. "I can eat the inferno eggs. Come back here."

"No. I don't want you eating something that you don't like. I see now I'll just have to heat you up slowly," he teased, turning back toward the door.

She pushed the covers back, put on her bathrobe, and headed for the kitchen. Zack met her at the bottom of the steps. "I bet you're hungry," she said, reaching for the cupboard. She poured dog food in his empty bowl, but Zack didn't touch it. "What's wrong?" she asked him.

Justin chuckled as he cooked eggs. "I fed him already."

Randa gasped and bent down to rub Zack's tummy. "You didn't?" she asked Justin.

"No, I didn't feed him those eggs." Motioning for her to sit down at the table, he walked toward her with a fresh plate of eggs, bacon, and toast. He placed a cup of coffee in front of her as well.

Randa liked it when Justin cooked. He looked like he belonged in her kitchen, and she could pretend that she had the life she'd always wanted—the one she'd missed out on when she was slaving away at F&G. Randa felt a strange sense of security but knew it was too fragile to get used to. Any second, the wrong thing could be said, they would have a shouting match, and she'd be throwing Justin out of the house.

She ate the new breakfast, then a second helping, and sighed. "That was excellent. I'm sorry my palate is not as strong as yours. How did you get into spicy food anyway?"

Justin leaned back on the counter, unknowingly flexing his muscles for Randa. "A few years ago, I was on a business trip to New York and a friend took me to a bunch of Indian and Mexican restaurants. I was hooked. When I returned home, Lisa wouldn't hear of having those kinds of meals so I only ate them when I was out of town. Since we separated, I have eaten something spicy every night in celebration." He grinned at her as he picked up her empty plate from the table.

"Justin, I didn't mean for you to bring up your marriage. I know how painful it is for you to talk about it."

He grabbed Randa's hand. "That used to be so, but not anymore. Since we've been seeing each other, the memories are still there, but they don't hurt as much." Justin looked into her eyes, then suddenly turned away.

He hadn't heard from Lisa recently, but he knew it was just a matter of time. He didn't want Randa to be caught off-guard or get the wrong impression when she arrived. It wasn't the right time to tell her then, he decided. When would be the right time?

"What would you like to do today?" he asked.

"Justin, I'm kinda tired from yesterday. How about a movie or something?"

"Okay." Suddenly he turned to the counter and grabbed his keys. "I have to get something out of my truck. Be right back." He rushed out of the kitchen.

Randa didn't have much time to wonder what he was doing. He rushed back into the kitchen with a large box.

"This is for me being a jackass," he said, handing her the box.

"Thank you, Justin." She hurriedly unwrapped the painting. "It's beautiful. The colors are so vibrant. It will make me happy every time I look at it." She stood and walked toward him, lightly kissing him on the lips.

He returned the embrace, overwhelmed by his feelings. "You are very welcome and very special," he said. He thanked her with a passionate kiss that let her know just how appreciative he was.

Randa was grateful for his accolades, but she noticed he didn't say anything about love.

SIXTEEN

"What was wrong with that one, Justin?"

Randa sat down in the seat in his office, recently vacated by the latest applicant. "She had good references, has worked in the marketing profession, and she couldn't quit staring at you."

Justin watched as Randa crossed her legs. She was so beautiful, and he could have stared into her eyes all day. But how was he supposed to do that if he didn't have her as his assistant? "I know. But something just didn't seem right. She didn't have your smile or your grasp of business. Maybe the next one will be better."

Randa shook her head, knowing that wasn't possible. "We have interviewed over twenty people for my job in the last week, and you've found something wrong with each and every one of them. Maybe if you tell me exactly what you're looking for, it will speed up the process."

"I want you. How many more of these are we going to do today? Maybe we could have dinner tonight?"

Randa took a deep breath, searching for patience. "Only if you tell me what you want in an assistant. I'm supposed to start my new job in three weeks, but I can't if you don't have a suitable replacement. So what do you want?"

"You."

"Justin," she pleaded softly.

He held his hands up in the air in a surrender motion. "I know. I made my bed, now I'm lying in it." He took a deep breath and sighed. "Okay, I want a male assistant."

"Why?"

"Because if it's a woman, I'll constantly compare her to you. I probably still will with a male. You have spoiled me for any other assistant." *Probably any other woman, too,* he feared.

She smiled her usual brilliant smile that jump-started his heart. "Well you just happen to be in luck, Justin. I have the impeccable résumés of two male assistants on my desk. You'll be seeing them this afternoon. So get ready." She scribbled in her notepad and stood.

He watched her straighten her short skirt and walk out of his office with an extra sway to her hips. How would he ever get used to her not being there?

Not picking an assistant would only delay the inevitable. She had to leave, and if she didn't do it soon, it would cause problems. Darius had also begun to question why it was taking so long to find a capable replacement. The tech department was anxiously awaiting her arrival, and Justin was the holdup.

"Justin." Randa's soft voice interrupted his daydream.

"Yes, Randa." He watched her walk into his office with a large brown envelope in her hands.

"This was brought in by messenger." She placed the envelope down and as she left the office, she said, "I'm going to lunch now. With Gareth." She stared at Justin, waiting for him to explode, but he was too occupied with her delivery to respond. Randa shrugged and left the room, closing the door behind her.

Justin looked at the envelope and sighed. It was

from Lisa. *Damn!* Evidently, she still didn't have his home address or else she would have sent it there. He opened it and laughed as he glanced through the ten-page letter inside.

He called his brother and informed him of the situation, then asked his advice.

"I say, let Lisa play out her hand," Jason said. "The worst that can happen is that she'll say or do something that will land her in jail. You know, you can still file charges against her for trying to forge your name."

"No, I just want her out of my life," Justin responded. "If I file charges against her, I'll be dragged through court, and I don't want that. I'm having enough problems right now."

Randa studied the menu, then looked toward her lunch companion. The atmosphere of the elegant restaurant was soothing, and she was happy to be out of the office. Justin was driving her batty with his refusal to pick an assistant. "What are you having, Gareth?"

"Lobster."

"I'll have the same." Randa smiled at him across the table as they waited for someone to take their order. "Okay, Gareth, what's the celebration lunch for?"

"You, silly." He toasted her with his water glass. "You know I always keep track of you, honey."

Randa gasped. He hadn't called her honey in over five years, mainly because Josh became insanely jealous the last time he did. "Gar, I only told a few people outside of work about my promotion. Did Karl tell you?"

"No."

"How do you know such intimate details about my life?" she asked, raising an eyebrow.

"Why?" he teased.

"Because sometimes it makes me feel uneasy. You're not my husband anymore."

"But I still love you."

Why can't the right person say that at the right time? she wondered. "Gareth, I love you too."

"Jessica told me," he admitted.

"You've been pumping my eight-year-old niece for information? I can't believe you would stoop so low." She laughed at the simplicity of it.

"Your brother and the kids eat at my restaurant all the time. They are all very proud of you, and so am I. After you were fired from F&G, you didn't wallow in self-pity; you pulled yourself up and found another start. Here's to the life you deserve." He toasted her with his glass again.

"What's brought all this on?"

The waiter came to take their orders and they passed him their menus after they gave their selections.

"Well, I had a meeting with my accountant the other day, and I need your signature on a few things."

"Why?"

"Because you and Josh are co-executors of my estate. You have controlling interests in my business; you know that."

"Yes. I know about the shares of stock, but what about the mess about your estate? I am not discussing anything relating to you not being here." She started to hum to drown out his voice.

"Randa, we need to discuss it," he said over her salute to the classics.

"No, Gareth. I don't like talking about it. Is there something you're not telling me?"

He was silent.

"I knew something was wrong when you wanted to have lunch today." She took a deep breath to calm her nerves. She hoped he wasn't sick. "What is it, Gareth?"

He hesitated before he spoke. "I went to the doctor the other day. It may not be anything, but they want to take some tests this week. I was hoping you could come with me."

"What kind of tests?" she cried out, fighting back tears. A defiant tear slid down her cheek. "Of course I'll go with you. What about Josh?"

"You know what a mess he is around doctors. I don't want him up there crying and acting all girly on me. He said it was okay if you came with me."

"What's wrong?"

"Well, there is a little problem with one of the valves around my heart. The doctor thinks it may be closed, but an X-ray or an EKG couldn't show anything. So, can you go?" he asked with a false nonchalance.

"Yes, just tell me when. I'll just schedule the interviews around it. Hopefully, Justin will have made a decision before you go."

"You're scheduling interviews for him now?" Gareth muttered a curse, then finished his glass of champagne. He didn't like Justin any more than Justin liked him.

"Yes," Randa explained. "The only way I can start my new job is to find him a suitable replacement. But out of the last twenty applicants, he has shot down each one. I'm beginning to wonder if he'll ever pick one."

"I think he's in love with you."

Randa nearly choked on her water. "I don't think so." Since the picnic, she'd thought Justin loved her, but he had yet to say it, so she wasn't entirely sure. The closest he'd gotten was when he told her that he cared for her.

"Randa, he always looks at me like I'm his competition," Gareth said. "Every time he sees us together, he looks like he could kill me. Doesn't he remember that I'm gay? You just tell him I'll always be around, so he'd better get used to it."

"You don't have to worry about him, Gareth. Justin and I have an understanding." *I love him and he's fond of me,* she thought.

"How's he going to react to you going to the doctor with me? He might try to find a reason for you not to go."

"He'll be fine. Don't worry."

That evening, Justin rang Randa's doorbell. He counted the seconds until she opened the door and left him speechless.

Randa stood in the doorway wearing a short strapless lavender dress and matching stilettos. The way the dress hugged her hips and emphasized her full breasts, reminded him that she was very much a sexy woman. He was beginning to rethink going out to dinner.

"Justin, are you okay? What's wrong?" Randa asked, ushering him inside and into the living room.

"You look great," he finally managed to say. "Are you sure you want to go out?"

She shook her head as she closed the front door. "Come on."

Over dinner, Randa told Justin she'd be out of the office at least one day the following week.

"Why can't your ex-husband's boyfriend take him to the hospital?" Justin snapped. "I still haven't chosen an assistant. Are you going to leave the tech department in a bind whenever he snaps his fingers?" He stared at the menu and tried to control his breathing.

"Justin, don't be a jerk. He's sick and asked me to go with him because Josh is afraid to go. That's much more important than you finding an assistant. Are you telling me you're a director and can't interview three people by yourself?" she taunted.

He took a deep breath and tried to calm down. He knew he was being irrational and should have known the guilt trip wouldn't work on Randa. Besides, this was supposed to be a romantic dinner, not an argument. "I'm sorry, you're right. Of course, I can interview them. I just hope everything turns out okay with Gareth."

She graced him with her winning smile. "Justin, I will be at the hospital with Gareth. If you need me, you can call me on my cell phone." She could see the lights going off in Justin's head and quickly amended her previous statement. "But only if it is a true emergency. Not to complain that you don't like how the prospective applicants looked or talked or that they didn't get your twisted sense of humor."

"Promise." He looked over the menu, raising his hand in a Boy Scout's salute. "I promise, I will not call you whining like some—"

"Don't you even think about saying that derogatory word! Gareth was also my husband, and I owe him that much."

"I understand." He wondered if she would be as understanding if he told her the things Lisa wanted from him that she outlined in her letter. "Call me. Let me know how things are going with his tests." He hoped it sounded like a gallant gesture, since he was feeling territorial.

"Thanks for understanding," Randa said before she recited her order to their waiter.

* * *

When Randa returned to work the day after she accompanied Gareth to the hospital, she was full of good cheer. Gareth was fine, and Justin had called her after she got home from the hospital to find out how Gareth was and to say that he'd picked an assistant. She saw his light on and walked to his office to congratulate him on his choice.

"Hey, you," she said from the doorway.

He looked up from the proposal he was working on and smiled. "Tell me about this new assistant. I talked to Bea last night and she said she's nothing like me," she teased. "I'm surprised. I thought you'd still be interviewing next week."

"I think she'll work out well, I do. How's Gareth doing?" he asked, genuinely concerned. If Gareth was still sick, Randa would just be spending more time with him.

"I talked to him again after I got off the phone with you," she explained. "He's fine and very relieved. He still has to have more tests to find out what the problem is, but they said it can't be anything too serious."

Justin blew out a deep breath. He didn't want to talk about his new assistant or about Gareth; he was more interested in talking about them as a couple. "Randa, what will happen to us when you move to your new position? I won't get to see you. How will I talk to you?"

She put her purse in his chair and went to close the door. When it was shut, she said, "There's this thing called a telephone. Also I hear something about a computer application called e-mail." She snapped her fingers and walked toward his desk, leaning over and giving him a bird's eye view of her full breasts. "And here's a wild idea: you could actually walk down the hall to my office." She laughed and headed for the door, picking up her purse on the way.

"I know. It just won't be the same," he said, watching her hips sway as she balanced on her stiletto heels. "I'll get used to it. I won't like it. But I'll get used to it."

"Why Justin Brewster, does that mean that you care?" she asked in a helpless damsel voice.

"You know I do."

Later that week, Randa yawned as she explained some of her duties to the new assistant, Delores Patterson. Justin had kept her up late the night before, much to her enjoyment. He still hadn't said "I love you," but neither had she. She didn't know where the relationship was going, but she was enjoying it while they were on a high note.

To Randa's delight, Mrs. Patterson caught on to the computer system quickly and seemed very efficient. She showed the assistant how to make a spreadsheet of Justin's meetings and smiled when she remembered her disastrous first day with him. "I program the spreadsheet for a week at a time because he has a habit of forgetting things, Mrs. Patterson," she explained.

"Please call me Delores. I also noticed he's not much of a morning person either. He barely speaks in the morning if you're not here. He smiles at you because he's got a soft spot for you." Delores rummaged through her notes. "What about meetings? Do I attend those?"

Randa was glad that Delores was businesslike and didn't pry into her affairs. "Only if he asks you. Sometimes you're needed, sometimes not. I took a tape recorder to make sure I took good notes."

Delores shook her head. "Oh, I'm a speed writer. Don't have no need for a tape recorder."

Randa laughed and leaned back in her chair, enjoying the moment with her replacement. Justin had made a good decision. Delores was a mature woman in her fifties and had keen insight. "Justin is your boss, and Curry is Justin's boss, but if Darius asks you to do something, he supercedes anyone else outside the partners. Any questions?"

Delores shook her head.

"Good. I'll let you make copies of last month's reports. Do you feel comfortable going by yourself?" She was confident of her replacement's answer.

Delores nodded and headed to the copy room. While she was gone, Randa wandered into Justin's office. She smiled as she took her customary seat and crossed her legs.

"How's training? Did I make a good choice by hiring her?" He smiled back at her, knowing her answer.

"Yes, Delores is very smart. She says you're not a morning person."

"She's too damn perky in the morning," Justin complained. "It's like she's had three or four cups of coffee by the time I get here."

"She's a happy person; be grateful. She could be moody. So many in her predicament would be bitter."

"What kind of predicament?"

"Well, her mother has been diagnosed with cancer. She's at a treatment center now since she's just starting radiation therapy, but Delores still has the chore of making sure everything is going according to plan. She's very upbeat about the entire situation."

Justin stared back at Randa. "I've been really blessed by having a healthy family. So many people my age have parents who have passed away or have a terminal illness of some kind." He reached across the desk and caressed her hand. "I also feel blessed that I know you."

"Thank you, Justin. I feel lucky, too." *Boy, was that the understatement of the year,* Randa mused. "I'd better get back before she returns, but I think she knows about us," Randa added.

"How?"

"She says you have a soft spot for me."

Justin leaned toward her, smiling mischievously. "The spot I have for you definitely is not soft. You can feel it if you want," he teased.

"Justin!" Randa cried in mock outrage. She huffed out his office, refusing to dignify his statement.

The following Monday, Randa exited the elevator and headed toward her new office.

"Good morning, Ms. Stone," her assistant greeted.

"Good morning, Anna." Randa smiled at the bubbly twenty-something-year-old as she walked into her office. *Her office.* She didn't know how much she missed having one until she got it back.

She sniffed at a vase full of long-stemmed red roses that had been placed on the edge of her desk. Plucking the small, white envelope from the bouquet, she opened it and discovered the flowers were from Justin. "Ooh, how sweet," she squeaked in a schoolgirl voice. It had been a long time since she'd been sent flowers.

Her joy was short lived as Danielle, her new boss, appeared at her door, summoning her for her first impromptu meeting. She chatted with Randa as they walked to the conference room.

"I realize you're still just settling in, but I've just been informed by Darius that we need to have the fiscal report done by the end of October, which is about five weeks away. The report goes to the board of directors, the investment coalition, the partners, and the shareholders."

"Of course," Randa spouted confidently. She'd only been in her new job a few minutes and already had a major project. She felt her adrenaline pumping with excitement.

They finished the walk in silence and entered the room. The partners, all males, stood and remained standing until the two women took their seats. Unlike at her old department meetings, Darius was the only friendly face she saw. No Justin. No Curry. Just the top execs at the company and Danielle.

"Randa, we're still getting the final numbers together for the fiscal year," Darius started. "But thanks to you and Joe's Pizza, along with some other projects, the firm has done very well. I was thinking we could use Joe's Pizza as the cover for the investors' report."

Randa nodded. "That sounds good. How about a little story about his business growth since coming to Sloane? Maybe we could add a direct quote or something?" Her mind buzzed with ideas and she noticed Mr. Sloane whispering to Darius, then Darius nodding in agreement.

It always seemed strange to her that the partners conferred so much with Darius, as if he were a partner, when he was only a vice president. "That sounds good, Randa. Of course, it will still need Darius's approval before going to print." Mr. Sloane shocked her by speaking, something that had happened only once out of all the meetings she had attended.

Randa nodded. *Just how much pull did Darius have?* she wondered. "Of course, Mr. Sloane."

"I'll need the report by the third week in October to preview it," Darius said. "I can have it back to you in two days so you can make any necessary changes. I do want your fresh slant to reflect throughout the report. I've gotten complaints that the investors' report has been, shall we say, boring."

He took out his organizer and began to scribble. The partners filled her in on a few more specifics for the report, and then the meeting was adjourned.

Randa closed her legal pad and rose from her seat. Darius was still writing in his organizer. When he heard her leaving, he looked up.

"Get with Curry before the end of next week for his part of the report. I'd catch him the early part of the week before he and my sister leave for Ireland next Saturday." He shook his head wistfully. "While they're gone, Cherish and I will be looking after their son. That boy is an energy ball, and he just started walking."

Randa heard the pride in his voice as he talked of his nephew and knew he was happy. She wanted the happiness that Darius was experiencing. Sure, she had Preston and Jessica, but she still wanted her own kids. Was it too late? Justin hadn't said a word about them having any kind of commitment and seemed to be happy with the way things were. Randa hoped there was still time and that her biological clock still had a few ticks left.

SEVENTEEN

After the meeting adjourned, Randa returned to her office. Anna greeted her with several phone messages, but one stood out from the rest.

"Mr. Brewster called and asked that you call him back immediately, Ms. Stone. He sounded quite upset that you weren't in. But I checked and double-checked your calendar, and you didn't have anything scheduled with him." Anna's apologetic voice tugged at Randa's resolve.

Randa interrupted the younger woman's apology. "That's okay, Anna. I'm sure it's nothing catastrophic."

After she took care of her other messages, she called Justin. She'd been at Karl's most of the weekend and she hadn't seen or talked to him. When she heard his baritone greeting, her heart fluttered with anticipation. "It's me," she whispered into the phone.

"Me who?"

"Randa, silly." Justin's voice charmed her even as he baited her.

"Hmm, Randa." He said her name as if he'd never heard it before. "I don't know a Randa. I knew one once, but I haven't talked with her or touched her in a long time. She's a high-powered executive now and doesn't have time for me anymore."

Randa threw her head back in laughter as she joined his game. "Well, I was hoping for a late night meeting with Mr. Brewster, but apparently I dialed the wrong extension. Maybe I'll baby-sit the kids tonight. Sorry to bother—"

"Wait!" Justin yelled into the phone. "Oh, you said Randa; I think I might know her. Why don't we discuss this over lunch?" His voice softened, rubbing against her strength of will like it always did.

Randa exhaled. She knew she'd have lunch with Justin, but she didn't want him to get used to having things his way. "I'll just check with my assistant and get back to you." She smiled as she hung up the phone and walked to her doorway. "Anna, do I have anything on for lunch today? Say, between eleven and one?"

Anna consulted Randa's calendar on her computer and shook her head. "You're free until three. You have an appointment with the printing company. Mr. Helbrandt with Express Printing is giving a presentation on the cost of printing the report."

Randa nodded and walked back into her office. Why, she wondered as she took her seat, would a large company such as Sloane not have an on-site printing facility? It would save the company millions in the long run. She would mention it to Darius and get his thoughts on it. She called Anna into her office. "Please block off two hours for lunch, call Mr. Brewster, and tell him that I can meet him for lunch."

"Yes, Ms. Stone." Anna returned to her desk.

Randa leaned back in her leather chair, imagining that call would get under Justin's skin. She resumed her work and waited for the call. It didn't take long. She had barely started working on the Joe's Pizza success story when the phone rang.

"What was that?" Justin demanded.

"What are you talking about?" Randa giggled. "I thought you'd appreciate professionalism."

"What I would appreciate," he drawled in a very

non-Texan accent, "would be a long lovemaking session with you." He knew she would enjoy that, too.

"Justin, is your door open or closed?" Randa gasped. She could easily imagine Delores's shocked ears as Justin started talking dirty.

He laughed that sexy laugh he had when he was teasing her. "Open. My super-assistant is at the copier. Is yours open or closed?"

"My door?"

"Your heart."

Randa yawned as Justin lay next to her, snoring loudly. Every since they had shared lunch earlier that day, her body had hummed with anticipation. Lunch had only been a prelude to their lovemaking. They'd shared a meal at the local diner and talked of the evening ahead.

As she snuggled closer to Justin, she heard Zack's familiar scratching at her door. He needed to go out. She stood up and put on her bathrobe, ushering the dog through the kitchen and into the backyard. "Sorry, boy, this will have do for now. Mommy's in heat," she laughed.

Zack stared at her for a moment before going to his favorite tree.

After he returned, she locked the door and headed back to her bedroom. As she entered the room she noticed Justin was still asleep. She took off her robe and got back in bed.

He rolled over, surprising her. "Where did you go?"

She smiled as he snuggled closer to her. Body against body, his very stiff erection was the only thing between them.

"I had to take Zack out," she gasped as Justin's fingers wandered over her body. "He was scratching at the door." She leaned toward his kisses. "Oh, that's right. You were snoring. You probably didn't hear him," she teased.

He eased her on her back, gently parting her thighs and kissing her as he moved to insert himself into her.

"Condom!" Randa cried out before he entered.

Justin reached into her nightstand and pulled out a gold packet. Rolling it over his length, he resumed his previous actions.

Randa heard him moan as he slid inside her and began to push against her favorite spot. The feeling of intense pleasure was mutual. Even if he never said he loved her, she knew he felt it. But was that enough? *Yes,* she thought as Justin's hard strokes woke every fiber of her tired body. *Yes! Yes! Yes!*

It was morning when Randa's eyes opened again. Justin was already gone. She walked to the bathroom and got quite a surprise when she opened her door.

"What are you doing here?" she said as she looked over Justin's muscular, nude chest. As her eyes glanced downward, she noticed he had wrapped a towel around his waist.

"Well," he started to unwrap his towel, "I was going to take a shower and was waiting for you." He let the towel drop to the floor and led her to the shower.

"Justin, we don't have time for this!" She hoped he would insist, since they were both naked and he stood at full attention. She would hate for that to go to waste.

He shook his head and gently pushed her into the shower stall. "Of course we do. We're both managers. We're just having an off-site meeting." He laughed as he joined her in the shower and turned on the water.

She stood behind him as he adjusted the water, admiring his build. Giving in to indulgence, she caressed him from his back to his trim hips, to his well formed butt, and watched him tremble. She held her breath as he turned and faced her.

"Well, are we ready for breakfast?"

Randa nodded and leaned against the wall, not caring if her hair got wet or not. She only wanted to feel his hands on her body, feel his tongue against hers, and to feel him inside her. This morning, he was determined to drive her crazy. Randa screamed in frustration as he rubbed his masculine length against her, but Justin only laughed. Finally, he lifted Randa and traveled inside her body. They both gasped in ecstasy and she immediately locked him in a possessive hold with her legs wrapped tightly around his waist.

"My, my. I thought you had enough last night," Justin moaned as he withdrew from her and entered her again. He repeated the process several times, grunting in delight with each surge forward.

Not giving any thought to the repercussions of being over two hours late for work, Justin exited the elevator and headed for his office. He was so happy, he almost felt like skipping the short distance to his desk. Whatever the costs, it was well worth the time he spent in Randa's bed, and her shower for that matter. He felt a connection with her, not just a physical one, which was spectacular, but something he never felt with Lisa. There was an emotional bond.

After their meeting in the shower, Randa surprised him by fixing an elaborate breakfast. "For a stellar performance," she'd told him as he greeted her in the kitchen.

A strange feeling stole over him as they ate

together. He belonged to her, and she to him. They talked about the news, stock tips, and the day ahead over breakfast, even compared how well their investments were doing. He liked that he could talk to her about anything. Well, almost.

He immediately went to his computer and e-mailed Randa when he reached his office. "Thanks for breakfast," he wrote. He toyed with the idea of composing some dirty limericks but was interrupted by an e-mail from Darius's assistant. Apparently, Darius wanted to see him.

Justin hurried to his boss's office and knocked on the open door. "You wanted to see me?" He tried to steady his voice. "If it's about me being late this morning, I can explain."

Darius smiled as he stood up and faced Justin. He towered over Justin by at least three inches. "No, Justin. I'm sure you had the best interest of Sloane in mind. What I wanted to speak to you about is Curry."

Why would Darius want to discuss his brother-in-law? "What is it? Is something wrong with his wife? His son?"

"No, nothing like that." Darius motioned for Justin to sit down. "He and my sister will be leaving for Europe for two weeks, and he's helping Randa with some of the stories for the upcoming investors' issue. I wanted you to assist her in his absence. Will you have time if you're needed?"

Justin smiled. Darius wasn't asking him; he was telling him. It was a polite command, more in the tone of *Do it and don't ask questions.* "Yes, Darius, I'll be happy to help her. When does Curry leave?"

Darius shuffled some papers about on his desk, his attention already diverted. "They leave next Saturday. I've already warned most of the staff that my wife and I will be watching little Christian while they're away. So if I'm grouchy in the mornings, he'll be the reason."

"Yes, I remember my nephews. For some reason, boys just must be a handful." He hoped he'd get the chance to find out with his own son. "Anything else, Darius?" Justin stood, knowing he was being dismissed, and turned to leave.

"There is one more thing I would like to discuss with you." Darius's smile was gone and he motioned for Justin to sit down. Darius walked to the door and closed it.

Justin knew that meant whatever he had to say was pretty heavy. He faced his boss as Darius took his seat.

"Justin, Randa went through some horrible episodes in her life just before she came to Sloane. I'm very fond of her and don't want to see her getting hurt, whether intentional or not. She reminds me of my sister before Curry blew into her life."

Justin nodded, not knowing exactly where this secret discussion was leading. What was Darius saying in his quiet yet commanding voice? He listened carefully as he continued.

"What I'm saying is that I know your ex is a piece of work. I know you took this job so far away from all your family and friends to get away from her. Lisa's called me personally, several times, trying to find out your salary, your work schedule, and whom you're seeing. I put her off as much as I could, but I know that she's not going to give up. I don't want to see Randa getting humiliated when your ex finally gets to you. I also don't want the name of Sloane damaged as well," he emphasized.

Justin's heart thumped loudly. He felt like one of those cartoon characters who spouted steam from their ears when they got upset. He couldn't believe

Lisa was calling his employer, embarrassing him at work. He also couldn't believe that Darius knew about him and Randa. How many other people were in the know? "Don't worry," Justin said. "She's contacted me as well and I'm prepared for when she finds me." He blew out a ragged breath and slapped his hands on his knees. "It's not my intention to hurt anyone."

"If you need any help, just let me know. I do know some people in the legal system."

"Thanks, Darius. I'll keep that in mind."

He made his exit after Darius gave him a satisfactory nod. He felt like such an ass. After making a detour to the break room, he walked to Randa's office. He hadn't been in there once since she'd taken her new position.

"Yes, can I help you, Mr. Brewster?" her assistant asked in that perky voice that annoyed him every time he called.

"Is Ms. Stone in?" He hated when Anna called him "mister." He aged ten years each time she did.

"I'm sorry, she's gone to lunch."

Justin muttered an expletive under his breath. He really needed to talk to Randa about Lisa. He wished he'd said something weeks ago. "Do you know what time she'll be back?"

"No," Anna said cheerfully. "She didn't say. I'll let her know you were looking for her when she gets back, though."

That would have to do. "Thank you, Anna. Please do."

He sulked back to his desk and waited.

EIGHTEEN

Randa sat back in her chair listening to Charles Helbrandt of Express Printing. After their initial meeting, she wasn't impressed by his offer and had rejected it. She granted him a second chance as a measure of goodwill only.

"Ms. Stone, you'll find that I have the best price around for the kind of report you want to print." Charles passed her an impressive dummy of the cover. "The color photographs, the lettering, the glossy finish—all those things add to the final numbers. You said you needed five thousand copies. That adds to the cost."

She ran her fingers over the cover. Jose's picture looked great on it. "You can't give us a break for ordering that number of copies? I've actually had another bid for the job, and it's about ten grand less than your final number. They can double our number of copies, and postage is included."

Charles leaned back in the chair, his Armani knockoff suit straining at the seams as it stretched over his arms. "But can they assure you the quality I can with that cheaper price?"

"Can you?"

"I'm not following you. I've had this contract for years, and no one has ever questioned my prices. Why all of a sudden are you looking at the specifications?" Charles was suddenly angry.

She watched him begin to squirm in his chair. "Because I'm like most people. I want more bang for the buck. In the five years you've had the contract, you have promised less and less each year, but you have charged more and more," Randa argued. He shifted positions again.

Charles let out a tired breath, sounding remarkably like a muttered curse. He reached for his bid and scribbled down a new figure, then passed the paper back to Randa. "I'll knock off twenty percent and won't charge the mailing fee."

Randa looked at the price and passed it back to him. "Charles, your price is still too high."

"I want to speak to the person in charge," he bellowed. "This decision should not be up to you. You shouldn't have that kind of power."

"Well, she has that kind of power, Charles," Darius said from the doorway, his massive physique filling the open door. "I would like to think you have a little decorum. Your prices have been through the roof, and with Randa's suggestion, we did a little checking. Your prices are double what anyone else would have charged us, had they been able to bid, of course. Just so you know, your friend in procurement has been released from our company."

Charles took a dramatic pause as if considering his options. He had none. He rose and stalked out of the office, muttering unrepeatable language as he brushed by Darius.

Randa's eyes widened in surprise. "I just thought he was overpriced, not a swindler," she said in disbelief.

Darius entered her office and sat in the vacated chair. "Well, like I said, we did some checking, and Charles has been sticking it to us for quite some time.

That was a good catch, Randa. I want to let you know that the board took your suggestion for an in-house printing department." He passed an envelope to her. "Hurry, open it."

Randa stuck her finger under the sealed flap and ripped it open. There was a card inside with a check for five thousand dollars. "Darius, I couldn't possibly," she gasped.

He nodded. "Yes, you can. By doing the printing in house, we will save over a million dollars each year. Thanks to you. Enjoy the bonus."

Randa walked around the room smiling after Darius left. She picked up the phone to call Justin and tell him her good news.

"Justin Brewster," he answered in a terse, baritone voice.

"Justin, you'll never guess what," Randa began, unable to keep the giddiness out of her voice. She was bubbling over with excitement, but Justin's dry, clipped voice threatened to destroy her mood.

"What Randa? I'm busy."

Randa held the phone away from her face and looked at it. This couldn't be the man she had just made love to that morning. "Never mind. I'll call you later." She hung up the phone.

Randa took a deep breath and relaxed in her chair, then called her brother and told him the good news. As usual, Karl was very proud of his sister.

"That's terrific, Randa," he said. "I knew that job would be perfect for you. Has Justin claimed his undying love for you yet?"

"No. Right now he's hovering between asshole and jerk." She sighed. "I was wondering if I could baby-sit for you tonight?"

Karl laughed. "Actually, we're going out to eat tonight. Jessica made me promise to take them to

Gareth's restaurant. Why don't you join us? We could celebrate your good news."

"That sounds great. I could use some cheering up."

Karl's cheery voice turned serious. "Randa, if Justin can't realize what he has in front of him, then he's stupid."

"I know," she said, "it's nice to be appreciated every once in awhile. Thanks, Karl. I'll see you tonight."

Randa hung up the phone and sighed again. *Think of something else, Randa.* She had to keep herself busy so her mind wouldn't drift to Justin. What was wrong with him? He had mood swings like a woman with PMS. Randa dialed Curry's extension to check on his end of the stories for the magazine.

As she listened to his voice mail stating that he would be out for the rest of the day, Randa decided she would do the same. She really couldn't do anything without his input anyway. Grabbing her purse and jacket, she headed for the elevator.

Justin simmered at his desk. Why did he snap at the one person he shouldn't have? He was going to have to get a grip on his emotions where Randa was concerned. To know that Lisa had contacted his boss several times had him in a rage. It was ironic, really: the one woman he wanted probably wouldn't talk to him, and the one he didn't want wouldn't leave him alone.

He walked down the hall to Darius's office. After he was invited inside, he closed the door.

Darius leaned back in his leather chair. "What can I do for you, Justin?"

Justin took a deep breath and sat down. "Remember when you said you had friends in the legal system?"

"Yes."

Justin glanced around the room, noticing the photos behind Darius. "Well, I might need some help with Lisa." He explained the details of her latest exploits, including a fraud charge. I've known for awhile that she was looking for me, but I need a better backup plan. Her behavior is more erratic that I thought."

Darius nodded. "I agree, Justin. It never hurts to have resources." He reached inside his desk drawer and retrieved a business card. "This is a good friend of mine. His name is Sean Cummings."

Justin took the card and examined it. "This says he's a psychologist. How can he help me?"

Darius nodded. "He can. He works in the legal system. You tell him the circumstances, and he'll be able to help you get rid of your ex once and for all."

Justin nodded his head, thanked Darius for his help, and left. Back at his desk, he looked at the card again. He decided to give Sean a call just to see what his options were.

Sean listened intently as Justin explained his predicament. He thought carefully before he answered. "I think you've got a few options at the moment. From what you're telling me, her behavior sounds like she has some sort of compulsive disorder. Honestly, I think the best scenario for everyone will be if she shows up here."

That was the last thing Justin wanted. "Hopefully that won't happen."

Sean laughed. "I know you might not want to deal with it, but she may need real help. What she's doing are not the actions of a normal adult."

As Justin pondered what would happen to his life when Lisa arrived, he knew he'd have to tell Randa right then.

He dialed her extension but got her voice mail. He pressed zero to be transferred to her assistant.

"Anna, this is Mr. Brewster. Is Ms. Stone in?" he said into the receiver.

"I'm sorry, Mr. Brewster, she's left for the day. She said if it's important, she can be reached by cell phone. Did you need me to call her for you?"

Justin didn't like the helpful tone in her assistant's voice, as if he were too feebleminded to dial a phone himself. "No, thank you."

After he hung up, he dialed Randa's home number and listened until her answering machine kicked on, signaling she wasn't home. He dialed her cell phone and got another voice mail service. Where was she?

He could call her brother. Karl might not be very helpful, but he figured it was worth a try. After searching for the business card Karl gave him months ago at Jessica's party, he finally looked in his Rolodex.

After playing twenty questions with the receptionist, Justin was finally allowed to speak with Karl. Randa always spoke of her brother as being helpful to no end, but that was to Randa, not him. "Karl, this is Justin Brewster," he began. "I was wondering if you knew where Randa was."

Karl's tone indicated he wasn't going to be very helpful. "Why do you want to know where my sister is?" he snapped. "She's over twenty-one and can take care of herself. Maybe if you were a little more considerate of her feelings, she would tell you where she was going."

"Okay, Karl. I take it she has talked to you. Yeah, I was in a mood when I talked to her earlier. But I can't say I'm sorry if I can't find her."

Karl laughed, irritating Justin even more. "Well, Justin, I won't see her until this evening when I pick her up."

He didn't want to sound desperate. "Karl, I need your help. I somehow keep screwing up with Randa. Could I meet with you sometime and have a talk?"

"Justin, I don't know if I could actually help you. Let me rephrase that. I don't know if I should help you." He took a deep breath, the amusement evident in his deep voice. "I think I can answer your questions right now."

"How?" Justin was clueless.

"I know you love my sister by the way you keep fighting with her when she doesn't have time for you. You're jealous of Gareth, the kids, me, and anything else that takes up her time. But because you won't admit that you love her, you think it gives you the upper hand or something. Justin, all it's gonna get you is alone. If you don't tell her, she'll think you don't love her, and then she'll be off with that pretty-boy doctor from the shelter." Karl threw that in just because he wanted to upset Justin. He knew perfectly well that the doctor was just a friend. "Randa's enjoying her new life, and I'm not going to let some guy who was put through the ringer by his first wife ruin it for her."

"You know about my marriage?" He shouldn't have been surprised that Randa told her older brother about his problems.

"Yes, I know. Look, we are dining at Gareth's restaurant tonight in celebration of Randa's bonus. Why don't you join us?"

"Randa got a bonus?" Justin smothered an expletive under his breath. That's why she'd called earlier. She wanted to share the good news.

"Yes, for some idea she had about printing. Oh, and Gareth will be there. We usually celebrate at his restaurant. The kids love that place."

"I'll be there tonight. Don't tell Randa." Justin hung

up the phone and sighed. Tonight would involve some serious groveling. He hoped there wouldn't be too many witnesses.

A few hours later, Justin walked into Worthy's Eateries in the art district of Fort Worth. The restaurant was decorated with Monet-style prints, and it reminded him of the art gallery he'd been to with Randa. Now he could see what she saw in Gareth.

A young woman dressed in black approached him. "Welcome to Worthy's Eateries. I'm Renee, your hostess. One for dinner?" she said, giving him a saccharine smile.

He shook his head. "I'm meeting a party here, Karl Stone and family."

The hostess instantly became genuine. "Oh, yes, they are in the Comfort Room. Gerardo will lead you back. Have a nice dinner, Mr. Brewster."

"How did you know my name?"

"Mr. Cornworthy said you would be attending, and all the other guests are here. Have a nice evening."

Justin nodded and followed the waiter to the private dining room. He expected to see Karl and his kids, but hadn't thought he would find several men fussing over Randa. When he entered the room, a deafening hush fell over the party.

"It's that man that came to my party," Jessica announced as she ate a plateful of pasta.

"Justin, what on earth are you doing here?" Randa asked. Preston jumped out of her lap and went to his father.

"I wanted to see you." He took a seat next to Gareth. Even though Gareth wasn't Justin's favorite person, he had to respect the friendship that Gareth shared with his ex-wife. Unlike Justin, who never wanted to see or hear from his ex again, Gareth was a decent human being.

"Why did you want to see me? I thought this would be the last place you'd come." Her annoyance was evident in her tone.

He gathered what he had left of his dignity and spoke. "Randa, could I speak to you privately?"

Everyone's glance went from Randa to Justin back to Randa. He probably shouldn't have tried to confront her on Gareth's turf.

"All right, Justin. Make it quick. We're having a celebration." She stood and walked to the door.

Justin followed her down the hall to the lobby.

She sat on the couch and folded her arms. "Just get this over with," she said. "I'm missing my celebration."

He sat beside her and took a deep breath. "Randa, when you called, I shouldn't have taken my frustrations out on you. I'm sorry."

"Justin, keep your 'I'm sorry' til the next time you yell at me for no apparent reason."

"I do have a reason, Randa." He told her about Lisa's most recent antics and his fear that it would jeopardize their relationship.

Randa placed her hand on his cheek, comforting him. "Why didn't you tell me?"

"I-I know you don't think I'm over her, but I am. I wanted to so many times, but there was never a right time." He put his hand over hers, smoothing his face into her other palm. "I'm sorry I wasn't honest with you. I-I—"

"It's okay, Justin," she said, pulling him into an embrace. "We'll deal with it."

NINETEEN

Randa settled in bed for an early night of rest. For the first time in the last week, she was finally able to watch the news alone. Justin had a late meeting, and Zack, who stared at her from the foot of the bed, was her companion for the evening.

She fluffed her pillows and turned on the TV, then reached for her favorite author's latest novel. She began to read and noticed that her throat was dry. Reaching for her bathrobe, she headed to the kitchen to make a cup of chamomile tea. As she waited for the kettle to boil, the phone rang.

"Turn on Channel 4 news," Bea yelled excitedly.

"What is it, Bea?"

"Just watch it!"

Randa ended the call and hurried to the living room to turned on the TV. She gasped as she noticed her former employers hiding, or attempting to hide, their faces from the news cameras. The caption under the picture read: "Ad agency closes its doors due to civil rights violations. Details to come." The screen went to a commercial.

"Oh my," Randa murmured to the empty room. She couldn't believe it. She reached for her cordless phone to call Justin, but after the phone rang five times, she remembered why he wasn't home. She called her brother. "Karl, turn on Channel 4!" she yelled, hanging up as the commercial went off.

The anchorman reported the top news story. "Fuentes, Gonzales, and Balmerston Advertising Agency closes its doors after it was reported the agency fired 30 employees because they weren't Hispanic. The Hispanic community is outraged by the agency's practices. In the last year, the firm has lost over 80% of its business. If you are a fired employee of this firm, please contact the Department of Justice."

Randa shook her head as the anchorman rattled off a phone number and e-mail address. She shut off the TV and went back to the kitchen. As she made her tea, she realized it had taken Fuentes and Gonzales less than a year to ruin a multimillion-dollar company. She walked back to her bedroom, thankful for the turn her life had taken.

Lisa Brewster walked through the Dallas/Fort Worth International Airport terminal feeling relieved. She had escaped Portland just minutes ahead of the police. She hadn't thought she would have made it this far without being caught. Hopefully, the cops would not think of her Texas connection.

After she picked up her bags, she quickly walked to the shuttle area. As the van drove toward Fort Worth, she thought of her plan. She knew Justin would take her back once he looked at her. He could never resist her charms or her looks and would be easy pickings, she thought. The van dropped her off at a cheap motel near downtown.

After checking in with her partner, who was still back in Portland, she went to bed. Tomorrow she would put her plan into effect.

The next morning, Lisa took a cab to the Jefferson

Building, a gold twenty-story building that reeked of success. She entered the elevator and pushed the button for Sloane, Hart, & Lagrone. When she arrived on the floor, she ignored the receptionist and headed toward the back of the office. *Nice*, she thought. She figured Justin had to be making a hefty six figures. She approached the woman at the nearest desk and asked for Justin Brewster.

"Do you have an appointment?" Delores asked.

"No, but he'll see me."

The woman looked at her, shaking her head. "And why's that?"

"I'm his wife," Lisa said triumphantly.

Justin thought the morning was going to be good, but a nagging feeling told him something was not right. After his morning meeting, he walked to Randa's office for a quick chat.

"Justin, what is it?" she asked, walking toward him as he entered. He looked like something was on his mind. "It's not Lisa, is it?"

He grinned as she came near. Her mauve suit fit her perfectly.

"Justin?" she asked, standing directly in front of him.

"Yes. I wanted to talk to you." He hoped the erection he was feeling wasn't too apparent. He slammed her door closed and locked it. Pulling her to him, he turned and pressed her against the wall, kissing her passionately. He slid his hands around her and caressed her bottom as she moaned in pleasure. "I missed you last night," he mumbled against her soft lips.

Justin backed up and looked at Randa's flustered face. "Good morning," he said.

She caught her breath and returned his greeting. Crossing the room, she sat on her desk and gave him a good look at her legs. "Are you here for pleasure, or do you have another purpose?" she teased.

"I told you. I just wanted to say good morning," he said with a very cocky attitude.

"Well, while you're here, let me ask you about the report. Darius told me that you would be helping in Curry's place. He's already excited about his trip," she said, changing subjects unwittingly. "I can't really blame him." Her hazel eyes gleamed with excitement.

"If I didn't know better, I would think you were going to Ireland instead of Curry and Darbi." He sat in a chair and leaned back.

"I wished it was me. It sounds so romantic." She looked at Justin, then quickly darted her glance away. "I'm sorry, Justin. That wasn't a dig at you."

"I know. I wish we could go somewhere, but there's just not any time we could both take off. If we could, you know we would."

"It's okay, I know work is your primary focus. There'll be other times." She smiled at him and switched subjects. "Have you had a chance to look at the report yet?"

"It's perfect, as far as I can tell. You did a great job."

Randa beamed at his compliment. She'd worried that he'd have some difficulty seeing her as a professional equal since he was used to calling all the shots, but so far he'd been great.

Glancing at his watch, he sighed. He stood and hugged her, kissing her softly. "I'd better get back to the grind. My assistant will be hunting me down again." He kissed her again and left her office before he gave in to his lusty thoughts.

Justin walked back to his office in a happy mood,

but it ended quickly when he saw the reason for his mistrust of women.

Exhaling a ragged breath, he walked inside his office and closed the door. "Lisa, what on earth are you doing here?" he hissed. He sat down and inhaled sharply. Gazing at her now, he couldn't see how he was attracted to her all those years ago. She still had her same slim figure, tight clothes, manicured nails, and coiffed hair. Now he preferred a woman with curves, sophisticated clothes that left something to the imagination, and natural nails. Lisa was too high maintenance, and she did absolutely nothing for his libido.

"I came to see you, Justin." She blinked her false eyelashes at him.

"Why?"

She crossed her legs, revealing more of them. Justin thought they were too skinny. "You know you've missed me, honey. I've missed you."

"You mean, you miss my salary. Are you here to spend more of my money or forge my name?" He leaned back in his chair and laughed.

"I have no idea what you're talking about," she said indignantly. "You know I came here with no money. I would hate to tell Darius Crawford that you sent for me and now you're acting surprised. Certainly, you don't want your boss to think that's the type of man you are."

Her high, squeaky voice grated his nerves. "Look. Lisa. You don't have to go to my boss," he said softly. "I'll take care of you. Don't I always?" He had just planted the seed for his scheme.

"Okay, Justin. I need a car, and I need money." Holding out her perfectly manicured hand, she waited for him to deposit something, either a credit card or cash, in her hands.

He would have to stall her. "Why don't we go collect your clothes and we can talk about us?" he asked. Lisa wanted Justin for his money, not his time.

"W-what about your job? Don't you have to work or something?"

"I'm taking the day off." He picked up the phone and called Darius, quickly explaining why he had to leave. After he finished, he escorted Lisa to the elevator.

Walking down the hall, Randa watched as Justin got into the elevator with a woman dressed in too-tight jeans. She was too thin, had on too much makeup, and she was hanging on to Justin like he was the last man on earth. She figured it must have been a new client or someone. The woman was nowhere near Justin's type. Dismissing her thoughts, she headed toward her old desk, but stopped when she heard the woman introduce herself to one of their coworkers.

"I'm Lisa, his wife," she said to the man getting onto the elevator.

"Ex-wife," Justin amended promptly.

So that was the infamous Lisa, Randa thought, watching the doors close. She was a breaker of bank accounts and Justin's heart. What was *she* doing here?

Later, as Randa walked into the weekly meeting, she noticed that Justin was not there. Neither was Curry or Darius. Actually, Darius was late, something that had never happened before.

"Sorry I'm late," Darius began, taking a seat. "I had to take care of a few details for Justin. He'll be out for the rest of the week." He darted a sympathetic look in Randa's direction. "If you need help with the report, I'll be happy to help you."

She felt her heart plummeting, but still found the

courage to speak. "Thank you, Darius. I just have to work on Curry's stories, and then I'm almost done."

"Great."

She nodded, not listening to the rest of the conversation. Her mind was on Justin. What was he up to? Why hadn't he told her Lisa was there when he was in her office feeling her up?

She needed to talk to Bea for advice. Was she overreacting? As her mind slowly went back to the meeting going on around her, she noticed Mr. Sloane was standing up.

"As you know, we're having a dinner in a few weeks. A celebration of sorts," he announced.

Randa looked around the room as he spoke. Curry was now present and sitting next to Darius. *When did he sneak into the room?*

Mr. Sloane continued his speech. "The name of our company will change in the next few weeks. Sloane, Hart, & Lagrone, will change to Sloane, Hart, Lagrone, & Crawford. Effective immediately, Darius will be a full partner. I know many of you have noticed the partners conferring with Darius on many occasions. He's been the backbone of the company and is responsible for much of our growth for the last few years."

"Curry will assume Darius's role as vice president of marketing as soon as he returns from his overdue honeymoon to Ireland. Justin Brewster will assume Curry's role as director of advertising when he returns to work next week." Mr. Sloane whispered something to Darius, then resumed his speech. "We hired a new director of marketing, Javier Spencer, formerly of Fuentes and Gonzales. As some of you remember, F&G was our biggest competitor. It has recently closed its doors since its unethical firing of so many key employees made the news."

Randa smiled at the thought of seeing Javier again. She knew him well as he was her assistant at F&G. They both could have a good laugh at the expense of their former employers.

One of the other partners tugged at Mr. Sloane's sleeve and whispered loudly. "Don't forget the baby."

Darius smiled as Mr. Sloane continued. "Also, Darius will be embarking on another venture in the near feature. He will be assuming the role of daddy in about seven and a half months. His beautiful wife, Cherish, is expecting their first child in June. Congratulations, Darius." He took his seat as the people began to applaud Darius's good fortune.

Randa was overwhelmed; she tried to hold back her tears of joy. She could only imagine what Darius felt. He had just made history at Sloane: he was the first African-American partner in the firm's fifty-year history *and* he was going to be a father.

After the meeting adjourned, everyone shook Darius's hand except Randa, who broke with tradition and gave him a hug. "I'm very proud of you, Darius. You deserve it!"

"Thank you, Randa." His broad smile turned serious. "Could you stay after a few minutes so we can chat?"

"Of course," she agreed readily. Although Randa had been at Sloane for a shorter time than any of the other managers, she knew one thing: Darius Crawford didn't chat. *What was going on?* She took a seat at the end of the table and waited for the sky to fall.

After the last person left, Darius closed the door to the conference room and sat across from Randa. He took a deep breath. "Randa, I wanted to discuss a few things candidly with you. There are no microphones and no hidden cameras, so we can be honest with each other."

She nodded.

He coughed and shuffled his papers around. "I don't know how to say this other than straightforward, so don't take this the wrong way."

Again, she nodded.

"About Justin. I know you guys are seeing each other."

Randa tried her innocent act. "I don't know what you're talking about, Darius." He smiled at her, and she knew she was busted.

"You have the same look as my nephew when he's done something wrong. You know very well what I mean. I also know his wife showed up at the office this morning without warning."

"Ex-wife," Randa corrected him. "They're divorced."

"Whatever. I know this woman is trouble. She's been asking around if he's been dating anyone. That's why I'm really glad that you guys kept it low key."

"What's this about, Darius? Do you think she'll cause me bodily harm?" Randa joked.

"Women like her are usually up to no good, and I suspect that she has a mental condition of some sort. I don't want you getting hurt or worse if Justin tells her he's been seeing you. Just stay alert."

Was he telling her to beware of a crazy person? Lisa didn't look menacing to her. The woman she saw earlier was no more than one hundred pounds and was only five feet tall. "Thank you, Darius. I'll be on the lookout."

He smiled at her. "I think you and Justin might be good together. I've noticed the changes in him lately. He's not as cold and untrusting as when he first came here. I've also seen changes in you." Randa nodded, not knowing what to say. "I've alerted security that she's not to come on the property after today," he continued.

Randa thanked Darius for his concern and stood to leave. His last statement awoke a fear in her. Was she in danger?

TWENTY

Randa watched Zack as he ran through the park. His pent-up energy brightened her dreary day. She hadn't talked to Justin since he left with his ex-wife earlier, but was slightly comforted to know that he had been caught just as off-guard about his wife's arrival as she was.

"Well it's about time you showed up," she said to Zack when he returned. She leaned down and patted him as his breathing calmed. "What do you say we go home and order some dinner? Mommy doesn't feel like cooking tonight." She attached his leash and walked back to her house.

As she approached her home, she noticed Justin's truck parked in front of her house. When she got closer, she watched him getting out of the vehicle and walking to her front door. Randa thought her heart was going to pop out of her chest as she joined him on the step. "Where's Lisa?" she spat as she took her key out of her pocket and unlocked her door.

"She's at my house."

Randa's heart sank at those four words. Justin had taken his materialistic wife back, and they would make their home in Arlington. "That's good. Why are you here? She might not like your being over here without her being present. Since now we're exes or whatever." She opened her door and led Zack inside.

Justin rushed in behind her. "Randa, I came over to explain. Not to give you the boot." He stood in her entryway and stared at her, daring her to make him leave. "I wanted you to know that I didn't know she would show up today. We need to talk."

"Well, this sounds like it may take awhile. I need to feed Zack." She walked to the kitchen to get the dog food. While she watched Zack eat, she ordered dinner from a Chinese restaurant, and then went back to the living room. She hoped Justin would state his business and leave.

Justin sat stiffly on the couch in deep thought.

"Okay, Justin, let's get this over with, shall we? I have dinner coming." Randa plopped down in the love seat across from him. "What was so all-fire important you had to sneak over here without your wife?"

He looked up at her with tired eyes. "First of all, she's still my ex. I wanted to explain the situation to you so there would be no misunderstandings, no claiming I misled you or anything like that. I don't want to make the same mistakes twice."

Randa sat back with her arms across her chest. "I know what you mean, Justin. You don't want two women running behind you. Well, that won't be a problem. I know this may be hard for you to believe, but I will be just fine without you, if not better." She hoped he believed that lie.

Her words stung, but Justin knew they were spoken in anger. "Listen to me, please," he pleaded quietly. He stood and paced the area in front of her. "Lisa just showed up today. I told you already that I didn't know she was coming. There are some things I need to take care of concerning her this week. So it's probably a good idea that we don't see each other while she's here."

"So she's still calling the shots? She wants you, so

you run over here with some trifling story about how we can't be together. And you gave me grief about Gareth?" The pitch of her voice rose higher with each statement. "You know, you deserve her," she said with disgust.

Justin sat down by her. "Randa, she was my wife. Am I supposed to kick her out on the streets? She showed up with no money, and I think there may be something really wrong with her. I think she may have mental problems. I just don't want her doing anything to you if she knows we're together."

"I'm not the one you need to watch," Randa declared. She opened her mouth to say something more, but the doorbell sounded. "Excuse me." She stood, but to her surprise, Justin stood also.

"I'll get it." He strode to the door and opened it.

Randa watched as he paid the delivery guy and entered the living room. He handed her the sack.

She carried the bag to the kitchen and returned to Justin with a plate for herself.

Justin smiled, and he knew he deserved her hostility. Scooting over, he made room for her on the sofa. She saw what he was doing and headed back to her spot on the love seat.

"Justin, why do think you need to protect me from Lisa? She doesn't look like she weighs a hundred pounds."

He watched her as she picked up a chicken wing. "Because you don't know what she's capable of, and I do. I've seen her do some pretty rotten things in the past to get what she wants."

"And apparently she wants you. I have been forewarned already, so don't worry. When will she leave?" The hostility had not left her voice.

"That's the tricky part. I know I'm asking a lot, but

I need you to trust me. There are some things that need to take place in the next few days."

Randa looked at him suspiciously and took another bite of her wing. "I'll try, but I'm not making any promises," she warned.

The next day, Randa breathed a little easier as Zack ran around the park. Justin wasn't leaving her for his ex, but the woman was still staying at his house. He told her they were sleeping in separate rooms.

Not seeing Justin was just fine with her. She had a lot on her plate at the moment, and the investors' report was taking up the greatest portion of her time. She had only a few days to perfect the drafts before handing her final copy to Darius for approval. She smiled as Zack made his way back to her.

Randa bent down and attached his retractable leash. "I think we both deserve a thick, juicy steak. What do you think?" She bent down to rub his back and got puppy kisses as a reward. "Okay, I think that's a yes."

As they started home, Randa noticed a car at the end of the street. The driver was using binoculars to watch her. Instantly she recognized the woman as Lisa. Randa panicked. *Would she do something to her now or would she just create an embarrassing scene in her neighborhood?* Telling herself to calm down, she continued walking as she regretted not bringing her cell phone to call the police.

Lisa stepped out of the rental car and walked toward Randa. The expensive silk suit she wore looked like something out of *Essence* magazine.

"Randa, I'm Lisa," she said in her high-pitched squeak. "Justin's wife."

"I know who you are."

"Good, I won't waste more time on pleasantries that we really aren't feeling toward each other. I know you have been seeing Justin."

"And?" Randa listened as Zack growled at Lisa. Her dog was never mean to anyone and usually loved strangers.

Lisa looked down her nose at Zack. "What a horrible little animal. You're one of those women with a house full of pets, aren't you? Justin hates pets."

"Did you come here to talk about my dog?" Randa challenged, rolling her eyes.

"I came here to tell you to leave Justin alone. He doesn't have the heart to tell you that it's over between you. We're going back to Portland as soon as possible." Lisa flipped a piece of her fly-away hairdo from her face.

"I'm not stopping you."

"Yes, you are, in a way," she squealed.

"What way?"

"Monetarily. I'm sure you'd want him out of your life as soon as possible, and Justin has told me that you have a little stash."

"What?"

"You give me, say, ten grand, and we'll be gone as soon as humanly possible. I know the company rule about dating. I'd hate to tell Mr. Crawford that you and Justin have been sleeping together, going against the policy."

Darius already knew, so what difference would that make? Since Lisa didn't know she held no sway, Randa saw no sense in telling her. "Why don't you let me think about it?" Randa said, walking off.

Lisa let out a disgusted sound. "You call me tomorrow. I'm at Justin's. You know the number."

* * *

Justin paced the town house. Lisa was gone in the rental car, and he had no idea of where she could be. Being used to her conniving ways, he had taken every precaution to make sure that Randa's name or address wasn't on anything that Lisa might come across.

He locked his office. As he walked into the kitchen, he heard the front door open. "Lisa?" he called as he opened a bottle of beer, preparing for the long night ahead.

"Yes," she answered, walking into the kitchen. "Did you miss me, honey?"

Justin watched her walk toward him with an exaggerated swing of her skinny hips. *What was I thinking all those years ago?* "Where have you been?"

She stood in front of him, batting her eyelashes like she had done so many times in the past. Reaching up to kiss him, she wrapped her arms around his neck. "You know, it could be like old times. You waiting for me to come home, then taking me out to dinner. Don't you miss our old life?" She moved her lips closer to his.

Justin turned his head and disentangled her arms from around him. "You mean, when you spent every dime we had trying to outdo your snobby friends. You mean when I had to sell my beloved Range Rover to cover most of our debts." He was definitely over her now. All he had for fifteen years of marriage was the bad memories of her spending.

Lisa shrugged her small shoulders and sat in a chair. "Justin, you act like you didn't know what was happening. All you had to say was no."

"I did say no. That only made you want something more expensive in its place," he raged. He took a swig of beer, hoping it would calm him down.

Lisa shook her head in disgust. "You know how I hate the smell of beer on your breath. Throw that away. It's not even an import. Justin, I've always told you if you had to drink that mess, it had to be an import. Throw that domestic crap out right now!"

A cold chill ran down his spine. He took a long drink of beer and stared at her like she'd lost her damn mind. "We aren't married, and this is my house," he said firmly. "I can drink what I please! If you don't like it, get out!"

Lisa's store-bought hazel eyes clouded with fake tears. "Justin, I only want what's best for you. I was just trying to help."

"Save the martyr bit for the next man, Lisa. It's not going to work on me anymore. Where were you?"

"Telling your girlfriend to leave you alone, since you seem afraid to."

He strode over to her, grabbing her hands and pulling her to her feet. "What? You've been at Randa's?!"

"Justin!" She wiggled her hands free. "You're hurting me! Yes, she was walking that disgusting animal," she said, brushing the wrinkles from her suit and checking for signs of dirt. "I told her we were back together. You know I always had to do your dirty work for you when we were married."

He tried to suppress his anger. It wouldn't do anything but make the situation worse. "How did you know where she lived?"

"Wouldn't you like to know?" she said.

"Don't you go near her again! Do you hear me?" he breathed through clenched teeth.

"All right, Justin." She smiled, settling back into the chair. "I won't go near your precious Randa, but it's going to cost you."

"What?"

"You'll find out tomorrow." She rose and walked toward the living room, then she turned and faced him.

"How much is it worth to you that Randa is protected and unharmed?"

He didn't like the way the conversation was going. The psychologist was right. Lisa was plum, dumb crazy. "What do you want?"

"Tomorrow," she squeaked, leaving the room.

Justin didn't like the smile of victory Lisa had on her face. He feared for Randa's safety, and he didn't want her to get hurt because of his mistakes.

After Lisa was asleep in the spare bedroom, Justin tiptoed down to his office. He wanted to call Randa but was afraid Lisa would overhear his conversation. He had to tell someone about Lisa's crazy behavior.

He e-mailed his brother. Luckily Jason was online and could instant message him back. Justin began typing his questions.

Can the Oregon police extradite her from Texas?

Jason replied: *Yes. They just need to know where to pick her up. But she does have to be handed over by the police. A citizen can't do it. Any ideas?*

Justin smiled as he typed his answer. *Yes, I don't want to tip her off. But I have everything in place. I'll call them tomorrow.*

Jason: I don't even want to know.

Justin: I know she's going to try to extort money from me, so I'm staying on my toes.

Jason: It's nice to know that she hasn't changed. Goodnight.

Justin smiled as he signed off his computer. He remembered to put on his password lock, hating to use security in his own house. He went back to his bedroom. As he settled in bed, he heard Lisa pacing in the room across the hall.

TWENTY-ONE

Justin called Sean Cummings early the next morning, ready to put a plan into action. "She arrived two days ago," Justin explained. "She's made it pretty clear if I pay her some money, she'll leave."

Sean rattled some papers. "How good of an actor are you?" he asked.

"Sorry?"

"Well, Justin, there's a way to be rid of her once and for all. But you'll have to be convincing."

Justin smiled. "I can be pretty convincing. If it will get rid of her, I'll be the best damn actor known to man."

Rich laughter filtered across the phone line. "Well, Justin what do you say to a trip to the courthouse with Lisa tomorrow?"

"You mean, marry her again? No, thank you. I don't see how that's going to help me."

"Well, you're going to have to trust me. You trust Darius, right?"

"Yes." He did, or he wouldn't be having the conversation with Sean right now.

"Curry?"

"Yes."

"Just trust me. Do you have someone that could make up some dummy forms?"

"I could probably convince my assistant to do it,

but why do I have pretend to marry her? Why can't I just drop her off at the police station like I planned to do?"

"If you turn her over directly to the police, she'll go to jail, but she'll never get the help I think she needs. If we can get her in front of my friend who's a judge and prove that she's unstable, I can get him to recommend some sort of leniency and mental help to Portland officials."

Justin sighed. This was turning into a complicated mess. "Okay, I'll get the paperwork together."

"Good. Then I'll see you at the courthouse tomorrow." Justin hung up with Sean and called his assistant at work to explain his plans. He hung up the phone, hoping tomorrow his hell would all be over.

As Justin drove to the office, he imagined that Randa would probably raise an eyebrow at his scheme. He decided he would stop by her office to explain.

He walked toward his office, pausing at his assistant's desk. "Hello, Delores. Do you have something for me?"

"Yes, but I have some reservations about this," she said. She handed him a thick brown envelope. "I also made copies and left one on your desk. I hope all this planning works for you."

"You're not the only one," he said. He walked down the hall to Randa's office, but the closer he got to Randa's desk, the more unsettled he became.

Justin strode past the assistant, heading for the door, but her perky voice stopped him.

"She's not here, Mr. Brewster. She had a family emergency."

"Was it her brother, niece or nephew?" *Or was it that needy ex-husband of hers?*

"I believe it was her nephew. He was involved in a car accident. I don't know when she'll be back."

"Oh, my gosh! When?"

"Early this morning. She's at Children's Palace."

Justin nodded and headed to the elevator. Children's Palace was Fort Worth's most notable hospital. Instead of looking like a hospital, it looked like a giant playground for kids. He hoped Preston wasn't seriously injured.

Justin walked to the hospital information desk, took a deep breath, and asked for Preston's room. He felt like it was his son who had been injured, and he didn't know what was going on.

The receptionist looked at him from her computer screen. "Are you a family member?" she asked.

"Friend of the family," he said, panic seeping into his voice.

"He's in intensive care. Fourth floor."

Justin thanked her and headed for the elevator. With all his heart, he hoped Preston would be okay. Sneaking a peek into some of the rooms almost broke his heart as he barreled down the hall. He saw children wrapped in bandages and hooked up to machines. His chest felt tighter as he reached the area where Randa's nephew was located.

A nurse greeted him as he approached the double doors. "Who are you here to see?" the tall blonde asked him.

"Preston Stone."

The nurse stood to one side and let him enter. "The car accident. Third bed on the left."

Justin walked to the bed, and the sight of Randa crying and the empty bed almost did him in. "Randa?"

She looked up, her beautiful hazel eyes drowning in tears. She stood and ran to Justin, almost knocking him over as she hugged him. "I'm so glad you're here. Karl is in court and can't be reached. Justin, I wanted to call you but I know Lisa's there."

He hugged her and let her ramble, knowing it was fear. Rubbing her back, he listened to her sobs as she calmed down. "Randa, you can always count on me. What happened?"

She took a deep breath and attempted to speak. After a few tries, she was finally able to relay the story. "The nanny was taking him to the doctor when a truck sideswiped her. T-the police said if he hadn't been strapped in the backseat he would have died." She looked at the empty bed.

"Randa, where is Preston?" He didn't like the fact that the room was missing one hyperactive little boy.

She wiped her face with a tattered napkin. "He's in X-ray now; then he has to take some more tests before they bring him back here. I know he's frightened and hurt. He's going to think he's alone. I want to be with him, and these people won't let me!" she cried.

Usually calm, independent Randa was on the verge of losing it in the hospital. Justin comforted her and spoke softly. "Honey, you've got to calm down. They're running tests. You'll upset Preston if he sees you like this. You'll have to be strong for Karl. How's the nanny?"

"She's in stable condition. She broke some ribs. I called the hospital across the street to check on her a little while ago, and she was asleep."

Randa held Justin in a death grip. He tried to put some space between them so he could look into her eyes, but she wasn't having it. "Randa, you need to sit down." He guided her to the chair, but she wouldn't let him go.

"Thank you, Justin." She finally freed him. "Sorry for getting clingy," she said, wiping her eyes. "I'm glad you're here. I know you have other things going on in your life. I appreciate the effort."

Effort? Justin was there because he loved her and wanted to ease her pain. "Randa, yes, I do have some major things going on this week. That's how I found out you were here. I dropped by the office." He wanted to forewarn her about the upcoming events, but now was not the time. It would only add to her troubles.

She glanced at him and wiped her eyes. "I'm glad you came. You've made this whole ordeal less frightening."

Slowly, she was returning to in-control Randa, the woman he'd fallen in love with. But he loved out-of-control, hysterical Randa, too. "I wanted to be here. I'll wait with you." He pulled a chair beside her and grabbed her hand.

"Are you sure, Justin? What about Lisa?"

"She'll keep," he said with a shrug.

Randa awoke at the sound of the door opening. She smiled as she nudged Justin from his sleep. The doctor walked in the room holding a chart. "Well, what's the verdict?" Rising to her feet, she prepared herself for the worst possible news.

"Well, Ms. Stone, since you are listed as a guardian, I can tell you. Preston has some internal injuries, and right now he needs to be still. He's strapped to the bed for his safety, and he has a broken arm. Needless to say, he's a little cranky. He'll be in the hospital for at least a few days. Do you know when his father will be here?"

"No, I don't. He's in court. I left a message with his office and on his cell phone." When Karl was in court, he didn't check his phone until after business hours. There were no exceptions to that rule.

The doctor smiled and left. Soon the orderlies wheeled Preston into the room; he was sound asleep. He looked like an angel sleeping.

Randa's eyes welled up with tears as she surveyed his damaged little body. She glanced at the tube that ran into his arm. *That'll hurt when it comes out,* she thought. The straps across his body were pulled tight so that he couldn't move. Gently, she touched his arm, relaxing as she felt movement.

Justin watched her as she silently stroked Preston's arm, and he went to her side. Randa turned to face him when he put his arm around her shoulder.

"I appreciate you being here," she said, looking up at him. She choked back the tears that would start the avalanche of emotions.

"Randa, you don't have to thank me. I did it because we're a couple, and I care about you. You mean a lot to me." He smoothed her hair away from her face and kissed her forehead. "No more thank-yous, please."

She sniffed back tears. "Okay, Justin."

He stood next to her. "I'll stay with you until Karl comes."

Had he read her mind? "Thank you." She smiled and stood on her tiptoes to kiss him. "I know I wasn't supposed to, but you really didn't have to, and you still offered. I'm grateful."

TWENTY-TWO

Randa watched as her brother rushed into the tiny room, making his way to his son. She suddenly felt uncomfortable as she watched him cry uncontrollably and caress Preston's arm. "Karl, I'll give you some privacy with Preston. Make sure he doesn't move around too much," she said, rubbing her brother's shoulder for comfort.

He turned to hug his sister. "Thank you, Randa. You are my lifeline. I don't know what would have happened if you weren't here."

Randa thought he was going to crush her body. "Karl, you know Preston is my heart. Let me walk Justin to the elevator, and I'll be right back. I'll tell you everything the doctor said."

Seeing her brother's tears brought new ones of her own. Justin grabbed her hand and they left the room.

As they walked down the hall hand in hand, Randa marveled at how warm, inviting, and caring Justin had been. But she remembered he still had issues he needed to take care of. "I'm sure Lisa is waiting for you," she said, looking at the floor.

He tilted her chin so he could see her face. "She is, and there's also something I need to tell you, but now is not the time. We'll talk later, when Preston is home." He kissed her gently on the lips, then suddenly pressed her body against his, deepening their passion.

"I'll talk to you in a few days to see how he's doing. If you need time off from work I'm sure Darius would be more than understanding," he said, pulling away from her.

She nodded, too afraid a sea of tears would fall.

He reached out to touch her arm. "If you need help with the investors' report, I'll be glad to help when I return next week." Justin took a deep breath as the elevator doors opened. "Be sweet." He stepped onto the elevator and pushed the button for the lobby, blowing a kiss to her as the doors closed.

Randa stood motionless in front of the elevator. She didn't even want to blink her eyes. The Justin that got on the elevator had to have been a dream.

"Honey, if you don't want him, I'll take him," a nurse chuckled as she walked to her desk. "He's one sensitive man. My husband would never have sat here all day with me, especially if it wasn't our child."

"Yeah," Randa agreed. "He's pretty special." With a sigh in her heart, she went back to the other important men in her life.

Taking a seat next to her brother, she saw Karl was staring at his son's limp form. She patted his leg. "How are you holding up?"

Karl shook his head. "I can't believe I didn't know my son was in the hospital until almost six hours after the accident. I could have checked my messages at noon, but the district attorney wanted to have lunch. What would have happened if you weren't here? There would have been no one to be with him and keep him calm."

She knew he would overanalyze the situation like he always did. *Maybe because he was an attorney and had to look at all the angles,* she mused. "Karl, your career is important to you. Thankfully, you have me listed as a guardian and I was able to be with him."

Karl shook his head, still not satisfied. "Randa, if anything happens to me, would you adopt the kids as your own? I've been thinking about it for a while and I know that you'll always have their best interests at heart."

Randa was shocked. "Karl, I never thought about it before, but yes. Of course, I will." She reached for his hand and held it firmly in hers. "Preston's going to be fine, okay? You're not a bad father because you didn't check your phone."

Karl nodded. "Where's Jessica?"

"I arranged for Jessica to go home with her friend Caitlin. I explained everything to Caitlin's mother, and she said Jessie could stay until we got things sorted out here. I'll pick her up and she can spend the night with me. I'm sure she'll want to see Preston so I'll see what I can arrange."

Karl kissed her hand. "See. What would I do without you? Now, what are his injuries? Where's the nanny?"

She took a deep breath and explained the child's injuries. Her eyes threatened to water again as he shook his head. "Karl, he just has to be still for a few days. That's why he's strapped to the bed."

"I thought he was playing vampire again and biting the nurses," Karl chuckled. "How about the nanny?"

"She's across the street, at St. John's. She should be released in a few days. She has some broken ribs."

"Oh, my gosh. Who will take care of him? I've got to check on her, too." He ran his hands over his head.

He looked like he did the day Preston was born and his wife of fifteen years died. He reminded Randa of a lost child. "The doctor said he'd be in here at least a few more days. I can work from anywhere. I'll watch him until the nanny gets better. Maybe you should hire someone new until she's fully recovered."

"You know how shy he is around new people. I can start working from home," he said, calming down.

"I'm sure between the two of us, we'll be able to work it out." Randa stood and grabbed her purse. "I'm going to get Jessie. I'll let her call you before she goes to bed." She kissed her brother on the forehead. "I'll see you in the morning."

Karl nodded again. He stood and walked to the elevator, and as they waited for the car to arrive, he said, "Thank you, Randa. I don't know what I can do to repay you for this."

"Karl, you don't have to repay me. We're family. Believe it or not, this little episode has made me realize how important it is."

"Bless you." He kissed her on the cheek as the elevator door opened.

"Where have you been all day? You can't answer your cell phone?" Lisa demanded.

Justin walked inside the house and dropped his keys on the table. "Can I at least get settled before you jump on me?"

Lisa sat down on the couch, wearing a slinky dress. She looked like she was going to a nightclub instead of continuing to lounge around the house all day.

She crossed her legs and spoke again in a much softer voice. "Okay, Justin. Why did you leave me alone all day? It's almost eight. I can't believe you deserted me."

"What did you do all day?" he asked.

"Waited for you. I missed you."

He instantly thought of Randa and all the pain she suffered that day. Not once did she sound as whiny as Lisa did at that moment. "I told you I had some errands to run."

"You didn't go in public dressed in those jeans and sweatshirt?" Lisa asked, clearly appalled. "You should have worn a suit, or at least a tie."

If he had forgotten all that was wrong in their marriage, those last statements were a stark reminder to him. "Yes, I did go around dressed like this. We're not married anymore, so my fashion mistakes are not your concern," Justin said, his annoyance clear.

Lisa turned on the waterworks. "Justin, I just want you to look nice and businesslike. You'll never make vice president if you don't look like you belong."

"Who said I was trying to make VP? I'm happy where I am. What about your job in the city? Any promotions in sight?" He knew she'd been fired, but he wanted to see what she'd say.

"Actually, I'm on an extended leave right now." She avoided his gaze.

"Why? You don't have kids. Your parents are as healthy as horses. You don't speak to your other siblings."

"Let's just say, I wanted to explore other opportunities." She stood and walked toward him. "Why don't you take me out to eat?"

He looked at her without trying to hide his frustration. Randa never made an ass of herself like Lisa was doing right now. Fifteen years ago, he might have thought it was cute and sexy; now he found it downright irritating. "I'll fix something here."

"Justin Brewster, I have been stuck in this house all day. I want to go out, and that's final!" she squeaked.

"Well, unless you're paying for dinner, I suggest you go to the kitchen, because that's where I'm going." He proved his point by leaving her in the living room alone.

As he took out some ground meat for a meatloaf, he heard Lisa walk into the kitchen. "I guess you were with Randa all day," she whined. She stood by a chair and coughed.

"I told you I had errands to run. Randa isn't an errand. What did you do?" He made no effort to pull the chair out for her.

"I told you. Nothing." She coughed again, then finally pulled out her own chair and sat down.

"You didn't use the phone?"

"I only called you."

"Really? I tried to call, and the line was busy for a long time. I trust you weren't calling your boyfriend?" He opened the cabinet, looking for his seasoning.

"When did you get into all this cooking? Does Randa make you cook? When we were married, at least we got to eat out all the time."

"Yeah, all the way to the poorhouse."

"How many times am I going to hear about that? You were right there, Justin; you could have said no to me any number of times."

It's going to be a long night, he thought. Crazy or not, he couldn't wait to get rid of Lisa tomorrow. After he put the meatloaf in the oven, he took a deep breath and sat at the table facing her. "Look Lisa, we could sit here all night and say this was your fault or it was my fault. Let's just get through a meal without trying to lay blame at each other's doorstep."

"All right, Justin." She batted her false eyelashes at him and showed him her saccharine smile. "The girls want to go to Europe next summer, and I plan to go with them."

"The girls" were attorneys, doctors, and lawyers.

Unlike Lisa, who was a receptionist, or used to be, they could afford to take extravagant trips.

Justin played along. "What kind of cash are we talking about?"

She took a deep breath. "Well, they want to spend a month. So I need enough for that long, plus plane fare."

"What about you finding another job?"

"I can't work. You're the director of marketing. What would the girls say?"

"First off, they work; why can't you? Second, we're not married!" Justin was losing his patience with her. He'd only been home fifteen minutes, and already he was at his wit's end. "How many times must I remind you? Remember the judge, the hearing? You tried to get alimony, and the judge told you to learn to live on what you make?" He remembered the judge's comments to Lisa, and at the time, he thought he would never be able to stand up to her like that. Now he had no problem doing it.

"Justin, you got me used to a certain kind of lifestyle. Am I supposed to go back to living alone and in an apartment? I miss my car."

Justin rose out of his chair and began to peel potatoes. If he didn't do something with his hands, they would soon be around her pretty little jeweled neck. He had never been a violent man, especially toward women, but she was pushing him. "You're not living alone; you moved in with Derek the night I told you to leave the house."

"He means nothing to me." Lisa wondered how Justin knew that.

"Like me, huh?"

"Justin, I love you."

"No, Lisa. You love Lisa, but that's okay. I did love

you once. That's what made me blind to what you were doing to me."

"I thought we weren't going to place blame," she reminded him sharply as she tapped an acrylic nail against the table.

Jessica accompanied Randa down the hall to her office. "Mom Two, why is it so quiet and dark in here?" she asked.

"Because everyone has gone home for the evening," Randa explained. "We can call the hospital from my desk, and you can tell your dad goodnight." Randa glanced at her watch. It was already after nine. It would probably be ten-thirty before she got Jessie to bed. Randa liked playing temp Mom and hoped it was practice for the near future.

She guided her niece into her office and let her sit in her chair while she dialed the hospital. After Randa got the customary lecture about visiting hours, she was finally connected with Karl. She handed the phone to her niece and began collecting things she would need to finish her project at the hospital the next day.

After Jessica hung up with her Dad, they finished gathering Randa's things. Seeing a light on in Justin's office, she stopped by to see if he was working. He wasn't there, but the lamp on his desk had been left on. She walked over to turn it off and saw a certificate on his desk. Randa picked it up and burst into tears when she realized what it was.

"Mom Two, why are you crying?" Jessica walked into the office and snatched the marriage certificate from Randa's hand.

"It's nothing, honey," she lied. "It's a joke from Justin." She hoped her niece believed her.

"Daddy always says that if it's nothing that makes you cry, it's something." She studied the paper. "Boys are awful, aren't they? My teacher says that boys grow up to be men, but they still act the same as they do when they're boys."

Randa tried to hold back her laughter as she remembered one of Jessica's teachers was going through a messy divorce. "That's pretty much true, honey. Except for your dad, of course."

Jessica nodded in agreement.

TWENTY-THREE

Sleep eluded Randa. With the day she'd had, it was no wonder. After she put her niece to bed, she could finally let her feelings out. She stared at the ceiling, trying to figure out the recent events. Why was there a marriage license for Justin and Lisa on his desk?

"Well," she spoke to the room. "I won't give him the satisfaction of seeing me cry or pine over him like some lovesick spinster." She sat upright and reached for her bedside phone. She couldn't call Karl since he was spending the night at the hospital with Preston. She called her other rock instead.

"Hey, I hope I didn't wake you or Josh," Randa said between quiet sobs.

"No, you didn't. Are you okay?"

Randa smiled at the concern in Gareth's voice. "Yeah, I'm having one of those days from hell. It's just getting worse by the minute."

She heard him rustling his covers, then mumble something to his life partner. "Honey, this isn't like you. What has that idiot done this time?"

"Actually, this time it was more than just Justin. Preston was in a car accident this morning, and he's in the hospital."

"Oh, no. How's Karl?"

"Well, he's doing pretty good. He's spending the night at the hospital, and I'm going back in the

morning so Karl can go to court. He's in the middle
of that huge trial."

"What kind of injuries are we talking about?"

Randa sniffed, trying to hold back tears. He was
being really great just listening to her talk about her
horrible day. Did she really want to start crying to
him as well?

Gareth answered the question for her. "Randa, it's
me, baby. If you want to cry, cry your pretty eyes out."

So she did. "I felt so all alone this morning. When
I finally got to see Preston, they were wheeling him
back into the room. They had to give him some
medication so he wouldn't thrash around and hurt
himself even more. Justin showed up at the hospital
and kept me company all day."

"But that's good, right?"

"It would be if his ex-wife hadn't showed up in
town this week wanting a reconciliation."

"Ouch. Did he send her packing?" He waited a
heartbeat before he spoke. "I guess not, huh? Or we
wouldn't be having this little conversation, would we?"

He knew her too well. "She's staying at his house.
He rented her a car. Justin keeps insisting that I trust
him, saying he has some plan to execute to get her
out of his life for good, but I don't know. I think he's
trying to play me."

"Play you? You've been watching those hip-hop
music videos again, haven't you? In any case, I don't
think Justin would know how to play you. You're just
going to have to trust him and let him take care of
whatever he has to."

She hesitated to tell him the last part; she was too
humiliated that Justin was leaving her for that
skanky Lisa.

Gareth spoke slowly, irritating her that much more.
It meant that he was about to say something that she

wouldn't like. "Honey, I'm sure it will all come out in the wash. Are you getting ready for bed?"

Randa was confused. "Yes, I'm dressed for bed."

"Well, I'm on my way over."

"You don't have to. I'll be fine." She wanted him to insist. "What about Josh?"

"He has given his approval. I'm on my way."

Justin sat across the table from Lisa, ready to put phase two of his plan into effect. They had managed to finish dessert without arguing, and he hoped Lisa was feeling especially materialistic that day. "You know, Lisa, I think you're right," he said in a chipper voice.

"About what?"

He coughed to hold back the disgust in his throat. "Me missing you. When I first moved here, the nights were awful. I could smell your perfume in my sleep."

His reward was her wide, toothy smile. "Oh, Justin. I told you, you missed me."

"Yeah, I didn't want to admit it. Now that I don't have Randa in my face, I remember how much you mean to me," he lied. "What do you say we give it one more try?"

"Do you mean it?"

"Of course."

"You would put me back on your credit cards and bank accounts, too?" she asked hopefully.

"Why wouldn't I? You'd be my wife. And you wouldn't have to work, either." He struggled to keep his voice steady; he was really on a roll. "I got a license while I was out earlier, and we can get married tomorrow. What do you say?"

Lisa looked at him skeptically. "Wouldn't I have to be with you to get a marriage license?" she asked.

"Uh, no. Since we were already married, you didn't

have to be there." He hoped she believed that. It was the best untruth he could come up with on the spot.

Lisa walked over to Justin and kissed him on the cheek. "I say I'll see you in the morning." She scooted out of the kitchen and ran upstairs to pretty herself for bed.

Justin sat in the kitchen staring at the refrigerator. The charade was almost over, and he would have his life back in a matter of hours. He could just imagine Lisa's surprise when she found out she was going back to Portland broke and in handcuffs.

Randa opened her front door and let Gareth in, laughing at his attire. He hadn't bothered to change clothes and had shown up in his pajamas. "What would have happened if you had car trouble? You were going to walk down the street in your PJ's?" she asked, ushering him inside.

"That Jag is only a few months old. I was trying to get over here as quick as I could. Your voice sounded awful. Like when your mom died," he said, throwing his coat over the back of her sofa. "I didn't want you to feel alone."

He grabbed her hand and led her around to sit on the sofa. Gareth sat down. Randa situated herself between his legs and lay with her back against him. It reminded her of old times. Not with Gareth, but with Justin. She wondered if he'd succumbed to Lisa's wily ways and was now sharing the same bed with her.

Gareth stirred against her, reminding her that he was there. "Hey, you feel nice," he told Randa. "It's almost enough to make me want to go straight," he joked. He reached for her hand and interlocked it with his. "Isn't this better than pesky old Justin trying to have sex with you?"

"I know what you're doing, Gareth." She took a deep breath. "You think I should trust him, but how can I? He says he's over his wife, but she's staying at his house," she said, her confusion evident.

"Say I lived in Maine. If I came to town broke, you'd put me on the street?" Gareth asked.

Randa sighed; she knew where this line of questioning was going. "Of course not, but you and I didn't have a rocky marriage. Everything was great until . . ."

"Just say it, Josh?" Randa nodded. "She's Justin's ex-wife. She may be evil, but he can't abandon her any more than you would abandon me. Plenty of people would say I'm evil because I married a woman and knew I was gay."

Randa was beginning to see his point. Deep down, she knew Justin was over Lisa. The real problem was that she didn't know how he felt about her. She sat up and faced Gareth. "See what you're missing by being gay. I bet you and Josh never have problems like that."

He smiled at her. "That's what you think. Gay relationships are just as hard if not harder. Josh is insanely jealous, and sometimes it gets old. He fears that somehow I will turn straight and toss him out."

"But you wouldn't. Right?"

"No, but sometimes it's a nice dream. Then I remember that I'm 45 and don't want to start dating again," he quipped.

Randa watched her ex-husband as he talked honestly about his life partner. "Gareth, I know that's hard, but in the long run he's worth it, just like Justin. He makes me so mad sometimes, but he has a good side underneath. I've seen glimpses of that side, and it has been warm, caring, and gentle."

"Really. Wow, Randa, maybe you should trust him," Gareth said sarcastically.

She realized he was right, which pissed her off. She picked up her pillow from the floor and tried to knock that smirk off of his perfectly tan face.

"Hey!" he shouted, wrestling her for the pillow. "If I wanted to fight, I would have stayed at home tonight."

Randa giggled as she settled down. "Thanks, Gareth. If Josh doesn't know it, I'll make sure he does—you're the best." She snuggled back against him.

Gareth kissed her on her forehead. "And I'll have a straight-to-gay talk with Justin."

The next morning, Randa felt something tapping her on her shoulder. She was too tired to open her eyes. Snuggling closer to a firm chest, she smiled. Did Justin sneak over last night? Randa forced her eyelids open and saw Gareth lay behind her, snoring. Then she heard giggling. *Jessica.*

"Mom Two, what is Uncle Gareth doing here? I thought he liked special men. Are you cheating on Justin?"

Randa sat up, her mind buzzing with the politically correct terms that would make sense to Jessica. "Uncle Gareth wanted to talk last night. So we had an adult pajama party. I thought you didn't like Justin."

Jessica shrugged her pajama-clad shoulders. "He's okay. Daddy said he'd probably be my uncle sooner or later. Can I call him Uncle Justin? Maybe Daddy Two, since we call you Mom Two," she pondered.

Randa's heart almost exploded with love for her

niece. "Well for now, let's stick with Justin. We don't want to scare him, do we?"

Her niece shook her head.

"Why don't you go get dressed for school and I'll go make breakfast? What do you usually have?"

"If Daddy is taking us, we go to McDonald's. The nanny makes us something."

"Why don't I make breakfast while you guys are getting dressed?" Gareth said, rubbing his eyes. "I can make my specialty: breakfast burritos."

Randa stood as Jessica left the room. "Breakfast burritos?" she asked Gareth. "You own a chain of gourmet restaurants all over the United States and you're fixing breakfast burritos! I was expecting something exotic," she teased, heading for the shower.

Thirty minutes later, Randa finished dressing, then went to check on Jessica in her room. She wasn't there, but Randa walked in and smiled at her niece's attempt to make her bed. Karl believed in personal responsibility and it reflected in his children. The room was as neat as it was the previous day.

Randa heard Jessica, Gareth, and Zack in the kitchen, and a strange feeling hit her. This was the life she wanted. She wanted happy noises in the house, not silence. That was one of the differences between a house and a home.

Walking into the kitchen, Randa saw Gareth at the stove making breakfast. Jessica was dressed in her school uniform, sitting at the table with a glass of milk, and Zack was busy lapping up water from his doggy bowl.

"I took Zack for his business in the backyard," Jessica said proudly.

Randa walked over to her niece and kissed her on the forehead. "Thank you, honey. Would you like to see your brother on the way to school?" She took a seat in the chair next to her niece. "I'll call your teacher and explain."

"Is Preston going to be okay?" Jessica asked.

"Yes, honey. He's just bruised up. He'll be home in a few days." Randa almost cried at the sight of tears in Jessica's eyes. She rubbed the little girl's back. "Just you wait, in a couple of months he'll be chasing you around the house like he always does."

That brought a smile to Jessica's face. "Thanks, Mom Two."

Mom. There was that word again. The more Jessica said it, the more Randa wanted it for herself. She wanted her own child, but she wanted her own husband first.

TWENTY-FOUR

Randa and Jessica walked into the hospital room quietly, so as not to wake Karl or Preston. Karl was asleep in a chair next to the bed, but Preston was wide-awake. He smiled as he saw Randa.

"Mom Two!" he yelled, stretching his one good arm toward Randa.

She immediately dropped her briefcase on the floor, walked to the bed, and gave him a slight hug. "How are you, honey?"

His eyes immediately filled with tears. "I want to go home. I don't like it here," he said in a little voice.

That sound almost broke Randa's heart. She wanted to take him out of the hospital. Randa watched as her brother woke up instantly when Preston's cries filled the small room. He smiled at Randa. "I'm so glad you're here. He ran me ragged last night." He hugged his daughter. "Good morning, Princess."

"Hi, Daddy." She kissed her father on the cheek.

Jessica soon left her father's arms and stood by her brother. Her tiny hands caressed the straps that held the toddler in place. Randa expected her to ask questions, but she didn't. She stood on a chair and kissed her brother on the forehead. "Okay, I'm ready to go to school."

Karl and Randa exchanged surprised glances.

Jessica was hiding her emotions well, just like her father. Randa whispered to her brother, "See. You should express more emotion in front of them."

Karl shot her a look that would have sent nearly anyone running except Randa. "I have no idea what you mean. Besides, she's behaving well."

Randa shook her head. "That's just it, Karl. She should be asking questions about Preston's condition. She should be begging and pleading to stay by his side. You know, show some kind of pure emotion. If it were you, I'd be doing that."

Karl nodded. "I know. I guess I've suppressed so much for so long, I'd forgotten how it affects them." He kissed Randa on the cheek. "You better hurry if you still have to go to Mickey D's."

"Gareth came over last night and he fixed breakfast this morning." She waited for his cross-examination of how unwise it was for her gay ex-husband to spend the night with her, especially with Jessica around.

"I could ask. But I'd rather you tell me." He stared at her with the penetrating brown eyes that usually made witnesses cower on the stand.

"I was upset and he comforted me. The end."

"Over Preston?"

"Well, actually, Preston and Justin, but we'll talk about it later. I'll be back soon; then you can go to court." She ushered Jessica out of the room.

After she dropped Jessica off at school and was satisfied that her niece wasn't turning into her emotionally retarded father, Randa returned to the hospital to relieve Karl. She began to look over the drafts for the upcoming report. Since it was her debut report as tech manager, she wanted to make sure she put her best foot forward.

A pair of small, scared eyes stared at her and Randa let go a frustrated sigh. "I know, baby. It really sucks being tied down like that. But it's just for a few more days." She stood by the bed and wiped his eyes. "Then we'll have lots of fun. Just you and me."

A smile was her reward. Soon the doctor walked in. "Good morning, Ms. Stone."

Randa looked at the young doctor, hoping he would bring better news today. He looked over Preston's chart as if it were the Declaration of Independence. "He's doing very well. But we're going to keep him strapped down for a few more days, just as a precaution. Little boys tend to be rougher than girls."

She nodded in agreement. "Yes, Preston usually has more energy than anyone else in the house."

"He responds very well to you. Last night, he threw a fit after you left. The nurses had to give him a sedative before he calmed down."

He was always her special little man. Randa smiled. Even if she couldn't have her own children, Preston and Jessica were as close as she could get without going through labor herself. "When do you think he'll be released?" she asked.

"Not for at least three days. I want to make sure there was no internal damage. He's doing very well." He replaced the chart in its holder and nodded to Randa before he left the room.

Randa faced Preston. "Sorry, honey," she said, rubbing his good arm. "Why don't I get you a book and read you a story?" She smiled when he nodded. "*Jack and the Beanstalk? Green Eggs and Ham?*" she offered. He nodded to both.

Randa grabbed her purse and stood. "I'll be right back," she told him as she prepared to go to the gift shop. After checking with the nurse to make sure someone looked in on Preston while she was away, she took the elevator to the ground floor. Since it was a

children's hospital, the gift shop was full of books.
Randa picked up the two books Preston had asked for,
along with several others and a stuffed animal.

As the cashier rang up her items, Randa decided
to call Justin to find out if he was really getting married. She listened patiently as the phone rang and
rang. Finally the voice mail kicked in. "Hi, Justin and
Lisa aren't home—"

Randa's cell phone slipped out of her hands and
crashed onto the floor. "Oh, damn!" she said. She
covered her mouth as soon as the words were out,
hoping no children had heard her. *So it was true.*

"Miss?" The cashier spoke, attracting Randa's
attention.

Her mind slowly came back to the gift shop. "I'm
sorry. How much?" Randa handed over her credit
card and bent down to pick up her cell phone.

The cashier handed her back her credit card and
the receipt for her to sign.

Randa smiled. "You can put the receipt in the
bag." She hoped the cashier didn't think she was
crazy or something. "It's one of those days," she explained as she picked up the sack.

The cashier nodded as if she understood perfectly. "Honey, I'm having one of those years!"

When Randa returned to Preston's room, he was
still wide-awake. She showed him all the purchases
she'd made, and he decided which book he wanted
to hear first. As intriguing as *Jack and the Beanstalk*
was, Randa's mind still floated to the sound of Lisa's
shrew-like voice on the answering machine. *How dare
Justin!*

"Mom Two?" Preston said, getting her attention.
She realized the room phone was ringing.

Randa nodded as she hurried to the phone.

"How is Preston?" Bea asked when Randa picked up.

"Fine, Bea. He'll be in here a few more days. How are things there?"

"Crazy. But don't you worry. Darius said not to work on that report unless you truly have time. They've pushed the publication date back a week to give you some extra time."

She relaxed as she hung up the phone and walked back to her seat. Randa opened the book, but she didn't resume reading just then. Instead, she gazed into space in deep thought.

At least, she didn't have to deal with the investors' report right now, she thought. Between Preston and this nonsense with Justin and Lisa, her hands were full. Most people could only take one disaster at a time, but Randa had two. But was Justin really a disaster? Or was it just the act of a man still weak behind his first wife? In any rate, did she really want to be bothered with Justin Brewster anymore?

It was over for good, she decided and resumed reading the book to Preston.

Justin adjusted his tie in the solitude of his bedroom. The day was going to be fast and intense. His reward would be Randa back in his life with no threat of Lisa returning. He smiled as he put on his jacket. "Yeah, Justin, this is your day," he said to his reflection.

He walked to Lisa's room to see if she was ready and overheard her talking on the phone, obviously to her boyfriend. He walked back to his bedroom and closed the door. Walking to the bedside phone, he picked it up as silently as he could.

Lisa was attempting to comfort the voice on the

other end of the phone, something she never did for him. "I know this wasn't in our plan," she whispered. "But this will work. I'll marry him, get him to put me back on his bank accounts, and take the money. Shouldn't take over a few months, tops." Her cold voice held no remorse for what she was about to do.

"But where are you sleeping?" the voice asked. "Even a dope like Justin is not going to let you just take that money and not want sex."

"Not every man is like you. Justin never demands sex. We're still sleeping in separate bedrooms and will continue as we are."

"I don't believe you," the voice taunted back. "Remember how I met you? You were in my bed that very night, and you were still married."

Justin couldn't believe it. His brother had told him about the rumors, but he'd still held on to the belief that it wasn't true. He had hoped Lisa at least respected their marriage vows while she was sending him to the poorhouse.

He quietly replaced the phone to the cradle and sat down on the bed. Justin took a deep breath; for all the pain she had given him, the end was in sight. Lisa would get the help she needed, and he would get her out of his life.

Justin walked down the hall to Lisa's bedroom a few minutes later and knocked on the door. "Lisa, I thought we could go out for breakfast before going to the courthouse." A heartbeat barely passed before she opened the door.

She was dressed in a designer suit, of course. Her face was covered with two layers of makeup, and her hair was lacquered with who-knows-how-many different gels and other kinds of goop. Instantly, Randa's now makeup free face popped into his brain, reminding him of the end result of the charade.

"Breakfast sounds good. It's not McDonald's, is it?" She glanced in her small compact mirror.

"I was thinking a restaurant closer to downtown."

Lisa was just happy that he was actually spending money on her. "That sounds nice, Justin."

He knew she was agreeable for only one reason. Justin thought he would push the envelope a little. "You know, I was thinking we could maybe spend the night at the Hilton in Arlington for our wedding night celebration." He walked to the garage with her trailing behind.

Lisa pulled the door to the house, making sure it was locked. "Are you sure, Justin? I mean, we should probably just go home. Instead of you spending the money on a room, you could buy me a present."

Justin opened her car door, and she slid into the seat. He whistled as he walked to his side of the truck and got in. "So you don't want to have sex with me, is that it?" He started the engine, and they headed in the direction of downtown.

Counting the seconds of silence, Justin laughed.

"Justin," Lisa started, "you know we hadn't had sex in quite some time before we split up. I thought you didn't like doing that."

He hadn't wanted to do it because Lisa had just lain there like a damp rag. "It wasn't that I didn't want to have sex; it was all the rules you set in place to make sure that I wouldn't. Even if you were as good as you thought you were, it was hardly worth the price of admission."

Fake tears instantly tumbled down Lisa's perfectly made-up face. "Justin, you always said sex was great. Now the truth is coming out!"

"You don't want to get married, do you?"

"Of course I do. Don't be silly," she said, immediately changing her demeanor. "We can work around the sex thing."

Justin watched her as he negotiated onto the freeway. "Meaning that we won't be having sex any time soon?" he prodded. He wanted her to get flustered so maybe he could hear a confession about the boyfriend.

She reached a perfectly manicured hand across to him. "Justin, of course we'll have sex. I love you."

"Really?"

"Of course."

He nodded, not wanting to overplay his hand. He finished the drive in silence.

"Let's just go to the courthouse now, then. There's no sense in us waiting. We can get brunch afterward. How's that sound?"

Lisa nodded. The sooner she could get her hands on Justin's money, the better.

As they walked into the judge's chambers, Justin smiled. Judge Harold Milner sat behind his desk, and Sean, who would serve as the witness to the fake ceremony, was seated in a chair.

Sean's gaze met Justin's and he winked at him.

"Please sit down. I have just a few questions," Judge Milner said.

Lisa sat down and crossed her legs, smiling at the judge like she was trying to play the part of the shy bride. Judge Milner looked over the paperwork and began speaking. "Lisa. How do you feel about Justin?"

Lisa looked at him and smiled. "I love him."

"I see that you two were married before. What was the reason for the divorce?"

Lisa had an answer for everything. "It was my fault. I spent too much money. I nagged him too much about advancing in his job," she said sweetly.

The judge laughed. "You know, you're the first woman in my chambers that acknowledged that a divorce was her fault. I'm impressed."

Lisa smiled and batted her lashes at him. "I know I was at fault."

"So when you convinced him that you needed a vacation home, a third car, or jewelry, you knew that you really couldn't afford it, but you wanted him to get them for you anyway."

"I deserved those things," she shouted. Seeing the judge's reaction, she changed her tone. "I know I have a competitive spirit," she said softly, using her small voice again.

"And, I see, a low-paying job?"

"I don't work there anymore. Justin is going to support me."

Justin watched her as she told the judge what she thought he wanted to hear. He knew he could never love her again; he didn't really see how he could have loved her in the first place. The judge continued his line of questioning.

"Are you acquainted with a Derek Hall?"

"Yes."

"What is your relationship with him?"

"He's a friend. He took me in after Justin ended our marriage."

"Rumor has it that he's your lover."

Lisa glanced at Justin. "No, sir," she said dramatically. "I belong only to Justin."

Judge Milner smiled at her. "Well, Lisa, it looks like you got yourself a husband. If you'll excuse me and my assistant for a moment, we'll be right back and we can get you two married." Judge Milner and Sean rose from their seats. Sean shot Justin a worried look that indicated this procedure wasn't part of the plan.

Lisa watched Justin as they were left alone in the judge's chambers. *He looks almost remorseful,* she thought. *Is he thinking about Randa?* Lisa would make sure that evil woman's name never crossed his lips again. She had turned her sweet, docile husband into an overbearing man with a backbone. Right after she and Justin were married, she planned to take care of Randa Stone for good.

"Justin, are you thinking about Randa?" Lisa asked. She had to know.

"Of course not, Lisa. Don't be silly. You're all I think about." He smiled at her as he glanced at the clock on the judge's immaculate desk. He wondered what was taking so long.

"I just want you to be sure. I don't plan on getting divorced again," she said.

If she didn't know better, she might have thought the smile Justin gave her was very sinister. But this was Justin; he didn't have a sinister bone in his body unless directed by her.

"Neither do I," Justin said. "This time when I say I do, it will be forever." He took her hand and held it, milking his routine for all it was worth.

Lisa almost jumped out of her skin when Justin's hand touched hers. He wanted to hold hands like a couple in love. He was expecting sex, she knew. Her mind was buzzing for a reason for them not to make love on their wedding night.

"My stomach is really upset today. I don't feel well," she whined.

"Don't worry, I know something that will make

you feel all better." He leaned over and kissed her on the cheek.

The feel of his lips on her skin began to irritate her. Why did she always find these touchy-feely men? "Justin, I'm really not feeling well."

"I'm sure you'll feel better later. But we can add your name to the bank accounts another time since you're not feeling well." It was a horrible thing to do to a crazy lady, but he liked watching Lisa squirm.

"No, we can do that after this," she blurted.

He gave her another sinister smile. "Well, let me put it in terms that you can understand. If you don't sleep with me, I don't add you to my accounts."

Okay, this was not the Justin Brewster she used to know. "You would actually use those accounts to get sex?"

His stomach lurched at the thought of actually sleeping with Lisa, but he had to keep up the act. "You're finally catching on! You thought I would just idly stand by, let you rob me blind, and not ask for anything in return?"

"Of course, I want to make love with you, Justin. I just don't feel good today. A caring husband would wait."

"I'm not a caring husband yet," he reminded her.

"I'm sorry, am I interrupting?" Judge Milner asked, returning to his chambers. He was accompanied by a uniformed officer instead of Sean. Justin began to worry.

"I apologize. My usual witness can't be found anywhere," the judge said. "Do you mind if Officer Barton is your witness?"

Lisa didn't like the feel of the situation, but what could she do? Going back to Portland empty-handed wasn't an option. Plus, she had no way to get there. "I have no objections."

The judge coughed and looked at Lisa with hostility in his eyes. "If you'll follow Officer Barton, Ms. Brewster." The officer unhooked his handcuffs and headed toward Lisa. What was going on?

She looked at Justin. He didn't have that sorry look on his face anymore. In fact, he was genuinely smiling. Something was not right.

"Nooooo!" Lisa squealed as the officer came closer. "I can't go to jail."

Randa took advantage of Preston's midmorning nap by checking her phone messages. The first message was from Justin. As usual, he was rushing and couldn't talk long, but he said he wanted to see her. *For what,* Randa wondered, deleting the message. The next message was from Gareth. His voice sounded frantic and he was asking her to call him on his private line.

His private line? Josh didn't even know Gareth's private number; this had to be major. Randa hoped it was nothing medical as she quickly dialed the digits.

"Gareth, it's me," she said when he answered. "What's wrong?"

"Honey, I'm swamped right now. How about I come over later and we'll talk?"

He ended the call, and Randa clicked off her cell phone. She didn't like the sound of that at all.

TWENTY-FIVE

Handcuffed, Lisa sat in the small room, waiting for the judge to explain to her what had just happened in his chambers.

The door opened, and Officer Barton and another officer in plainclothes walked in. "Lisa Nicole Miller Brewster, I have a warrant for your extradition back to Portland, Oregon," the second officer said.

Her heart sank as he read the list of charges. Just then, she realized Justin, of all people, had outfoxed her. He was the one man she thought she could always manipulate. Had the few months he had been in Texas toughened him up that much? She knew it was that damn Randa. She let the tears flow, hoping the arresting officer would take pity on her, but he was determined to finish reading the charges.

"You will be held in the city jail for twenty-four hours, then transferred to the Portland facility," he continued.

"Can I speak to the judge that married me?"

The officer smiled. "He didn't marry you, ma'am. You didn't quite get to that part. If you'll allow me, there are still more charges to be read."

"You don't have to," Lisa said pathetically. She tried her toothy smile, which always worked.

"No, ma'am. I have to read all the charges to you and make sure you understand them before you speak to anyone," the officer told her. "These are your Miranda rights."

There was that name again. She was sick of hearing it. "Randa, Randa, I'm so sick of hearing her name," she muttered. Lisa began to cry. "At least this crap is over. Just take me away," she begged the officer when he was finished reading her rights.

Justin and Sean watched the scene play out through the two-way mirror. Lisa was led out of the room, and Justin wondered if it would be the last time he ever saw her. He certainly hoped so. Turning to Sean, he asked, "Did something go wrong with the plan? You and Judge Milner were gone a long time."

Sean looked at Justin sympathetically. "He told me that he didn't feel comfortable recommending a lesser sentence for Lisa. He didn't think she's crazy."

Justin looked at him quizzically. "Would a sane woman act the way she does?"

"I don't think she has mental defects either. From what you told me about her behavior, I thought she might have obsessive-compulsive disorder, but she's actually just a selfish, vindictive woman."

"So she'll go straight to jail?" Justin asked. She had treated him awfully, but he still didn't want her to suffer. That just wasn't the type of man he was.

"She would have gone to jail anyway when she got back to Portland. There was already a warrant for her arrest, and she fled. The courts wouldn't let a flight risk out on bond anyway." Seeing the puzzled look on Justin's face, Sean tried to comfort him. "From what Darius tells me, this woman ruined fifteen years of your life. I know you care what happens to her, but remember that she came here not caring what happened to you."

Justin nodded, taking in Sean's words.

* * *

Randa smiled as she finished the final edits of her report. *It may actually get to the presses on time,* she thought. That would be quite a feather in her cap if she could manage it, especially if she didn't have to get Justin's help.

The ringing phone startled her. She rushed over to get it before Preston awoke from his afternoon nap. "Hello?" she answered.

Bea's voice greeted her again. "Hey, how's it going?"

Randa listened to Bea talk, and she realized something was wrong; she could hear it in her voice. She put her hand over her heart to slow down the rapid thumping she was sure was going to wake Preston. "Okay, Bea. Out with it," she said.

Bea took a deep breath and rattled some papers at her desk. Another bad sign. Bea was usually straightforward and pulled no punches, except for the time when she'd had to tell Randa that her mother had died. Randa took another breath. *He's not worth it,* she chanted. "What is it, Bea?"

"This morning, Delores had some problems with the reports." Randa inhaled again, waiting from the bomb to drop. "I went down to help her. She appeared really nervous, like she was hiding something. Then I saw it. Sitting on her desk as plain as day."

"What?" Randa felt that Bea was taunting her by drawing the story out.

"I saw a copy of a marriage license for Justin and Lisa. I asked Delores about it, but she wouldn't tell me anything. She just kept talking like one of those old detective shows, saying stuff like 'all will be revealed in good time,' you know?

Randa breathed a sigh of relief. "I already knew about that, Bea. I stopped by the office earlier this week to pick up my things and saw it on his desk. I don't know what to think about him anymore." Randa's life was slowly crumbling all around her. "Gareth says I should trust Justin since he spent the day with me when Preston got hurt."

"What does Gareth know? He's a man. Yes, he's a gay man, but an idiot with a penis nonetheless."

Randa laughed. "Bea, I can't believe you sometimes. Gareth also wants to talk tonight."

"Don't tell me he's thinking of changing teams again?"

"I doubt that very seriously."

They talked a few minutes more before Bea said, "I didn't call to rattle you, girl. I just wanted to give you a heads-up about the marriage."

"Thanks, Bea. I think that little whatever-it-was is over and I'll just have to move on."

Justin walked out of the courthouse a free man. Lisa was finally out of his life, and now he could focus his attention on Randa, if she was still speaking to him, that is.

As he drove to his town house, he tried to call Randa's cell phone and got her voice mail. He realized that she had probably turned it off in the hospital. Justin exited the freeway and got back on going the opposite way, headed in the direction of Children's Palace.

He walked into Preston's hospital room and found Gareth in the chair by his bed. Gareth looked up from his magazine and barely gave Justin a glance.

"Randa isn't here," he said, burying his nose in the pages.

"I can see that. Where is she?"

"I don't know if I should relay that information to

you," Gareth said, anger rising in his voice. "Tell me, Justin, what does it feel like making the same mistake twice?" Gareth said, anger rising in his voice.

When Gareth had come by the hospital to relieve Randa from her shift, he'd found her in tears. She finally told him about Justin's marriage and how devastated she was.

Okay, she knows about the marriage license, Justin thought. He wondered if she also knew it was a ruse. Judging from Gareth's more-hostile-than-usual demeanor, she didn't. "That's something that should be discussed between Randa and myself, Mr. Cornworthy."

Justin chastised himself all the way to the elevator for letting Gareth know that he'd gotten under his skin. That was not the best way to handle the situation, especially with Gareth and Randa being so close. Randa would definitely be angry when she found out that he was there and had upset Gareth.

He walked back to the room to make amends. Gareth hadn't moved.

"She's not here," Gareth said, releasing a dramatic sigh. "But then, we just did this, didn't we?"

Justin sat down. "Yes, Gareth, we did. I'm sorry for snapping at you. I've been through an incredible day and need to talk to Randa. Can you tell me where she is?"

Gareth put his magazine down and faced Justin. "Well, Justin, she went to get Jessica and to drop some things off at the messenger service. How's the new wife?"

Justin was ready to spill the beans, but Gareth stopped him.

"You know what really rips my boxers about you? I defended you to Randa. I told her she should trust you and not ask what you were up to. Then you up and marry the same woman that put you in the poor-house the first time. You know, Randa is executor of my estate, a partner in my business. She's her own person; she doesn't need you for anything."

Justin really didn't like the last statement. "What are trying to tell me, Gareth?"

Gareth crossed his legs and stared directly into Justin's eyes. "Well, Justin, I spent last night with Randa, and you know what?"

The word stuck in his throat. "What?"

"I don't want her hurt anymore. Yes, I hurt her a long time ago, but that hurt helped us grow. Now I will not stand by and let you drag her through the mud all over again. Whatever I have to do to keep her happy, I'm going to do it."

"I assume that means sleeping with her?" he prodded.

"If that's what she needs, I will," Gareth said defiantly.

Justin stood up and walked out of the room.

"Did I miss anything?" Randa asked Gareth as she and Jessica walked into the room an hour later. "Did Preston give you any trouble?"

Gareth smiled as Randa checked Preston to make sure the straps were still secure and that he was asleep. "No, nothing," Gareth said, still flipping through the magazine.

Something about the way Gareth looked neither at the magazine nor at her face when he spoke alerted her that he wasn't telling her everything he knew. "Why does everyone make me drag things out of them?" Randa blurted.

He looked at her and rolled his eyes. "Justin the

Horrible came by and we had a discussion. I'm assuming he'll call you later."

She shook her head. "He doesn't have to." She sat beside Gareth as Jessica stood beside the bed.

"Why is he always sleeping?" Jessica asked, her voice full of concern.

"Because he has internal injuries and needs to be still," Randa explained.

Jessica sat in Randa's lap and hugged her. "I miss him chasing me around the house. When will he get to go home? I'm tired of coming here."

Randa comforted her niece. "Honey, that's your brother. There are a lot of things in life that you don't like to do, but you do them because it's for your family. How about tonight we order pizza?"

"Is Uncle Gareth staying tonight?"

"Oh no, honey. Uncle Josh will miss him too much."

Gareth coughed. "Actually, I was thinking I could have something delivered from my restaurant, and I could spend the night. I still need to talk to you."

"Okay, you win," she said cautiously.

Gareth smiled as he stood. "I'll meet you at your house later." He kissed Randa on the lips and left the room.

Randa watched him go. He hadn't kissed her like that in over five years. Something was going on, but she didn't know what. Jessica sat in the chair that Gareth vacated. They waited in silence until Karl arrived to take the night shift.

Once Randa and Jessica had gotten settled in at Randa's house, the food showed up. Randa gazed at the small delivery van that had delivered more food than she could eat in two months. She questioned the delivery driver about the amount, but he only smiled and nodded his head.

"Yes, ma'am, I'm sure all this is supposed to go here. Mr. Cornworthy was very specific. He said to tell you he'd be here shortly." He winked at her and refused a tip as he left her doorway.

Randa smiled, knowing that Gareth was up to something. She would just have to wait and see what it was.

She didn't have to wait long. Gareth arrived dressed in one of his Armani suits. Randa led him to the dining room, where Jessica was waiting.

"Here, enjoy some of your food," she said, placing a stalk of broccoli on Gareth's plate. "Just whom are you trying to feed? This is too much."

He shrugged his broad shoulders and sat down at the table. "I thought you might be too distracted to cook for Jessie, and I wanted to make sure both you guys had something decent to eat." He winked at Randa's niece.

They dined on steak, potatoes, and broccoli. Gareth was right; Randa knew she wouldn't have had time to cook this kind of meal. "Thank you, Gareth. You are a lifesaver."

"We'll talk later."

That little phrase was beginning to get under her skin. *What was this about?* But she decided to relax and enjoy the savory meal. She needed something calm in her life for a change.

Later, after she put Jessica to bed, Randa saw that Gareth had made himself at home in the room down the hall. She would have loved to have the security that he'd given her the night before, but she preferred to have Justin's arms around her instead. She released a weary sigh as she made her way to the bedroom.

Randa had just settled under the covers when she

heard a knock on her bedroom door. Assuming it was Jessica, she called for her to come inside.

"Randa?"

She looked up to see Gareth standing over her bed. She scooted over to give him room to sit.

Gareth took a deep breath, and Randa could see that something was troubling him. "You're sick again, aren't you?" she asked, her eyes immediately welling with tears.

He shook his head. "I wanted you to know that last night was great. It reminded me of why I married you in the first place. I think I love you, Randa."

"I know you love me, but you don't love me like a lover, Gareth," she pleaded.

"Yes, I do. I want to give us another try."

Randa shook her head. "You're gay," she reminded him, since he'd apparently forgotten.

"What did you want to talk about? Outside of your indecision about your sexuality."

Gareth laughed, and his voice comforted her in the dark, like it had during every one of her crises in the past. "I know I'm gay. I just want you to be happy. It's apparent that Justin isn't the one for you."

"What are you going to do, leave Josh and come be my husband again? Gareth, I want you to be happy, too. I've already come to terms with the fact that I won't be a wife again and I'll never be a mother, but I have Preston and Jessica, and I'm okay with that," she lied. "So what if Justin's an idiot and remarried that money-hungry woman—that's his fault."

"That's what I mean, honey," Gareth said, handing her a Kleenex from the dresser. "If you want a baby, I can provide. I can donate, or we could do it the old-fashioned way." She blew her nose, and he took the dirty tissue and threw it in the trash can on his side of the bed.

Randa was touched by his willingness to give her what she wanted. "I appreciate the offer, but I want it all: a husband, a home, then kids."

Gareth leaned down to kiss her. He knew his offer was a long shot, but he felt he owed Randa as much for ending their marriage. Not wanting to admit that he was yearning for children as well, he made light of their heavy subject matter. "Okay, remember my offer when they tell you menopause is around the corner," he teased.

Randa reached to hug him and smiled when they embraced. It was good to know that he still cared. "I will. I love you, Gareth."

Gareth awoke very early the next morning feeling overjoyed and relieved. After he took a shower, he walked down the hall to Jessica's room and found she was still asleep. He walked into the kitchen to begin preparing breakfast.

There was something about being in Randa's house and making breakfast that just seemed right. His mother would be proud. After he and Randa divorced and Josh moved in, his mother decided that she liked Randa; it was a classic case of too little, too late.

Zack walked into the kitchen and headed straight for his bowl. The dog looked at Gareth with big, pleading eyes when he found it empty. Feeling sorry for the puppy, Gareth walked to the cabinet to retrieve his food. "I can't believe Randa buys you this expensive dog food," he muttered, shaking the contents of the bag into the bowl. He rubbed Zack's back as he dug in to his meal. "I guess you deserve it. Randa loves you."

The phone rang, distracting him. "Who could that

be calling this early?" Gareth said out loud, looking at the clock on the stove. "It's not even seven." He walked to the phone and answered, "Stone residence."

The caller did not speak, but Gareth could hear someone on the other line. He tried again. "Stone residence."

"Gareth?" a male voice asked.

"Yes."

"It's Justin. Where is Randa? Why are you answering her phone?"

Gareth tried to keep a close rein on his temper; a heated conversation would only lead to either he or Justin doing something stupid and hurting Randa more in the process. "Randa is still asleep. Why are you calling, anyway? Shouldn't you be leaving for your honeymoon or something?"

He heard Justin take a deep breath. "As I said before, there is something I need to discuss with Randa. Put her on the phone."

"Well, I have decided that Randa should get her rest and get rid of idiots like you," Gareth taunted. "What did the ex do? Say she loved you and you took her back, just like that?"

Justin ignored his questions. He knew Gareth was trying to get under his skin. He asked the question that was foremost on his mind. "Why are you at Randa's house this early in the morning?" He hoped Randa and Gareth had not reconciled while he was busy getting rid of Lisa.

This is going to be fun, Gareth thought. "Well, if you must know, I stayed over last night, and the night before that, too. Randa and I got to talking about babies and stuff, and it was really late when we finally went to sleep." Gareth smiled at his embellishment as he'd neglected to tell Justin that he'd slept in the room down the hall.

"You are trying to get her, aren't you, Gareth?" *I knew he wasn't really gay,* Justin thought.

"Unlike some people, I have not remarried my ex-wife," he shot back. "Why don't you leave Randa alone? You are not what she needs. Randa deserves a man that loves her and can't be swayed by a materialistic, manipulating woman. I love Randa. I don't know who you love," Gareth yelled, hanging up the phone. Afterward, he walked to the refrigerator to gather the items he needed to make breakfast.

TWENTY-SIX

"Son of a bitch!" Justin yelled, slamming the phone down and sinking into the closest chair. Randa's ex-husband had just flushed his plans down the tube. He let out a loud sigh and propped his head in his hand. What could he do? Justin decided to stake out the hospital and talk to Randa when she arrived to visit Preston.

When he arrived at Children's Palace, he literally ran into Randa's brother, who was just leaving Preston's room. Justin gained his composure before he said, "Hi, Karl. How's Preston?"

Karl looked at Justin as if he were a stranger, indicating that he knew about the marriage certificate as well. "Preston is fine," he said curtly. "He may even get to go home sooner than expected. Not that you really care. Why are you here, Justin?"

"I came to talk to Randa," he explained.

"About your wife?" He motioned for Justin to take a seat in the hallway, then sat beside him. "What I don't understand is why you had to come here. Randa already knows you remarried your ex-wife, and right now, she's numb about it. Don't you think you've done enough damage? What more do you need to do to feel more like a man?"

Justin was dumbfounded. How had he let this situation spin so far out of control? He never wanted to hurt anyone, especially not Randa. Now her entire inner circle had rallied to protect her. "Karl, it's not what you think." He wanted to tell Karl the truth about the marriage certificate, but he didn't want Randa to get that information secondhand.

"You could have told her that you were still in love with Lisa. You asked her to trust you, and she did, and you broke her heart." Karl lowered his voice when he saw several nurses looking down the hall to determine the cause of the shouting. "You could have been a man and told her that you wanted your ex," he hissed.

Justin shook his head at Karl. There was no convincing him of his intentions. "I would never hurt, Randa. Ever. I-I—"

Karl heard Preston stirring in his hospital bed and walked away from Justin midsentence. He'd had enough of the blubbering fool that sat before him. "Excuse me, I have to tend to my child," he said.

Justin fumed. Just once, he wished someone would hear him out and not make rash judgments without knowing the facts. "I know Preston is your main concern right now, but I really need to have a talk with Randa."

A nurse walked in before Karl could respond. "Mr. Stone, Dr. Phillips is on his way. He's got good news." She smiled at him, unstrapping Preston as she spoke. "This little fellow might get to go home as early as today."

"Really?" Karl said, taking a seat in the chair next to Justin.

The nurse nodded. "It's only been a couple of days, but he's much better."

Justin watched the relief spread across Karl's face. He couldn't begin to imagine what Karl was feeling. Justin waited until the nurse left and Karl had checked on Preston before speaking again. "Do you think I could have a few minutes of Randa's time before you guys switch duty?" he asked humbly.

Karl wiped his eyes, thinking Justin wouldn't give up any time soon. "Any other morning, she would have stopped by with Jessie, but today they aren't coming. She won't be here until this afternoon."

Justin swore under his breath. Seeing the look on Karl's face, he immediately wished he could take the word back. "Sorry," he offered.

"Obviously, she needs some time for herself. She's been going through her own private hell these last few days."

"And I haven't helped one bit."

"No you haven't," Karl said firmly, rising from his seat and crossing the room to stand in front of Justin. The two men, each one over six feet tall, stood toe to toe. "If you hurt her any more—" Karl began.

Justin cut him off. "I would never hurt the woman I love."

Randa eased into the soothing hot water in the Jacuzzi and exhaled. Slowly, the tension from the last week eased from her body. Karl was right; a day at the spa was already making her feel much better. Now all the insane things that were now her life made more sense. She already had a handle on Justin and had decided she would forget about him in time. Randa loved him and it wouldn't be easy, but her heart would eventually mend. She really didn't have a choice in the matter, since he'd married Lisa anyway.

Sitting in the bubbling water, Randa thought of all the things she should be thinking about instead of Justin—the report, Preston, her job duties. While she liked her new position as tech manager, she was always working late and on weekends. Maybe after the report was done, everything would go back to normal. She sighed in disgust. "It's happening again," she said, sinking into the water.

Randa arrived at the hospital that afternoon feeling refreshed. She walked into Preston's room and was surprised to find that her brother wasn't there. Justin, however, was.

He sat in a chair in Preston's room, with puppy-dog eyes that tugged at her heart. She strengthened her resolve not to give in to him. After all, he was a married man.

"Where's Karl?" she asked harshly, walking to the bed and noticing the straps were missing from Preston's body. Her nephew actually looked like the little boy she knew. She saw color had returned to his cheeks.

Preston outstretched his good arm so that Randa could hug him. She also noticed his bed was tilted at an angle instead of flat like it had been the last few days. She scooped him up and rubbed his back.

"Where's your dad?" she asked.

He shrugged.

"He had to go to the office and asked me to stay until you got here," Justin reported. "He was a little reluctant about leaving, but the nurse assured him that she would look in on Preston as well."

Randa sat in the chair next to Justin. She didn't want to look at him. Tears would start if she did; they were already threatening to erupt from just hearing his deep baritone voice. "You can leave now, Justin."

"Randa, I'm not here to baby-sit Preston. I was

going to wait for you no matter how long it was going to take you to get here. I need to explain the events of the last few days."

She was determined not to let him see her cry. "Justin, you remarried your ex. Nothing you can say or do will change that. Now that I've seen how easily Lisa can manipulate you, I don't like you anymore anyway. You're obviously not the man I thought you were," she said bitterly.

"You're not going to let me explain, are you?"

"No. There's no need. You know how you always tell me about my icy throne? Well this is why I have one." She fought back her tears. "We both have to attend Darius's celebration dinner next Friday. I hope that you and your wife can act in a civilized manner. I know I will."

She heard him mutter something, then he stood. "You're not the woman I thought you were, either. I asked you to trust me, and you said you would. Now that I know you can't, I guess ending our relationship is for the best. One day, you're going to see how wrong you and your family are about me." He left the room without another word.

Randa looked to Preston for support. "I thought he'd never leave," she said, feeling the tears creeping down her face. She made no effort to hide them from her nephew. "I don't want you treating women like this when you're older."

Preston looked at her, nodding his head like he understood.

Randa dried her eyes as the doctor walked into the room. "Good news, Ms. Stone. I will be releasing Preston in the morning. He's healing well, and his injuries aren't as extensive as we initially thought." The doctor walked to the bed and rubbed Preston's head. "He's been a good patient."

"That's wonderful," Randa said, wiping her face with the back of her hand. "Will he need special care when he's home?"

The doctor nodded. "Just try to keep him still for the first few days. Let him set the pace when he's ready to start playing."

Randa nodded, thanking the doctor as he exited the room. "How about that, Preston? Tomorrow night you'll be sleeping in your own bed."

When Preston was released from the hospital, Randa and Zack moved in with her brother. Even though she missed her bed, she was happy to be at Karl's because it made her feel like she had her own family. She realized that she would have to go back home eventually and knew she would miss the arguments between Jessica and Preston over who got to sit next to her or who would walk Zack.

Even though Preston was supposedly still healing from his injuries, sometimes she found it hard to believe he wasn't all better. He ran through the house, up and down the stairs, terrorizing his sister all evening after she got home from school.

After Bea got off work on Wednesday, Randa met her at the mall with the kids in tow. Although she already had several formal dresses, she wanted a new dress for the celebration with her coworkers, which was in two days. Picking up a long blue gown, she almost passed out when she saw the price tag. "I knew there was a reason I always bought formals out of season," she said to Bea.

Bea laughed. "Yeah, like you were worried about the price." She flipped through a few of the dresses. "I like this one," she said, handing Randa a strapless aqua gown. "I bet you will knock Justin's eyes out of his head."

"I'm not dressing for Justin. He married his ex last week, remember?" She stepped back to look down the aisle at Jessica and Preston. They were sitting in the husband chairs next to the waiting room.

"He hasn't been acting very happy since he returned to work," Bea said. "He's been more withdrawn, you know, like when he first got there." She stood closer to Randa. "Rumor has it that the ex was extradited back to Oregon for an old forgery charge."

Randa's mind whirled. Were Justin and Lisa not married? She reminded herself that she had seen the marriage license. "It's just a rumor," she said nonchalantly.

"And the Oscar for best performance for an ex-lover is Miranda Stone," Bea chimed as she started clapping. They both laughed and continued looking for a dress.

Bea continued. "I hear that the marriage was just a ruse. But I'm sure he explained all that to you, right?"

"No, not exactly."

"Well, what exactly?" Bea picked up another gown. This one was a mauve strapless number with an A-line cut.

Randa held the dress against her and smiled. "I like this one. What do you think, guys?" she asked, walking over to Preston and Jessica with the dress.

As promised, they were as quiet as mice and waiting for their reward: a trip to the food court.

"It's pretty. Can we go eat now?" Jessica asked.

"I have to try it on first. Then we'll see."

Jessica sighed but nodded. "Okay."

"Stay here with Aunt Bea, and I'll be right back," Randa said, heading for the dressing room.

After she was satisfied with the fit of the dress, she walked to the counter to pay for it.

"I take it you like that one?" Bea said, walking to meet her, with Preston and Jessica trailing behind.

"Yes, it fits great. It accents me in all the right places." Randa laughed as she reached for her wallet.

"This is a great dress," the saleswoman said as she rang up the purchase. "Did you need any alterations, ma'am?"

Ma'am. Oh, that hurt. "Yes, please," she said, grimacing at the title. "I need the waistline taken in two inches, and I need it delivered by Friday."

Randa took a deep breath. Friday was going to be the true test of how strong her heart was when it came to the subject of Justin and Lisa Brewster.

TWENTY-SEVEN

Randa walked into the ballroom, determined to have a good time. She glanced around the room, waving at Darius and his wife when she spotted them. There was a crowd congratulating the couple on Cherish's pregnancy. Randa followed suit and walked over.

"Congratulations, Cherish," she said, trying not to appear envious.

Cherish returned her smile. "Thank you, Randa. You look wonderful as usual." She nodded at her gown.

Fearing she'd become a mass of tears, Randa excused herself to the ladies' room. As she washed her face, her mind drifted to Justin. So what if he went back to his ex? "You can move on and have a productive life," she said to her reflection. "You'll be just fine without him." With her dignity intact, she left the ladies' room.

Bea stopped her before she could rejoin the party. "Randa, what's going on with you? I saw you scamper to the bathroom. You know, Justin's here," she said, handing her a handkerchief.

"Is he alone?" She dreaded the answer.

"He is, but I could still knock him over the head with a champagne bottle. Then we could—"

"Bea, have you lost your mind?" Randa laughed at

her friend's silliness and gave Bea a hug. "My mother always said there was no man worth crying over."

"Amen!" Bea said, leading her to a table. Darius soon joined the women, taking a seat next to Randa.

"Randa, I hear everyone loves your work in the tech department. I want to thank you for getting the investors' report out during such trying circumstances. It looks great," he complimented.

"Thank you. It helped me keep my mind off of my nephew while he was in the hospital. I didn't want to let you down after you had recommended me for the job." She grinned at Darius. Although this was his night, he'd still made time to talk to her. Justin hadn't so much as looked in her direction.

Darius excused himself from the table, and Randa watched him as he mingled with the other partners. "Darius is so nice," she said to no one in particular. "Why are the good ones always taken or gay?"

"I'm neither," Justin said, sitting in the chair Darius had vacated. He wore a black tuxedo and white shirt. He looked amazing. "Can we talk? Alone?" he added, addressing Bea.

"Bea is staying," Randa said. "So whatever you think you have to say to me, you can say it here. Better yet, why can't you just leave me alone? You've made it quite clear that you don't want me, and I won't bother you anymore. Do you and your wife take some sick pleasure out of seeing how many times I'll fall for the same line?" She took a sip of champagne to calm her nerves.

"What the hell is going on?" Justin asked, his frustration getting the best of him.

She didn't answer. She finished the remainder of the champagne and signaled the waiter for a refill. After the waiter left, she gulped down the bubbly liquid, then she sat the empty glass on the table. "Justin, you remarried your ex. I know you did. I saw the papers on your desk. You could have told me. I'm not one of those desperate women that wouldn't have let you go," she hissed. "As you see, I've had no problem doing just that."

Justin looked at her incredulously. "Randa, do you really think I would marry Lisa after all I told you about how awful my marriage was?" he bellowed.

"Didn't she stay with you while she was in town?"

"Yes."

"You rented her a car?"

"Yes."

"I don't think we have anything else to discuss."

Justin played with the glass in front of him. "I think we do. Not once did you ask me why I did those things."

How much more of this am I supposed to take? she wondered. "Okay. I'll bite," she said tiredly. "Why, Justin?"

"She had an agenda when she came here, and she showed up with no money," he explained as calmly as he could. "She was wanted for forgery in Portland, and she came here to escape. I thought she was having a mental breakdown or something. I couldn't throw her out on the street, Randa.

"Yes, I rented her a car. I had to make her think I would take her back or my plan wouldn't work."

"What plan?"

"When she first started calling me, demanding money, I knew I didn't love her anymore, but I also knew she was going to show up here. I thought she was losing her grasp on reality." He explained all the twisted logic behind the marriage license and the rules of extradition. Randa listened attentively. He hoped she believed him.

She did. Randa felt like an idiot, but she wouldn't

let it show. Justin continued. "She's been charged with forgery and credit-card fraud. Randa, since I met you, you have showed me how things could be, should be, between two people who love each other," he said passionately.

She wiped her face with a linen napkin. "But you don't love me, Justin."

"Randa, weren't my actions proof enough that I love you? How many times did I feed your dog? Take him for a walk because you were too tired? I went to your niece's birthday party," he reminded her.

"Well, I would like to hear it," she said. Her heart was a ball of confusion. She had had so many ups and downs with him, and those three little words would make everything better. They would make her heart be still.

Justin took her hand and held it against his heart. "Randa, you are the most beautiful, intelligent woman I have ever met."

She cut him off. "That's not enough for me, Jus—"

He put his free hand to her lips to quiet her.

"And I love you," he said, looking into her eyes. He brought the hand he held to his chest to his lips and kissed it gently. Justin wanted to wrap her in his strong embrace and show her how much she meant to him, but he knew she would object.

"I love you, too," Randa said, thinking she would melt right there in her chair.

As the band began to play, Justin invited Randa to the dance floor with him. As he held her against his large body, he whispered in her ear. "Do you think your life is full, Randa?" he asked.

She pulled back and looked at him as they swayed in time to the music. "It is now. Why?"

"I want to give you everything that you want and need."

Randa stopped dancing. "What are you saying, Justin?"

He grabbed her to him again and moved her to the beat of the music. "We'll talk later," he told her.

Uh-oh, Randa thought. *That never meant anything good.*

After the party, Randa allowed Justin to follow her home. Zack was being looked after by Jessica and Preston at Karl's house, and though she loved her family dearly, she was thankful for the silence.

She sat on the couch, sipping a glass of wine, as Justin massaged her tired feet. High heels had always been her shoes of choice, but they wreaked havoc on her feet.

"Oh, that feels so good," Randa moaned as Justin's hands worked their magic. She wanted to ask if he'd put those expert hands in other places, but he hadn't told her what it was he wanted to talk to her about. She wondered if she'd still want him touching her after he divulged his thoughts.

"Are you ready to spill the beans?" she asked.

Justin exhaled a ragged breath. He pulled Randa toward him, so that she was situated between his legs with her back against him. Her stomach tightened with fear. They'd finally confessed their love for one another, and Randa was afraid that what he would say would sabotage it.

"Randa," he began. "You know you are very special to me, right?

She nodded. *Where is he heading with this?*

"And you know that I love you and care about you a great deal," he continued.

Again she bobbed her head up and down.

He put his arms around her and held her tightly against him. Nuzzling against her ear, he said the words Randa had never thought she'd hear again.

"I'd like you to do me the honor of becoming my wife."

Randa bolted upright, shocked at Justin's proposal. Tears streamed down her face as the emotion of the moment overwhelmed her. "Justin, are you sure? You got over this whole thing with Lisa?" Randa wasn't entirely sure that she wasn't the rebound woman.

"I love you, Randa. I have for a long time, but until I thought I'd lost you for good, I didn't know how important it was for me to say it. So many things were wrong in my marriage that I didn't even know about. I didn't know being in love was supposed to feel this good and secure. For the first time I feel safe. I'll do whatever I need to do to be with you," he said into her ear.

Randa turned to face him and saw the sincerity in his eyes.

He reached into the inner pocket of his tux and produced a small, black velvet box. Justin held it out to Randa and said, "I'm not asking you on a whim. I've had this for awhile. I knew I wanted you to be my wife. And the mother of my children."

She opened the box and found a three-carat solitaire diamond inside. Randa was speechless. Justin took the ring out of its case and put it on her finger. It was a perfect fit. "Are you ready to give me your answer?" he asked.

He thought his heart would pound out of his chest as he waited for a response. A fresh set of tears streamed down Randa's face, and he didn't know if that was a good sign or a bad one.

"Yes," she cried, throwing her arms around his neck. "I'd be honored."

EPILOGUE

One Year Later

Justin walked into the conference room, which had become a makeshift baby shower. He could barely contain his happiness. All the managers were present, except for the honoree. He took his seat next to Curry and waited for Randa to arrive.

Curry watched as Justin nervously tapped a gold pen against the oak table. "Congratulations," he said, watching the father-to-be.

"You, too. I didn't know you guys were planning on another one."

"It was unplanned, to say the least," Curry replied, laughing nervously.

Justin could understand Curry's nervousness; he'd felt it himself for the last six months. "I understand completely. I'll feel better now that Randa won't be working anymore. Since this is your second time on the maternity go-round, how do you get Darbi to take it easy?"

"I don't. I just make sure I'm there when she finally says she's tired."

Justin looked around the room and gazed at the presents adorning the wall. There were both baby-shower presents and Randa's going-away presents. It was her last day at Sloane, Hart, Lagrone, & Crawford.

They had been married less than a year, and she was twenty weeks along in her pregnancy. With all the complications that came with being pregnant and over forty, Justin had wanted her to quit the minute she missed her first cycle out of fear for her health. But she disagreed, claiming that she felt fine and nothing could go wrong. He reluctantly agreed.

Even though they were more than fine financially, Randa wanted to work until the last possible minute of her pregnancy to keep herself active. Justin proved to be crafty in enlisting the help of Karl, the kids, Bea, and Gareth to convince Randa it was time to quit and take it easy. After all of their prodding, it was the sonogram that made up her mind. As she lay on the examination table with Justin holding her hand, she saw her future on the screen.

Justin laughed as he remembered the many nights Randa had kicked him out of bed in her quest for a comfortable position. If it were anyone else, he would have thought them bossy, but he looked at Randa with love. No sacrifice was too great. If that meant he had to sleep in the other room, he did. Usually she joined him in the wee hours of the morning, claiming she was lonely.

The door opened, and Randa walked in. She looked radiant in her blue maternity suit, and her belly protruded proudly. Since her pregnancy, her shoulder-length hair seemed fuller and her hazel eyes, more sensual. Even at twenty weeks, she still turned him on in a crowd of people. The men stood as she entered the room and took her seat next to Justin.

"Sorry I'm late," Randa said. "Trying to tie up loose ends." She took her husband's hand and grinned at him.

Bea nodded. "I'm sure you left nothing for your

replacement to do. I'm sorry that you'll be leaving, but I believe you are at the place you want to be."

Randa rubbed Justin's leg. "Yes, I'm very happy. Although I was outvoted by my husband and family about working, I'm happy about my next role as a wife and mother."

Justin was so excited about the birth of their child, he thought one of his shirt buttons would pop off with pride. This marriage was nothing like his first one—starting with their honeymoon at the Disney World Resort. He squeezed Randa's hand under the table, then pulled it to his lips. She had made him the happiest man in the world. He leaned over to whisper in her ear. "I love you, Randa, more than words can ever express."

She smiled that smile that always made him weak. "I know, Justin. You tell me every day."

Dear Reader,

I hope you enjoyed Justin and Randa's road to happiness. Texas is my home state, and I love it for the nonchanging of the seasons. I hope you enjoyed the North Texas setting for this story as much as I enjoyed writing about them.

Randa and Justin are a very special couple to me because of their ages and the setbacks they incurred. I hope each obstacle placed in their path to happiness only made you root for them more, just as I did.

I welcome any comments about the characters, setting, or anything else. Please e-mail me with your comments at celyabowers@comcast. net.

Much happiness,
Celya Bowers

ABOUT THE AUTHOR

Celya Bowers was born and raised in a small rural town in Central Texas. Reading became her hobby at an early age, followed by "closet writing." She attended Sam Houston State University in Huntsville, Texas, majoring in journalism. After relocating to Arlington, she worked in corporate accounting for several years before picking up writing again. She loves to travel and attend cultural festivals. Her dream is to finally get a stamp in her passport.